# DEADLY

# DEALS

# DEADLY DEALS

A BEYOND THE VEIL NOVEL

## M. W. MCLEOD

Deadly Deals
Deals of the Damned Book Two



This novel's story and characters are a work of fiction. Any resemblance to actual persons, places, or events is purely coincidental. Certain long-standing institutions, agencies, and public offices are mentioned, but the characters and situations involved are wholly imaginary.



ISBN (eBook):          978-1-957257-05-1
ISBN (paperback):      978-1-957257-04-4

Version 2021.06.11

Disclaimer: When summoning the Devil himself from the pits of Hell, it is recommended to call him by any monikers with only the darkest of connotations. The King of Hell, Prince of Darkness, Lucifer, and Satan are all acceptable. Use of the name Samael or Lightbringer will end badly for all involved parties barring the fallen angel whose wrath was incurred.

To firnds and griendfriends –
May autocorrect treat us all better.

Your personal and creative journeys continue to inspire
every day.

# 1



Ellyria looked up from her book at the last of her study group. The holidays and finals were taking their toll on their usual group of five. Today it was just the two of them. "I'm having trouble concentrating today."

"I blame the weather," Tucker said, leaning back in his chair. He looked out the window at the snowy Harvard campus scenery and yawned. "Today is just dragging on."

She sighed. "Maybe we should just call it for the day."

"If you want to." He shrugged, sitting upright and looking at her. "We already made a decent dent in the study guide." He sounded like he was forcing himself to sound as positive as possible about the situation. They had a lot of studying to do with finals breathing down their necks over the next couple of days.

"Yeah. I think I just need a mental health break." She smiled, packing up her things.

He returned the gesture and stood up, grabbing his things as he did so. "I'm thinking about food. What about you?"

"I don't know. I've got plenty at home." She shrugged, avoiding the commitment.

"Coffee then?" he asked. His tone became more urgent and simpering than before.

Ellyria thought about his suggestion for a moment. Tucker had always been nice, but she got the feeling he was more interested in her than she was in him. She saw how he looked at her and couldn't help but think about how handsome he was as well. There was just so much in the way of her ever having any sort of relationship with normal men. They were so breakable, and she had so many secrets. After weighing her options, she decided that coffee wasn't too bad an idea on such a wintry day. "Sure." She smiled, picking up her bag.

"Sweet." He smiled widely as he led her to the campus coffee shop. "So, what do you like to do in your spare time? You never seem to talk about yourself," he asked as they walked.

Ellyria sighed. "Because there's not much to talk about. I don't have much family, and in my spare time, I like to read." She didn't bother to mention the fact that the things she read most often were magical grimoires and ancient Latin.

"Reading is pretty interesting. You can get lost in your own little world." He kept his voice conversational until his expression soured a bit, and his tone became lower. "That sucks about family. I'm sorry. So, I take it you live alone then?".

"No, I have a roommate. Rent is way too expensive up here to not have one."

"That's good. Yeah. The rent can be bad, I guess. I have a scholarship, so it isn't that big of a deal for me," he said, looking ahead a bit. "So, what is your roommate like, then? Do you two get along well? I've heard the horror stories."

"I rent off campus, so the scholarships don't pay for it." She shrugged. "He's a good guy. We have some ups and downs, but that's just life."

"That's good." He nodded at her. "You must both work hard to afford the rent, then. That's an excellent trait to have."

She shook her head. "I'm a full-time student. I pay other ways. He works his ass off and still complains when I try to do the dishes."

Tucker turned and gave her a strange look. "Oh. You two are a thing, then. Got it." He looked upset and took a step away from her as they walked.

"Okay," she said, trying not to snarl as she got angry. She stopped and reeled around on him. "Not that it's your business, but I'm paying for rent with my Mom's life insurance money. I do *not* pay for rent like that."

He jumped a bit at her outburst. "Sorry!" His expression grew dismayed. "It just sounded that way. Even if you did, there is nothing wrong with that. And-" He let out a long sigh, looking defeated. "Sorry about your Mom," he said before he reached into his wallet. He pulled out a five-dollar bill. "You can go get the coffee. I've already messed this up. Sorry." He turned around and walked away with haste.

Ellyria took the bill with a little surprise and couldn't summon the nerve to respond before Tucker was already long gone. "Smooth as a dull butter knife," she said to herself, not knowing if she meant herself or him. She swung by the coffee shop before heading back to her house. "Hey, Zane."

"Hey," Zane said from behind a computer screen as she entered the house. "How did today go?" he asked as he typed away.

"Classes were fine, but it was just me and Tucker at our study group. Of course, he hit on me."

He made a face at that news. "I don't like him," he said as he continued working. "Something about him is off."

She moved over to give him a peck on the cheek. "That's because he makes your witch uncomfortable."

He shook his head at her and chuckled. "No. It is because there is something wrong with him. I just don't know what. Yet." He grumbled something she couldn't hear under his breath. He finished up what he was doing and closed the laptop. "I am guessing you are hungry?" he asked, standing up.

"Getting there, but I can cook. You're busy making us money, Mister Stockbroker." She laughed.

He chuckled and made his way to the kitchen. "I'm done with that for the day." He smiled at her. "Might have bankrupted a few companies today, but they had it coming. Never embezzle in South America."

"I'm not sure I even want to know." She shook her head. She pulled off her heavy jacket, revealing a sweater. "I'm never going to get used to this cold."

"Lucky me, I can tolerate it." He chuckled at her as she took off her jacket. "Then you want to go to New York for a penthouse."

She nodded. "It'll be just as cold." She paused. "Now there's a question I never thought to ask. Is it hot in Hell?"

"Depends on the layer, or if the Dark Prince is feeling spontaneous."

She looked at him and made a face. "There's a frozen over one, isn't there? Just to prove a point to us foolish mortals."

"Yup," he said, popping the 'p'. "The look on their faces is priceless." He laughed.

Ellyria kicked off her shoes and sipped on her coffee. "I don't think I know what to do with myself without the study session this afternoon, but I couldn't focus any longer. So, I think I need a break."

"There is nothing wrong with that," he said as he made her a snack. "Besides, your tests are almost done, right?" he asked idly.

"I've got three more this week." She sighed. "One of the frat houses on campus is having a big party to celebrate finals being over on Friday."

"Do you plan on going?" he asked her as he handed her the snack of pita chips and hummus.

She nodded. "It's been a while since I've relaxed for a bit."

"Well, I can't stop you." He sighed a bit. "I guess I will be there too."

"You know, you can ask me to not go. Just say the words."

"I know I can, but I also can't. There is a code I *have* to follow."

"I can order you to tell me how you feel."

"I think parties are stupid. Anything you can do there, you can do here," he said. He did not want to get ordered around.

"Thank you." She smiled at him. "And you're right. They are stupid. I just don't know what else to do with myself. Things are feeling- stale? I don't know. I need better hobbies."

"There is always knitting."

"I would rather take up becoming a serial killer," she deadpanned.

He shook his head at her. "That is too much work. You wouldn't have enough hours in the day to do that and law."

"Oh sure, but I can take up knitting." She giggled. "Maybe it's time we bought that gaming system."

He thought it over for a moment. "I would recommend a computer for that, to be honest," he said with a serious nod. "It would cost more, but there are far more games you could play then."

"As long as you can play, too. I want to watch you play games where you steal cars and cause chaos."

"Then we get two of them. They have a game about robbery?" he asked.

She nodded. "Along with just about every other crime."

"I'm in." He smirked evilly. "Oh, so much destruction."

"You want to buy them, or should I?"

"I will take care of it. What color would you like the lights?" He chuckled.

Ellyria thought for a minute. "Assuming they don't have purple, blue."

"Red it is for me," he said, walking back over to the laptop and getting the computers ordered.

"You might enjoy some resource management and strategy games too. World domination and conquest."

"I didn't know that they offered that as a recreational activity," he hummed to himself. "I think I might." He smiled at her, going back to the screen for a moment. "And ordered," he said with a dramatic click.

She glanced at the screen. "Ugh. I shouldn't have looked at that price."

"Don't worry. Six grand is nothing." He waved it off. "There is plenty more where that came from."

"I really need to pay more attention to the finances." She winced.

"I can help with that," Zane said. "The hard part is dealing with the money and making sure it all goes into the correct accounts. Otherwise, it is straightforward all things considered."

"I think I might hold off until I graduate." She frowned. "That sounds like a lot."

He shrugged. "It is more and less complicated than I make it out to be. By the time the deal is done, I will have you set for life."

She nodded. "Thank you."

"Don't worry about it. It is my job." He returned the gesture.

She ate her snack and turned on the television. "I want to see what happens next with Geralt and Yennefer."

Zangrunath looked at her and shook his head. He already knew the ending. "Enjoy," he said a bit on the sarcastic side as he went to get started on dinner.

Ellyria began watching the episode, but had to pause it when her phone went off with a bunch of text messages. "Oh, for Lucifer's sake," she said, looking at her messages and groaning. "Tucker-"

"What is it?" Zane asked from the kitchen. "Is he apologizing like the worthless peon that he is?"

"He might be drinking." She handed him the phone. "I'm going to expect X-rated photos soon."

Zane glanced over at the phone, muttering the texts under his breath. "I love you. I'm sorry. You are my world." He sighed after a moment. "There is something wrong with him."

"Well, he's not prince charming. That's for sure," she said. "I should've taken the chance this afternoon and told him we were together."

"That would have at least made this easier to deal with. You should just tell him that and make it easier on everyone," he said, going back to cooking again.

She took her phone back and texted Tucker. 'Thanks, but no thanks. I'm in a relationship.'

'I thought you said that wasn't the case? What happened?' A text fired back almost as quick as she sent it.

'What I said is that I don't have sex for free rent. Not that I wasn't with my roommate.' She growled as she hit send.

There was a pause in the text. The three little dots at the bottom of the thread appeared and disappeared multiple times. 'Prove it.'

She looked up at Zane. "Do you show up in photographs?"

"Yes, why?"

"Can you be Zane for a minute, please?" she said, turning on her camera.

He turned into Zane instead of Zangrunath and walked over to her. "What do you need a picture for?"

"Proof, I guess," she said, kissing his cheek and snapping a picture.

He looked at the picture and shook his head. "At least make it worth it." He stole her phone and kissed her on the lips as he took a picture of them. He handed her phone back to her. "There, that should make him believe you."

She smiled and sent the picture. "I hope that's good enough."

"Hopefully. Otherwise, proving the point will be much different." He smirked, standing up and going back to make dinner.

"I can arrange that for us," she said.

He looked at her for a moment. "Once dinner is done." He smiled at her. "I refuse to let food get burned."

"That's fine." Despite herself, Elly smiled. She noticed her old quartz necklace around his neck and walked up to touch it. She channeled more magic into it. "I should really read into this."

"Into what?" he asked, looking over at her.

"Why this stone prefers people other than me?"

"It probably has something to do with emotions." He smiled back at her. "I'm no expert on crystals, but doesn't each one help with different aspects?"

She nodded. "Yes, they do." She paused. "I have a book on it, actually." She ran off towards her room to grab it and came back, frantically flipping through pages.

"I wasn't expecting the enthusiasm." He chuckled at her.

"Well, it's the first idea we've had about it for a while. Here it is. Quartz. Draws away negative energy and neutralizes it." She looked at him. "Do you feel any different in that regard?"

"Maybe a little less bloodthirsty," he said, shrugging a bit.

"Balances and revitalizes. Cleanses and enhances. Aids in concentration. Unlocks memory. Stimulates the immune system." She sighed. "Well, that's not helpful."

"Does it say who it helps?" he asked her as he plated food for her.

"It implies the wearer most of the time." She shrugged.

"Then it could imply what your concentration is on, right?" he asked, placing a healthy Greek chicken wrap in front of her.

She thought about it. "Are you saying that this stone likes to jump around to the people I concentrate my energy on?"

"No. What I'm saying is, what if the energy you put into it makes you concentrate on it more? Like focusing on a part of yourself."

She thought about that as she took her first bite of the meal. "Can you turn invisible and move around?"

He did as she asked and walked around the living room and kitchen while she couldn't see him. "Is it working?" he asked from behind her.

"Yeah." She smiled. "I can sense it. You can stop now."

"Maybe I enjoy being sneaky," he said into her ear, letting his breath tickle the skin there.

She shivered as his breath tickled her ear. "Oh."

"Finish your food first," he said as he appeared, moving around the island to get the dishes done. "Then fun." He smirked.

She continued to eat, and her phone buzzed. "Oh, son of the Dark Prince."

"What is it now? Why did the antichrist get involved?" he asked, sounding annoyed. He didn't even bother asking who it was sending the text messages. They both already knew.

She unlocked her phone and looked at the message. "Just more drunk texts." She shut her phone off. "Screw this."

"Just tell him to fuck off tomorrow," he said as he finished the dishes in record time.

She finished eating in short order and sighed. "Thank you. It was delicious, as always."

"You're welcome," he said, looking her over with lustful eyes.

"You don't have to be Zane, you know."

Zangrunath kissed her and turned into his true self. "If that's what you want." He smirked before he kissed her and showed her the many perks of being with a demon.

During their magical evening together, Ellyria growled at Zane, saying, "Mine," on repeat, knowing 'love' was a word seldomly, if not ever, used amongst demons. For the time being, she was okay with it. She liked their closeness, and for her, that was good enough. She wasn't ready for marriage and kids and all of that, anyway. For right now, she was more than happy with what she had with Zangrunath. As they rested towards the end of the night, Ellyria held onto him. "I like this."

Zangrunath smiled at her and gave her a kiss. "Good. I'm glad you enjoyed the new things that we tried," he said as his fingers trailed random patterns over her skin.

"Dangerous question," she said as she laid back, enjoying his tenderness.

"What is the question?"

"Do you want this witch after this is all over?"

Zangrunath grew quiet for a few moments, thinking her words over. He thought about their relationship so far, and he enjoyed it. But he also remembered their contract and how it worked. "If I could stay with you, I would. I want to see what you will become after you have that dream of yours come true."

"And after I join you in Hell?" she asked, not expecting that answer.

"It would be nice to have you at my side." He smiled, stealing a kiss. "It would make it far more bearable."

She kissed him. "Good. I've become attached to you." She was still careful not to use words like love around him, but attachment and possession. Those were safe. "Mine."

He smirked back, tracing the seal on her back. "Mine."

She shivered, seeing goosebumps come up on her arms. "I didn't know that was sensitive."

He smirked and traced a different pattern on her back. "It has its uses." He started getting some ideas about how he could show her all the nuances of the seal and its benefits, but before they continued their fun, he asked. "I assume that you're missing your finals tomorrow?" He had a smile on his face and a dark chuckle rumbled deep in his throat.

"Will you go in my place? I just want to be close with my Zangrunath tonight. I already know all the material." She looked up at him with a tired smile. "For now, it's late. I'd like to rest, if you don't mind."

Zane nodded and laid Ellyria down to rest in his arms, cuddling into her closer than they had before. He stroked her back and gave her soft kisses as she grew closer to sleep.

Ellyria breathed deep and slow. She floated in consciousness for quite some time. Her tiredness didn't make her cranky tonight when it might do so on others. Tonight she decided that simply enjoying the comfort of Zangrunath's arms was enough. She would fall asleep when her body was ready. Exhaustion washed through her, and she spoke without thought. Her words rang true even though she would hold them back under normal circumstances. "I love you."

Zangrunath heard her words and shook his head. He understood the concept of love. His demonic mind and nature made it so that he could never grasp it as he could in life. He wasn't sure why Elly would love him. He was just doing his job.

He watched over her as she fell asleep next to him and rested a hand on her. He did like Ellyria. She was better than the other witches he had been bound to over the centuries by a considerable margin. Ellyria was smart and powerful, and those things appealed to him. She was the strongest witch he had ever met. He wasn't sure if he could love her in the way she seemed to love him, but he knew he could and would protect her in every manner possible. He vowed to keep her safe, and he would die and reform as many times as it took to keep her safe. When it came down to it, he wanted to see her succeed in every aspect of her life.

He looked over her form under the covers for a long moment before he leaned in to give her a kiss on the cheek. "Sleep well, Ellyria," he said, knowing that she was already asleep.

## Thursday, December 8, 2022

Ellyria awoke to an empty house late in the morning. She was still exhausted, but she smiled. Last night was fun. She hoped Zangrunath gave Tucker Hell today as she made herself breakfast.

After Zangrunath finished Ellyria's test, he walked towards the car before Tucker approached him. "Hey. Sorry about last night. I was drunk and stupid and-" he said before Zangrunath cut him off.

"Don't talk to me again," he said in Ellyria's scariest tone. "No one should have to deal with what you did last night." He tried not to smile and laugh after he delivered the rejection. This part of his job was always fun. His serious tone must've come across, given how fast the young man stepped away, looking crushed.

Tucker deflated. His shoulders slumped as he looked down at his toes. "Sorry, I," he said, trying to explain himself before being cut off again.

"Sorry, nothing. You are just a pathetic man who doesn't have the backbone to do anything about it," he said, giving Tucker a serious look. "Stay away from me and never come near me again." He flipped Ellyria's hair and marched to the car to make his way back home to the real Ellyria.

A few minutes later, he walked into the house and turned into his demonic self, looking over to see Ellyria resting on the couch. "So, how are you handling today?" he asked, leaning over the back to look at her.

She hummed as she lounged in her pajamas with a book in hand. "I'm the most relaxed I've been in months, to be honest. Maybe since Samhain."

"Good." He smiled at her, looking her over. "Are you hungry? It is getting close to noon," he asked, heading towards the kitchen.

She rolled over to watch him. "Maybe for a snack. Somebody let me sleep in."

"You needed it." He smirked back at her. "You were exhausted." He chuckled, making her a light snack.

She nodded. "I was and still am. Good thing I can heal myself if need be."

"You say that like I might take offense."

She shook her head. "No. I'm just enjoying the afterglow of a fun evening."

"The fact you liked what we did makes me savor that time together even more." He smiled, walking over and handing her the snack. "Dig in."

"Thanks." She smiled, picking up a piece of pear from the fruit cocktail and crunching into it. She hummed in appreciation of the delicious treat. "Yum. Anything to report for the day, or was it pretty boring?"

He sat down beside her and wrapped his tail around her midsection. "Tucker tried to talk to me, and I told him to eff off and not speak with you again. Other than that, it was pretty boring."

She turned to look at him better. "Well, so much for my study group." She sighed, feeling lonely. Zangrunath was really all she had for company. "It's okay, though. They were asking questions I don't want to answer."

"Like us and family?" he asked, looking down at her.

"And what I do in my spare time." She shrugged. "Can't exactly say occult rituals."

He chuckled at her. "Well, you can, but then you will have to come up with a different answer when they think you are joking."

"I don't think I have the charisma in me to pull it off." She smiled, eating a cherry.

"You can be very charismatic." He smiled in return.

She wiggled with his tail around her waist still. "You're right. I convinced a demon to be in a relationship with me."

"Convince and asking are two different things," he said, squeezing her with his tail. "Thanks to the ritual, you could ask me to fulfill your deepest desires."

"I like to think that there was convincing involved, even though I know the rules about you taking care of me. I've read the code, but I never asked or ordered anything." She took a piece of peach and ate that next. Her mind somewhat wandered to the mystery of how she'd gotten a copy of the demon code into her grimoire, but once again, decided that it was a problem for another day.

"You still could have. I don't mind being ordered by you," he said, looking her over with interest.

"Still, I don't like to. You know that. I could've gone and done the test today. I should have. You know I don't like the master and servant thing." She finished her snack.

He watched her for a moment and took the bowl from her. "I just want to help you get what you want," he said as he took the dish to the sink, "in every aspect of life."

"I know." She followed him to the kitchen and wrapped her arms around his middle. "I know." She closed her eyes as she held him from behind, trying not to cry as she was once again reminded that what they had between them was on a timeline.

He turned around and held her for a moment as he looked down at his special witch. "It's not that I have to help you. It's that I *want* to help you," he said, giving her a small squeeze. "You're better than the other witches."

"Thank you. I know you don't have to do some things you do for me, like investing money."

"You're welcome. I am making sure you have the funds to fulfill your wants and desires in whatever way you see fit."

She smiled up at him, giving him a kiss. "I already have enough for the penthouse. Don't I? I know how aggressive you've been with trading."

"Pretty close." He smirked back at her with arrogance and kissed her in kind. "Give me another few years and you can afford it without batting an eye."

She shook her head. "That's insane. We started with like, what? Four hundred thousand from the house and the life insurance."

"Yup." He nodded. "And now you have close to two million dollars. It wasn't hard. Just pattern recognition."

"I- excuse me?" She shook her head. "What?"

"You have close to two million dollars. Yes, you heard me correct."

She kissed him again. "You're amazing. Shoot. I don't qualify for scholarships anymore. Do I?"

"On paper, you do." He smiled at her. "I have it in a separate account under my name that I will give you access to when you graduate. I didn't want to ruin free money."

"You thought of everything." She smiled.

"I try. Now we just need to wait for the computers to get here."

She nodded. "Can't wait." After holding him a moment more, she let go. "I'm going to meditate. I feel like I'm so close to something." She sighed. "Like my eighteenth birthday, but different."

"Don't tear the house apart."

"Oh, hilarious." She giggled. "I know how to control that now. I can unmake things just as fast I remake them."

He chuckled. "I know. I have seen what you can do."

"I know." She grinned. "I promise not to saturate the gold market."

He made a face. "Please don't. We have too much riding on that," he said with a serious expression.

"I can always break into Fort Knox and turn the gold to lead." She chuckled.

"Please don't." He looked like he might wince in pain at the thought alone. "They do tank training there."

"At least, I'm not the Grant that suggested taking their seventeen-year-old daughter to a nuclear testing location." She laughed, but rolled her eyes.

"Thankfully, that didn't happen." He chuckled. "You're the Grant that is going to be a terrifying lawyer."

Ellyria smirked, kissing him before walking off to meditate in the warded spare bedroom. "For Hell."

"It will be fun to have you by my side." He grinned, watching her saunter off to go meditate.

She swayed her hips a bit as she turned the corner. "Eternal damnation never sounded better."

Ellyria sat down in the spare room, all alone. She sensed Zane moving around the house thanks to the quartz stone around his neck, but instead of focusing on that, she turned her focus inward. In and out, she breathed. She could hear her heartbeat for the longest time until that too became background noise. Once it happened, she erupted with power. Her body floated, not that there was anybody to see or sense it. When they moved in, she'd warded the room well for her meditations. She was missing something, but she wasn't sure what. She guessed it had something to do with Zangrunath interrupting her meditation on the day of her eighteenth birthday, and she had sought that elusive power ever since.

Zangrunath completed a few chores and went to watch Ellyria meditate. He wasn't sure what it was, but just seeing her with that much power made him want her more. As he stepped into the spare bedroom, he felt a blast of natural energy. He closed the door behind him before sitting off to the side where he could enjoy the show.

Like years prior, she delved to the point where she'd discovered the manipulation of matter. She'd been here many times since then, but what came next, she still didn't know. It almost made her afraid, except this was her magic. Ages ago, her father taught her she never needed to fear her own magic. She pressed forward into her own consciousness, magic, and body. To her, it might have been minutes. Hours passed. She was close. Almost there.

He watched as her hair became pointed and the surrounding air pulsed with energy. He knew he was safe from her, and she wouldn't hurt him. A good bit of time passed since she'd started this. She seemed to search for something that he couldn't see tangibly there. He watched as her eyes stared off into the distance. Even he couldn't tell what it was.

At the furthest depths of her consciousness, she found it, grasping it desperately. It had defied her for too long, but no more. It tried to move from her grasp, so she used her other power to rein it in, taking it for her own. Her eyes opened, still pulsing with the power inside of her.

He looked into her eyes, which were alternating between different colors. "Did you find what you were looking for?" he asked with a smile.

She floated down to the ground. "Yes."

"Good," he said, leaning back against the wall. "What was it?"

She thought for a minute. How could she demonstrate? "You can make fireballs, right?"

"Of course." He chuckled.

"Throw one at me," she said, and her words resounded in him as a witch's order to her demon.

"You know I can't do that." He reminded her. "I can't harm you."

She looked back at him without batting an eye. "I'm telling you it won't."

A curious look crossed his face. He sighed, conjuring a small mote of fire before throwing it at her like she asked.

When Zangrunath threw the ball of fire, she focused for a second, not even moving, as the magic fizzled out of existence before it could hit her. "See?"

He looked at her and then at his hand in shock and curiosity. "What was that?" he asked, baffled by the newfound ability.

"I guess I can unmake magic." She pursed her lips. "What are my parents?"

He blinked several times before he shook his head. "I have no clue," he said, looking over at her. "They must've been the two most powerful casters to exist."

"And then they had me," she said, sounding somewhere between sobered and staggered. She looked at him with fearful eyes. "Sometimes my magic even scares me."

"It shouldn't," he said, moving over and leaning down next to her. "It's your power. You use it as you see fit."

"Not that." She sighed. "I trust my magic. It wouldn't hurt me, but I could hurt so many people."

He looked at her seriously. "Do you want to hurt people?" he asked, lifting her chin up to look into her eyes.

She looked back into the abyss of his black orbs. "No, but the temptation is there. It's so, so easy, Zangrunath. I could see myself at the pinnacle in months if I ever decided to take it, and with you-" She barked one laugh and snapped.

"You focus on what you want to do, and I will focus on the hurting," he said. "You just dissipated a fireball without moving a muscle. Try not to worry about hurting people. If you can do that, you can do anything. You will get to the top. I know you will, but I also know you are going to do it your way. Not my way."

She smirked at his words and kissed him. "You should talk me down from genocide more often."

He smirked at her as she kissed him. "If it means more of this, any day of the week," he said, pulling her chest against his so that their faces were inches from each other. He rumbled with a possessive growl as he held her close.

She grinned, looking down at him. "Should I prepare myself for you to take the rest of my finals this week?"

"Do you want to take any of the finals?"

"Not a single one." She grinned.

Zangrunath lifted her up and moved them into the living room, where they began a fun winter break together. He helped her discover some new things to do with each other, forgetting the outside world altogether, as well as the open blinds to the living room. They wrote off any lights coming from outside as headlights from the cars passing by or a rude neighbor.

# II



Zangrunath roused Ellyria, and moments later, one of his duplicates offered her breakfast in bed. She yawned, taking the coffee first. "What service this place has," she said with blunt sarcasm.

"Consider it a prize after last night." He smirked.

"You flatter me." She blushed. "We need to cool it with the late-night fun."

He chuckled at her. "I just deliver what you want."

"You kept me up past midnight." They could both hear how half-hearted the complaint sounded.

"It's my fault that you enjoy it?" he asked with a smirk. "I am making sure you get what you want, however you want it."

She snorted and held her nose. "Coffee up the nose is not fun! Look, not that I'm complaining, but I didn't mean it quite that way when I started things last night." She looked at him with a level gaze.

He sighed. "Fine. We will be less physical with each other. Happy?"

"No." She moved the tray of food out of the way, gave him a hug and cuddled into his chest. "We're still going to have fun, but we need to respect my sleep schedule for school." She kissed him before getting up. "I have class soon."

He looked up and watched her as she walked away. "Fine. Curfew will be ten." He smirked.

She moved into the walk-in closet as he said that. "Thank you for helping me keep a respectable schedule for school, even though you're half the problem."

He gave her a look of annoyance and intrigue. "If I remember it right, which I do. You smirked, bit your lip, and said, I will be your dessert."

She came out of the closet fully dressed, deciding to drop the subject for now. "How do I look?"

"Wonderful. Like someone who wants to own the world."

She giggled, preparing to deliver to him the corniest line in her repertoire. She sauntered over and took his head down to her level before whispering in his ear. "But I already own the entire world. I have you."

He smirked and gave her a kiss. "All you need to do is say the word, and it's yours."

"The word," she said with a grin. She waved a hand. "With both of us, the world is too easy. Let's aim for something much more challenging- politics."

"That's why you take the classes." He chuckled, looking at the clock. "You get to school. I have businesses to ruin and money to earn," he reminded her, moving to work on the computer.

She gave him a quick kiss. "Thank goodness today is just the one class this semester. I'll see you by lunch." She grabbed the car keys. "Come on Shelby, baby. Time to go make the men weep."

He laughed as she said that. "Trust me, you don't need the car to do that," he said as she left the house.

Ellyria made it to campus before she realized what day it was. She groaned as she parked and rested her head on the steering wheel. "Why does every school have to celebrate this day?" she asked herself as she locked the car and made her way into a now snow covered and glittery red and pink campus. She'd tested out of most of her math courses, but this one wasn't quite math. It was business and accounting. She hated it on principle, but she needed the credits. As she walked into the lecture hall, she found the room covered in pink rhinestones and sequins. She glared at the decorations, taking a seat seconds before an envelope was all but shoved in her face. She grabbed it, if only to remove the nuisance from her sight. "What's this?"

"It's a letter," Tucker said, retreating to a different row in the classroom.

She ignored the letter, shoving it into her bag as the class started. She could see Tucker trying to steal glances at her all period, but she ignored him. When class ended, she made her way to Shelby before opening the envelope as she sat behind the steering wheel. She read and hyperventilated as anger took over.

*My sweet Ellyria,*

*After our blow up back in December, I decided I needed to see you. I had to explain what happened and why I did what I did. You were difficult to track down, but I was persistent. At least, your car is easy to recognize.*

*I parked in front of your house, and I was going to go knock on the door. The problem was that it was past dark. I didn't want to bother you if you were eating or something, so I waited. I was glad I did.*

*Enclosed is a photograph of you and your roommate in a compromising position. If you'd like the SD card, meet me in the library at noon.*

*Tucker*

Ellyria looked at the photo of Zane and her on the couch together. It had to be taken months earlier since they decorated the house for the holidays. "Fuck," she said aloud before switching to her mental voice. "Zane?"

"Yes?" he said, hearing anger in her tone.

She looked at the picture and sent him the image she was seeing. "Help."

Ellyria heard a mental wail, which made her wince before Zangrunath appeared in the car a few seconds later in his human disguise. He looked at her for a moment. "Who do I have to kill?"

"Tucker."

He released a growl and nodded. "I will be back," he said, getting out of the car and making his way towards the library.

Ellyria sat in the car, locking the door behind him. She couldn't believe the nerve of this jerk. When a knock came at her window, she jumped. She'd gotten so distracted by emotion that she hadn't thought to pay attention to what was happening around her. She growled both aloud and through mental communication as she saw him. "Tucker."

"Hello, Ellyria," he said with a crooked smile. "Did you like the picture?"

She pushed her car door open, forcing him to step back out of her way. "What happens between me and my boyfriend on our property is our business."

"I know. I wasn't on your property when I took the picture, so it wasn't trespassing." He smirked, looking her over with a lustful gaze. "Though I wasn't expecting you to be into some of those things," he said, blushing a bit.

"We were experimenting." She gave him more information, hoping he would keep talking.

"Well, I'm glad you two like to be so creative," he said, turning and walking away.

Ellyria didn't think. She reacted. She made the soles of his shoes so dense that he couldn't lift them. When he fell to the ground with a crack, she knelt beside him. "I'm going to make you pay for everything you think you saw."

He looked up at her, shocked by his sudden inability to move. "You can't do anything to me," he said in return.

"Why do you think that?" she snarled, using a simple non-detection spell as she used her abilities to throw him into the car and immobilize him.

Tucker looked around, and fear overtook him. However, he didn't scream or cry out. He was too interested in whatever Ellyria was trying to do. "Because the internet is a Hell of a place for a video to get uploaded, isn't it?"

Ellyria remembered that weekend and knew what he'd seen. "And where did you upload it?" she asked as she screamed on the inside. Did this cretin even understand how illegal revenge pornography was?

"I haven't. Yet," he said with a wide smirk. "I just want you to myself."

She leaned into the back seat and started the car. "Oh buddy, you just got it." She maneuvered the car towards the nearest ley line.

"Where are we going?" Tucker asked, seeing them drive away from the campus.

"A place where we can park for a while," she said. A brief pause hung in the air as she telepathically said to Zane, "I'm going to kill him. You get his stuff."

"Already on it."

She looked back at the pervert pinned to her back seat. "What do you want me to do to you?"

"I want to do what he did. It would be beautiful to see you that way in person."

She shivered with disgust as the surrounding area became more forested and she turned down a small outlet road. "What do you want, exactly?"

"I want to do it all, but we can start off slow."

"You have a phone on you?" she asked.

"Of course. Who doesn't?"

She waved a hand and took the phone from him, floating it out of his pocket. It shut off with another wave. She made sure she didn't touch it, throwing it on the dash with a little more mental force than she intended. "There are some things you should know about me if we're going to do this."

"What's that?" he asked, eyeing her from the back seat in his helpless predicament.

She could feel Zangrunath's rage, and she borrowed it for a moment, making her eyes glow with fire. She turned to look at him. "I'm a demon, and to have sex with me, there's a contract that sends you straight to Hell."

He tried to recoil in terror, but couldn't do so. He shivered in his place as he gazed at her with longing. "Sell my soul for a night with you?" He sounded nervous.

"Yep," she said as she parked the car. She yanked him out of the back seat, feeling the ley magics enter her. She appreciated the calming sensation of the magic for a brief second. Her body pulsed with power as she looked at Tucker with disdain. "What'll it be?" she asked in a mocking tone. "My body or your soul?"

He looked up at her and saw the power within her. His expression settled on awe. "Take it. I want you."

She kissed him spontaneously for a second before she used her magic to create spikes from the earth below her that ran through his body. She heard a squelching sound and watched as the light left his eyes in an instant. Blood splattered on the snow, and she looked away. A lump of emotion settled like a rock in her throat. It felt almost painful. She stood up and wiped her mouth, heaving with frustration and anger. She killed a man, but she'd almost done something even more stupid. "I think I almost made an actual deal there."

Zangrunath appeared next to her and dropped the electronic and other digital contents of Tucker's dorm room onto the ground next to her. He looked at the blood covered area, the corpse, and towards Ellyria. "Do not make a deal with anyone," he said with a possessive growl.

"I don't understand." She shook a bit as the adrenaline from the entire debacle wore thin.

"You are mine," he said with firm finality. "I will allow no one to have you but me," he pulled her close as possessiveness washed through him.

"Yours," she said as he held her. "His cell is on the front console."

He nodded and grabbed the phone. He tossed it into the pile with the rest of his things. "Do you want to do it?" he asked, looking her over and wiping a bit of blood from her face.

She nodded once, waving a hand and starting an inferno where the gore and technology rested on the ground. She looked at him, trying to ignore anything else. "Order window coverings next day delivery when we get home."

"Of course." He nodded, looking back at her. "No one but me is seeing you like that again," he said, putting an arm around her and holding her close.

"I feel like an idiot." She sniffled. "I should've stopped it before it got this bad."

He looked into her eyes and placed a hand on her cheek. "No, you are not. We got surprised," he said, watching the incinerating remains, which smelled like fried bologna. "He was a twisted individual."

"That's just my luck. Take me home, Zane."

He nodded and led her to the car. "Of course I will," he said, helping her get into the car and shutting the door. He walked around the vehicle and got into the driver's seat.

Ellyria looked at him. "I used my powers for evil."

He reached over and held her hand. "It wasn't so bad, was it?" he asked in a gentle voice.

"He made it so damn easy," she said, as her voice cracked.

"Of course he did," he said as he started Shelby. "He was a bad person. It made it easier to bear."

She held his hand and squeezed it. "I'm glad you were here."

"I am always with you," he said, squeezing her hand in kind.

She laid down on the bench seat and rested her head in his lap. "Happy Valentine's." Even though the words were sarcastic, she meant them.

He chuckled at that and stroked her hair as he drove. "Happy Valentine's Day."


**Thursday, May 16, 2024**

"I cannot believe that you convinced me to walk for graduation. You're the only person who cares," she said as she did her hair for the event.

"You would be upset one day if you didn't. You should walk for one of your graduations," Zane said as he helped her get ready.

She lifted her robe and handed it to him. "I should've put this on before doing the hair."

He chuckled and helped pull the robe over her head, making sure to not mess with her hair. "There. Now you are all dressed up for the part." He took a step back and looked her over.

She smiled, picking up the cap to go with her gown and pinning it into her hair. "I'm assuming that I need to order you into the audience, or can you be a football field away from me now?" She laughed at her own terrible joke.

"Just tell me to be in the audience. I'm not that powerful."

She smirked and kissed him. "When we get there, go sit in the audience. What distance are we up to now? I never remember to ask."

"One hundred feet." He shrugged. "It takes time, is all."

"It's been like four years." She thought about that. "It would take my lifetime for it to be a football field."

"No. It just takes a while." He smirked at her.

She leaned over to the bathroom counter, picking up a medal and a tassel. She placed them around her neck. "Summa cum laude. Eat your heart out, Harvard Law."

He gave her a kiss. "You are going to be terrifying."

"I already am." She grabbed the keys to the Shelby and tossed them to him. "Let's blow this pop stand."

He snatched the keys from the air and moved to the side. "Lead the way."

She sauntered out the door with Zangrunath in tow. "You set our reservations for tonight?"

"Of course." He nodded, getting the door for her. "I set it for six."

"Should be enough time, I think. How are we getting there so fast?" she asked. "New York is a long way away."

He laughed at that and sat in the driver's seat. "I am one Hell of a driver." He started the car, looking like the epitome of demonic mischievousness.

"Doesn't the ceremony start at three?"

"And doesn't this car have a turbo?" He revved the engine to punctuate his sentence.

She frowned. "I better not have to repair it," she said, with eyes squinting in his direction.

"You won't. This car will be fine."

She rubbed the dash with a hand. "Good. I promised to take care of her." She looked over at him. "Let's go get me a diploma!"

"Let's." He backed out of the driveway, hitting the gas and launching the car forward towards the ceremony.

She closed her eyes and enjoyed the feeling of the speed and power of the vehicle. Her head rested back on the seat. "Miss Ellyria Grant. Bachelor's in English Literature with a minor in Latin Language and Literature."

"The most powerful person I know." He smirked at her, shifting the car into a higher gear.

She smirked over at him. As they got closer, the roads got congested with such a sizable group of people all going to one location. She bounced her knee as impatience overtook her. "This is why I was fine with them mailing it." She sighed.

He sighed and slowed the car down, glancing over at her. "Calm down. We will make it there on time."

"I know. Just anxious. Sorry."

"I've noticed. You need to relax more."

"I don't know how to relax. Not before all of this. There's so many eyes."

"Are you giving a speech?"

She shook her head. "No."

"Then don't worry about it. All the people there are looking for their offspring. You just worry about yourself and relax. It will be over before you know it," he said in a calming tone.

"I'll just think about having a nice moonlit dinner with you." She smiled. "You agreed to eat an overpriced meal with me, after all."

He grinned in return. "Of course, you are graduating from college. The least I could do is have dinner with you. You deserve a reward."

She thought about that. "I'll have to think of something fantastic for graduating from law school."

"We can move into the penthouse," he said with a wink.

"Or go overseas." She chuckled. "Rent a private jet and see what a certain club is about."

"If that's what you want," he said, not looking upset at the idea in the least.

She smirked. "Not going to lie. Seeing you nerd out visiting old battle grounds sounds like a good time."

"I wouldn't mind giving you a private tour. I would be the best guide to give them over some jackwagon who read some words on a page." He scoffed at the thought, looking proud of his accomplishments on the battlefield for a moment. "I think I like that idea."

"It would be nice to take a month off to go see the sights and relax after all of my schooling is over." She glanced over at him. "You just tell me where you want to see some battle grounds, and I'll tell you which museums we're visiting."

He chuckled. "I did most of my business in Europe, so any battles there should be enough," he said, turning off the highway and onto the main roads.

"As long as we get a vacation, I'm happy. I already can't wait."

"You just want to lounge around on a beach."

"Given that I've never been to the beach, that would be accurate."

He thought it over in his head for a moment. "Then I would recommend the Bahamas for that. The water is nice most of the year."

She hummed, "So to Europe for a couple of weeks and to the Bahamas after that."

"That sounds good." He smiled and a few moments later, the stadium came into view. "As long as you are happy, that is all that matters to me."

"Well, I want you to enjoy yourself, too."

"Oh, don't worry about me. I will always find a way to entertain myself." A devilish grin appeared on his face.

She laughed. "Chaos. I know."

He nodded and pulled the car into the packed parking lot. He got out first and moved around to get the door for her.

"Here you are, miss Ellyria." His voice was formal, yet lighthearted, as he offered her his hand.

She took his hand and feigned innocence. "I do declare, Mister Zangrunath. I didn't know that chivalry was alive and well."

"It never died. It was just hiding amongst the plebeians," he said, as he helped her out of the car and shut the door behind her.

"I like that word." She giggled. As they started walking to the building, she saw all the graduates entering at a different door. Pausing, she gave him a kiss. "I'll look for you in the audience."

He gave her a kiss in kind. "I will wave," he said. Zangrunath watched her go off to join the other students before he made his way to the seating area. He sat down in the numbered seat from his ticket. Annoyance struck him a few moments later when a couple sat beside him. They wouldn't stop talking, and the woman's voice was grating. He did his best to tune it out. He just watched and waited to see his Ellyria make her way up onto the stage.

Ellyria saw a lot of familiar faces, which she realized she didn't know. The last four years had been a whirlwind of emotions, studying, and Zane. She smiled, thinking about him. He was her rock, and it killed her. She wouldn't always have him there to rely on. She got in line by last name and waited for her name to be called. As she walked across the stage, she shook hands with the dean of her college and a couple others she wasn't familiar with, moving her tassel before going to sit and listen to the speeches, and of course, Zangrunath broke the 'polite clapping' rule. That was just his way.

Zangrunath didn't care about the looks he got from the claps. He was more focused on the person on the stage. His Ellyria. Once she moved off the stage, he waited as best he could for the rest of the whelps to be finished. He got bored, however. So, all too soon, he said, "Good job. You looked beautiful."

She jumped a bit at the telepathic communication. "Thank you and don't think I didn't see the flash from the crowd. I want a pretty frame to go with it."

"Of course. I will make sure it looks good enough to show the world."

She tried to pay attention to the proceedings, even listening to the obligatory Latin speech that she guessed only a handful of people in the crowd cared about or understood, but her attention turned to Zangrunath again. "Let's sneak out."

"If that is what you want. Let's," he said, happy to get out of the crowded auditorium.

She cast the non-detection spell on herself and carefully maneuvered around the many bodies, unnoticed or otherwise ignored. When she pushed through the outside crash bar door, she found Zane there. She paused for a moment, admiring her love before holding up the package with her degree enclosed. "Let's lollygagging out of here," she quoted an old movie.

He smiled and gave her a kiss. "Let's. We have a dinner reservation to get to." He wrapped an arm around her, leading her to the car.

She smirked. "I don't even want to know how much tonight costs."

"Not as much as you think, but more than what a person should spend on a dinner." He chuckled.

"On a rooftop in New York?"

"Of course. You ask for it; I make it happen."

She shook her head as he helped her into the car, removing the graduation gown from over the top of her nice outfit. "My guess is several thousand, but don't answer that."

He shook his head at her. "Not that much." He laughed. "The bill will be a few hundred dollars, but not that disgusting."

"Okay." She nodded. "Not that it matters. Still haven't bought the penthouse."

"I am working hard on that," he said as he drove towards the restaurant. "Penthouses are not cheap, but it will be worth it."

She smiled at him. "I know you will make sure it's perfect. Just like our current rental." She gave him a pointed look and made air quotes.

"Of course. I will always get you what you want," he smiled, "even if on paper you own the house."

"I own a house in Cambridge." She shook her head. "How did I not notice? I'll never know."

"I am going to make sure that you are set for the rest of your life when our deal is done," he said in a soothing tone. "Not that you would need it. Lawyers make a pretty penny."

As she tried to control her emotions, she held his hand and looked away. She knew he loved her in his own way; she knew love wasn't a feeling that demons had, but the fact that he wanted her to be okay after he was gone proved it to her. She didn't say the words. Instead, she said with a thick voice, "Mine."

He held her hand in kind and squeezed it. "I am yours, and you are mine," he said. He knew she was feeling a mix of emotions right now. His arm moved around her and pulled her close to him as he drove. "Don't worry. Everything will be fine."

"It's just another step forward until you're gone, and I-" She turned into his shoulder and let the tears fall.

Zangrunath felt wetness come through his shirt, and he pulled to the side of the road. He turned to her and held her as she cried. "You are the strongest witch I have ever met," he said as he rubbed her back in soothing, gentle circles. "You will be fine without me. I know you will keep going. You are strong."

She looked up at him with teary eyes. "Thank you for always taking care of me."

"Of course," he said, resting his forehead against hers. "I will always do the best I can to help you."

She kissed him in a moment of desperate passion, and when she pulled away, she looked into his eyes. "You don't have to say it back, but I love you."

He looked at her and kissed her like she'd done him. "You are mine, and I will do anything to help you feel better."

She leaned into him and closed her eyes. "Let's start by going to dinner," she said as she sniffled a bit. Her hand rested on his thigh as she cuddled against his form.

He looked down at her and kissed her head. "Let's get you fed." He wrapped an arm around her and drove the car towards their destination.

"I think I'd like you to show me how my finances work this summer. It's time I understand all of that."

"I will," he said as he rubbed her shoulder. A smile pulled at his lips. "I promise to explain it in simple terms. You will not get too confused."

Ellyria nodded, wiping her eyes a bit. "When this is done, I can't summon you again, can I?"

Zane released a sigh before shaking his head. "No," he said in a straightforward tone. "The deal doesn't work that way."

"Can I summon you on Samhain?"

He made a face. "Demons are not applicable to that."

She nodded. "I guess I'll just have to be ready when it happens. I have no other choice."

"I'm sorry." He rubbed her shoulder. "I would stay longer if I could."

"It's okay." She sighed. "I'm not sure I wanted you to watch me grow old." She shivered. "All while you're still-" She waved a hand over his form. "I'd look like your grandmother."

"I can look like anyone. I can even make myself look older."

"You'd be my silver fox, then." She giggled.

"I would be okay with that," he said with a small smile. "And I could be there to take you to Hell."

She held his hand and squeezed it. "I thought that was death's job. You can't take me if you're already there?"

"I just want to cut out the middleman. If anyone is going to take you to Hell, I want it to be me."

"I can be yours there?" she asked. "Do you have enough sway as a general for that? I don't understand the pecking order. You still need to teach me about that."

"I'm not the highest ranked general, but I don't think there would be a problem." He smiled at her. "You could be mine forever."

"Yours."

His smile grew wider, and he squeezed her hand. "Forever."

"You would make damnation worth it. The biggest problem would be if you got summoned."

He rubbed her hand with his thumb. "It takes a lot to summon me. The only way that would happen is if World War three started, but we dodged that bullet so far." He chuckled.

"And could I get summoned?" she asked.

"If you get made into a demon, yes," he said, thinking that idea over. "Given your strength, it would take a world ending power to do that." He laughed at the ludicrous idea.

"Do I keep my powers at all?"

"Some of them, but that depends on what they decide you would do best in your afterlife." A thoughtful frown dominated his expression as he spoke.

She looked up at him and made a face. "What are the options? Where do you think they'll choose?"

"I'm not sure." He sighed. "Given your power, I think they would choose to make you a general like myself."

She thought about that. "I would have been fine being in your legions."

"I would like that." He smiled.

"Having to obey your orders," she added with a smirk.

"Of course you would enjoy that." He moved his hand to rub and squeeze her thigh.

Ellyria let out a little surprised yipping sound when his touches tickled her. "So would you."

"Yes, I would." Zane smirked at her as they entered the outskirts of New York City.

She looked up at the skyscrapers and lights and felt peace. "I love this city."

"It is nice." He smiled, watching her for a moment as he drove them to their destination.

"And so much sin for you to create chaos with," she said with a little chuckle.

"It would be too easy." He chuckled. "I would just need to walk down a street and say a few words."

She smiled. "Living here will be interesting."

"It will," he said with a nod. "You won't be able to open up Shelby as easily on the streets."

"We'll just have to take trips for that."

He smirked at her, and when he turned to watch the road again, he saw their destination close by. "Oh, we will." He pulled the car into the parking garage, shutting the car off after pulling into a spot. Then he walked around to help Ellyria out. "Shall we go eat?"

"Yes, we shall." She took his hand, strolling beside him.

He gave her a kiss and led her towards their destination, past a sign that he made sure to walk by fast. Once they reached the elevator well, he hit the button for the sixty-fifth floor. "I hope you enjoy the view. There are very few buildings you can't see while up here."

She leaned into him. "I can't imagine not enjoying this."

"I am hoping. I rented the whole restaurant," he said as the doors opened, revealing the elegantly decorated Manhattan restaurant. The room was large and open, with windows looking out over the New York skyline. The smell of bread coming from the kitchen was delightful. As they stepped into the main foyer, a well-dressed server appeared.

"Welcome and good evening. You must be the reservation for Grant?" he asked with a smile, giving a slight bow.

"Yes." Zane smiled at the man before looking towards Ellyria. "Ready?" he asked.

"Ready." She grinned as they followed the server.

The server led them to the rooftop section and helped seat them. "Are there any drinks I can get you?" he asked the two of them.

"I'll take a vodka soda with squeezed lemon and a splash of sour mix."

"Of course, miss," the server said, writing her drink order down. He turned to Zane. "And for you, sir?"

Zane looked at the menu. "Let's go with the gin and tonic."

"Of course, sir. We will have those out for you in just a few moments." The server smiled, leaving them alone out on the magnificent, starry rooftop.

"I didn't expect you to rent the whole place!"

"I thought you would like the quiet. This place gets pretty busy."

She blushed. "I do. You spoil me. That's all."

"Alright then. Next time, we will choose something with a drive through."

"Not for my graduation from law school!" She covered her mouth as embarrassment struck.

He laughed at her. A goofy smile gracing his features. "Never stop being you."

Ellyria nodded, waving over herself. "Ta-da."

As she did that, the server came back and placed their drinks on the table. "Here we are. Are you two ready to order, or do you need a few more minutes?"

"I think I need another minute," Ellyria said, looking at her menu now.

"Alright, I will return in a few moments." The man nodded before leaving them to ponder the menu.

"It all sounds great. Well, the stuff that I recognize."

"I have heard good things." He smiled at her, placing his menu down. "I know what I am having."

She looked up. "Oh?"

"I'm going with the dry aged New York strip. Seems simple enough."

"I was looking at that." She chuckled.

"Two of them then?" he asked her seriously. "Make it easy?"

She nodded. "Sounds like a plan." She paused for a minute. "And the strawberries and cream for dessert."

"Sounds good to me." He smiled, waving over the server.

The man came over, taking their orders and giving another bow as he left them be again. As he strode with purpose, it was almost like he was dancing throughout the restaurant.

She gave Zane a look. "Is he normal? He gives me- a feeling-" she hummed. "I didn't make sense, did I?"

The demon chuckled at her. "No, it made sense. He made a deal."

She looked from Zane to the server. "I can't tell what for. Maybe theater given the area."

"I have no clue." He shrugged, looking at the man before looking back at her. "Doesn't concern us either way."

"Do people with deals know they made a deal?" she asked.

"I would hope so. Otherwise, there would be problems."

She shook her head. "I'm an idiot. Forgot about the code."

"It's fine. There is a lot to it." He smirked, taking a sip of his drink.

"I should know it, though. I might need to live by it."

He reached out a hand to hold hers. "You have plenty of time. For now, enjoy tonight. We can worry about that later."

She nodded. "I know." She looked around and up at the sky. "This is beautiful."

"Yes, it is." He smiled, gazing at her.

She looked at him and saw him watching her instead of the scenery. "Oh, you." She blushed.

"What can I say? I literally cannot lie to you." He smiled at her.

She took his hand from across the table and held it. "Sometimes, I wonder how I got so lucky."

He rubbed her hand with his thumb. "Sometimes, I wonder the same thing. I have done this countless times, and this one has been different in every single aspect. No wars and no real bloodshed. No backstabbing or deceit. Just helping someone become successful."

Ellyria didn't realize that she'd leaned in to hear his words. She sat up a bit. "I can't even fathom where that scared, sad seventeen-year-old would be now had you not shown up. By far, you are my biggest and best mistake, and I would never change it."

"Same," he said with a sincere smile. He was going to speak before the food came to the table.

"Here you are, folks. Enjoy," the server said, placing the food in front of them.

"Thank you. It looks delicious."

"Thank you," Zane said, looking at the food and smiling.

Ellyria took her napkin and put it in her lap before picking up her utensils. "Not going to lie. It's kind of odd to see you eat after all this time."

He smiled and cut into his steak. "I can eat," he said, taking a bite. "I just don't need to."

She cut into her perfect steak and took a bite. "Oh, this is delicious."

He nodded, enjoying the taste for a moment. "The cook might have made a deal."

She laughed. "I'm fine with never knowing." Her eyes closed as she chewed the melt-in-your-mouth meat.

He smiled and watched her eat for a moment before he cut into his own entrée again. He took a sip of his drink. "This is nice, not having to cook."

She took another bite. After a minute, she said, "Thank you for always doing that. I know you know I can cook."

"It's fine," he said, waving her off. "You are busy becoming the world's best lawyer."

Ellyria gave him a soft look. "I can't wait to learn legal writing and business law. Hearing about it from you is great, but I want to hold a conversation and understand it all. No offense."

"None taken. It deals with clear language, expectations, and making sure both ends of the deal are achievable. That and taking care not to give too much power for too little in return," he said, taking another bite of his meal.

"I wonder who I'll work for."

"I'm not sure, but knowing you, anywhere you choose to work." A mischievous and knowing smirk formed on his lips.

She thought for a while as she chewed. "I think I'd want to start off at a firm."

"Smart move. It helps get your foot in the door and experience," he said with a nod of approval.

"Then I think I'd like to work for a company, maybe a talent agency or a book publisher. Something that would be a bit more specific and detailed."

"I can help arrange that," he said with a nod. "As long as you know what you want to do, we can make whatever vision you have a reality."

She looked down at her plate, trying to ignore the sour thoughts that Zane might not be there for all of it. "I do." She smiled, but it didn't reach her eyes.

He set his fork down for a moment and held her hand. "No matter what, you will always be mine," he said for her and her alone

"Yours."

"Now and forever."

She finished her plate a moment later. "This has been the best night of my life."

He finished his plate at about the same time as Ellyria. "But we haven't even had dessert yet."

"Oh, trust me, I didn't forget." She smirked.

The server walked over and took the empty plates. "Are we interested in dessert?" he asked the pair.

"Yes, please." She looked at Zane. "Do you want to share?"

"Yes, please," he playfully parroted her words.

"What would you like?" the server asked, enjoying the cute couple's flirting.

Ellyria looked over at him. "The strawberries and cream, please."

He nodded. "Coming right up. I will have that out for you in just a few moments."

Ellyria held Zane's hand. "Are we going home tonight, or did you have plans?"

"My only plan was to come here and have dinner with you. Where we go next is entirely up to you."

"I don't know." She thought aloud. "Hotels are nice, but the beds aren't as nice as ours."

"Then we should head straight home." He chuckled.

She looked him up and down. "I am more than fine with that."

"I figured you would be," he said, looking back at her in kind.

As they were eyeing one another, the server came back with their dessert. "Here you are. Enjoy." He smiled, leaving them alone again.

Ellyria grabbed her dessert fork and took a small piece of the decadent looking fruity dish before offering it to Zangrunath. "A sweet for my sweet."

He looked at her offering and took a bite. He chewed the bite of food. As he did, he said, "You will regret that later."

"I'm counting on it." She winked.

He winked back at her and took a piece of fruit, offering it to her in kind.

She took the bite and hummed in appreciation. "Oh, yes."

He chuckled. "You are too easy to figure out." He smirked, stealing a small piece of the strawberry.

She took another forkful for herself. "Zane?"

"Yes, Elly?" he asked, hearing the little telltale pitch in her tone.

She glanced over at the server, who was watching them intently. "You're not going to propose to me, are you? The waiter is watching like you are."

He chuckled at that. "No. We are fine the way we are. Besides, marriage doesn't work the same with demons." He offered her another piece of fruit.

She nodded. "Oh, thank goodness. I don't think I'm a marriage and kids sort of person, and if I am, I don't think I'm ready for that yet. Not by a long shot."

"Also, marriage involves churches. No, go for me."

"Even if I wanted to get married, it would be in court." She smiled, taking one last forkful.

"Are you ready to get out of here?" he asked, already knowing the answer.

She took his hand. "You bet your ass."

"Can I bet on yours?" he asked, waving the server over to get the check.

Ellyria nodded. "Sure."

Zangrunath paid before leading Ellyria back down to Shelby. "Let's get you home." He smiled, pulling her close to him.

She leaned against his side. "I think I'll take a nap so we can have fun times later."

"By all means," he said with a wink, leading her to the car.

She smiled. "I want to get in the hot tub together, too."

"Will do." He helped her into the car. "I will make sure you are nice and relaxed."

# III



Ellyria sat at the dining room table, looking over a document. She looked away from her assignment to see Zangrunath. "Can I talk this over with you?"

Zangrunath nodded and pushed the vegetables he was cutting to the side. "What is it?" he asked, walking over.

"I'm supposed to write a document using Bluebook citation." She showed him the assignment. "I need to make the best deal for the imaginary company that I work for. At first, I thought I'd outline the money changing hands, but that is already pretty clear. It would take me a paragraph at most. Would it be wrong to make the bulk of the content about control of assets that are changing ownership instead?"

He looked over the assignment with a critical eye. "That would work as long as you define what the assets are. One person might think it is the money, while another might think it is the stock in the company or equipment," he said, giving an example.

She nodded several times. "Okay. That's about what I was thinking. Thank you."

"No problem," he said, smiling and going back to working on the dinner he was making.

She wrote fast, mind going a mile a minute while her hand struggled to keep up with her stream of thoughts. "I'm going to be a bit."

He waved her off. "Take your time. I just started making dinner. It will take a while."

She took out a red pen and started marking up the document, registering when Zangrunath brought her dinner. Then, she ate and wrote. While multitasking, she worked deep into the night. She looked up at the clock when she finished, yawning. "I sleep too early. Eleven thirty-four is late for me nowadays."

He walked over to her and wrapped an arm around her. "That's because you work like a maniac," he said as he guided her to bed.

"I just," she yawned yet again, "don't want to revise on the weekend."

"If you do, it won't be much after all of that," he said as he lifted her up and brought her to bed. "You work hard. I know you will be fine."

She curled up into him. "Goodnight, Zane."

"Sleep well, Elly." He smiled at her, giving her a kiss as he tucked her in for the night.

**Wednesday, April 22, 2026**

Ellyria came back home around six at night with a wide grin. "Zane!" She jumped up and down as she offloaded her belongings and pulled a document out of her backpack.

Zangrunath blinked a few times as she ran into the house. "Yes?" he asked, watching her enthusiasm with infectious joy. "What makes you so happy?"

"I got the legal writing essay from Friday back!" She held up the documents to reveal a red '100%' circled.

He smiled. "Good job," he said, pulling her in for a hug. "You are doing great."

Ellyria hugged him back. "Thank you. Thank you. Thank you!"

"For what?" He chuckled. "Giving a small bit of advice?"

"Everything. Ever."

He held her close for a moment longer. "Well, thank you, but you did most of the work," he said in a simple, matter-of-fact tone. "You're already pretty smart. You just need to be nudged in the right direction, is all."

"It's all coming together." She smiled, kicking her shoes off near the door.

Zane waved a hand and moved to put her shoes in line with the rest of them before looking at her. "It was always there. You just needed guidance."

"With a lot of things."

"You would have figured it out. It would have just taken longer," he said, moving into the kitchen. "I bet you are hungry."

"Yes, I am," she said. After a minute of waffling between going to get changed and just staying in the living room to chat, she sat down at the kitchen bar. "Things are getting competitive."

"No wonder you are back home so late," he said, glancing at the clock as he made her dinner. "You like to win; you are competitive like that."

She nodded. "There's this internship over the summer, and there's a lot of politics kicking in."

He let out a sigh. "Ugh. I hate politics. So much they said, we said nonsense. That's why I prefer deals. It's an even divide where everything gets laid out." He smiled. "Easy."

"I'm not even sure I want it, but the temptation to get ahead is there, and it's strong." She sighed, rubbing her temples.

"Then go for it. It will get you closer to what you want."

"So much for our summer vacation." She frowned. "I enjoy distracting you while you try to concentrate on video games."

"As do I." He smirked at her before he released a sigh. "We will manage. It will just be one summer."

She sighed. "I guess. It's time that I become the lawyer and not just Ellyria."

"You will still be my Ellyria," he said as he placed her dinner in front of her.

She picked up her utensils and looked up at him. "I can't believe I'm saying this. This is not who or what I thought I'd be one day, but I need a wardrobe upgrade and a stylist."

He smiled and released a self-assured chuckle. "And why do you think I am here?"

"You what now?" she asked, feeling baffled by his suggestion.

"Wardrobe upgrade? Easy," he said without pause, waving his hand at all of her. "As for a stylist, I have been bound to enough women to know what trends will never go out of style." He smirked at her. "This is nothing."

"Well, make me a lawyer." She shrugged, digging into her meal.

He looked her over with a critical eye, but not because he needed to. "It won't be difficult."

"I didn't think so, but I still dress and carry myself like I did in high school and college. I need to be ready sooner than I thought."

"Don't worry. I will whip you into shape in no time," he said, crossing his heart.

She rolled her eyes at him. "In the least sexual way I can summon, make me a woman."

He chuckled and gave a little shrug. "Walking and talking will take time and practice. As for clothes, the internet."

"I don't even know where to start." She giggled, getting a little excited about shopping. "Any suggestions on clothes you wouldn't rip off?"

"I would rip them off of you all the same," he said as he thought. "Well, I think several department stores will have what you're looking for. There must be a website for this. Either way, I think a black-on-black look will suit you well. It is slimming and formidable as well as easy to clean."

"I know for a fact that I want a pencil skirt. They look so powerful on TV and in movies," Ellyria said before she groaned. "I'm going to have to start dry cleaning things."

"You can have people do that for you." He waved the concern off. "The number of things you can have done for you in this day and age is astounding."

She nodded. "I guess it's not so bad if I'm paying them," she said. "This whole, I play and you work thing has never sat right with me."

"I have plenty of playtime." He chuckled. "It is fun getting gaming profiles banned."

"Yeah. I never expected the love for first-person shooters, but you get to torment kids." She shrugged, though she still looked like she was thinking about the previous conversation of major wardrobe purchases.

"If you are worried about the money, don't be. You are going to be fine. Besides, lawyers are loaded. I know you will become miss money bags before too long."

Ellyria finished her meal and looked at him. "Thanks to you, I haven't been worried about money since high school."

"It was my job to help you," he said in a serious tone. "You having no worries is a good thing."

She stole a kiss from him and cleaned her dish. "I have an essay to write for Friday." Her frustrated groan filled the room.

"You can do this," he said, his voice almost chipper by comparison to his usual timbre. "It will be a cakewalk."

"It's for the internship. Yay." She waved her hands with her lack of enthusiasm.

"Then make it fun," he said. "Just because it's work doesn't mean you can't enjoy it."

She nodded. "Dear Parker, McDonough, and Hannon, please choose me because I'm witchy. Thanks."

He shook his head at her and released a scoffing snort. "Not like that." He sighed. "Dear Parker, McDonough, and Hannon, I am a strong and independent woman who is more than capable of working at your company. I have language and social skills which make me well suited to helping your clients. Knowing this, please consider me to work for you."

"Well, it's not a full letter, but it's a start." She smiled.

"It's all about the word play." He smiled at her. "It's the difference between eating with grandma and eating grandma. Word choice and punctuation matter. If you get it, I'll make it worth your while."

She giggled at his example. "Oh, you. How am I supposed to concentrate while thinking about that?"

"First, you need to get accepted, so you better work hard."

"Eff me," she said, averting her eyes from the literal demon who was enjoying taunting her far too much. She grabbed some paper and a pen from her backpack, sitting at the kitchen table and thinking for a moment before writing.

"If all goes well, I plan on it." He chuckled, watching her get to work.

*Dear Parker, McDonough, and Hannon,*
*Please accept this letter as my formal request for entry into your summer internship program.*

She looked at him reading over her shoulder. "No pressure or anything."

He chuckled and walked away. "Just wanted a brief idea of what was ahead."

"Sure." She sighed. His distraction made her lose track of where she was going with the letter.

He whistled as he left the room so she could work. She just needed a goal, and he knew what she wanted.

She looked back at the paperwork and started again.

*As a female embarking in a male dominated industry, I feel that it's of the utmost importance that I take every opportunity to put myself in a position to be ready for the future. It takes a certain amount of strength and dedication to be in this industry. It also requires subtlety, attention to detail, and that certain electric something that you can't quite express with words.*

*Energy. Energy is something I have in spades, and one thing I've learned about energy is that energy is power.*

Ellyria looked at the document, grumbling her frustrations under her breath. "This is way too much information. I'm telling them about my life story in the most bass-ackwards roundabout manner there is."

"Then tease them with what is coming!" Zane said from the other room in a playful, singsong manner.

She tossed the draft in the bin.

*Dear Partners,*

*Did I get your attention? I hope it did. My name is Ellyria Grant, and we'll be working as partners in a firm together one day, but the first step requires that you take the chance to hire the strongest, most independent future lawyer that you've ever met.*

She hummed. "Okay. This one I like."

*The most important thing you should know about me is that I have a certain magic about myself. Sometimes, I can just make things happen out of nowhere when things are stuck.*

She smiled. "Thank you!"

"You're welcome."

**Thursday, April 30, 2026**

Ellyria wore her new black blouse with a rounded neckline and a black pencil skirt with a pair of heels. She paced back and forth in the living room as she wrung her hands together. She saw Zane out of the corner of her eye, but ignored him in favor of her worry. "Everybody else has interviews tomorrow. Why was I invited to dinner tonight?"

Zane looked at her for a moment and chuckled. "Oh, I think I have an idea." He gave her a knowing smile. "Who are you meeting tonight?" he asked as he watched her pace.

She looked at her shoes. "Mister McDonough's assistant, I think."

"Then why do you think he invited you to dinner, to show you his baseball card collection?"

"To tell me that my letter had balls, but not just no but Hell no."

He chuckled at her. "Calm down. Everything will be fine." He walked up to her and rubbed her shoulder. "I will be right there next to you the whole time."

"Invisible," she said with a sigh. "I can do this. I can do this."

"Yes, you can. If not, I know you will give them Hell."

She nodded. "I would kiss you if it wouldn't smear my lipstick."

"You can save that for later." He smiled. "Just go get the job first. I can wait."

She smiled and grabbed her purse and the keys to Shelby. "Let's do this."

Zangrunath smiled and disappeared. "Break a leg," he said with telepathy as they left.

She hopped into the car after locking the door. "Thanks. Time to go eat an expensive dinner." She sighed as she punched the gas, accelerating towards the restaurant. When she arrived, she parked, putting her keys in her purse before walking with purpose towards the building. Her heels clicked on the pavement, and she held her head high despite her worries. She smiled at the hostess. "Hello. I'm here for the McDonough reservation."

"Hello, Miss. Mister McDonough is waiting for you. Right this way." The hostess smiled before leading her to a private table.

Ellyria tried not to cringe, and said in her head to Zangrunath, "Did she just say Mister McDonough? I thought it was supposed to be his assistant."

"She did. That is odd. Why would a partner want to see you?"

"I guess we'll find out." She offered her hand to Mister McDonough as she approached the table. "Good to meet you, sir."

He stood up as she approached and took her hand. "Hello, Miss Grant. It is good to make your acquaintance." The gentleman with a stylish crew cut smiled. His brown hair looked somewhat red against the navy blues of his suit.

She returned the smile as she took her seat across from him. "I'll admit I'm surprised. I expected your assistant."

"That was the original plan, yes." He chuckled, taking his own seat. "But I figured he wouldn't be able to do a proper interview."

She nodded, but lied when she responded. "I understand. Thank you for taking the time out of your busy schedule to see me. I believe that most of these meetings are taking place tomorrow at the University." She still didn't get what was happening here and wanted more information.

"That is one reason my assistant couldn't make it, yes." He chuckled. "But for you in particular, he wouldn't be able to understand your- innate ability." He smiled, waving the server over.

The server came over and took their drink orders. When he left, Ellyria looked towards Mister McDonough, feeling a bit baffled. "How so?" she asked, trying not to gulp loud enough for him to hear.

"Well, I look over all prospective new interns. I like to make sure I know who I am hiring. I was a little curious after seeing your background check. It seemed quite mysterious. Unnatural, even."

She hummed a little. "Oh, I'm sure it's all easy to explain. What was it that was in question?"

"Your senior year of high school."

She frowned in false upset. "That was a rough year for me, but my grades remained high despite everything."

"You did well, considering you had issues with Section Seven," he said, meeting her eyes as the drinks arrived.

She froze as she took her drink from the server. She looked up at the man and saw the dazed look on his face. Magic. She leveled a gaze at McDonough. "I handled it." On the inside, she screamed at Zane, "What the Hell?!"

Zane didn't respond.

"Zane?" Her head tilted to the side.

"You look like you are having some trouble there. Is everything alright?" Mister McDonough asked with a straight face.

She nodded and lied through her teeth. "Oh yes, of course. Thinking about Section Seven just makes me think about my parents. I'm sure you can understand." She didn't bother to mention that her constant companion was being maddeningly silent.

"I can understand. Losing those close to you can be tough. Not being able to hear them talk back can be nerve-wracking." He took a sip of his drink after he finished taunting her.

She raised an eyebrow at him. "Mister McDonough, sir, may I ask the real reason you wanted to meet me?"

"Of course, but I will answer that when we have food and the room to ourselves," he said, waving the server over. "You will thank me for the discretion later."

She ordered her meal and waited for him to order his before looking towards him again. "Do you speak Latin?"

"Fluently." He smirked at the suggestion.

She switched over to the language. "*So do I.*"

"*I had a feeling you would.*" He chuckled.

"*Why is that?*" she asked. She was enjoying this, which further proved that there were things wrong with her.

"*Well, at first I wasn't sure. But after seeing the timing of certain events and how well you took care of things, I figured you might also have friends in low places.*"

She nodded. "*That would be accurate. Care to explain why he's being uncharacteristically silent?*"

"*Because mine talks way too much.*" He sighed. "*I needed to think.*"

"*So, you turned off the volume, or are they having their own little tête-à-tête?*" she asked, taking a drink.

"*Turned off the volume. They can still hear us, but unless they show themselves, we won't be able to hear them,*" he said, taking another drink as well.

She eyed him carefully. "*So, you wanted to meet me because of him and not because of my internship letter?*"

He shook his head. "*Not quite. My actual intent was to learn more detail about your deal. I wanted to make sure that you and I won't butt heads with one another. That would be problematic for the both of us,*" he said as he sloshed his wine around in his glass a little and took a whiff.

"*Without going into details, I'd like to be a respected business and contract lawyer.*" She smiled.

He looked her over with a guarded and curious expression. "*Really? You sold your soul to become a lawyer.*"

"*That is an embarrassing and complicated story.*"

He nodded. "*I understand that.*" He sighed before he regarded her with a more serious expression. "*So, you want to be a well-respected lawyer, that's it? No plans for world domination or money?*" he asked, half-joking.

"*If I wanted to take over the world, I could've done it years ago. It would've been easy and money isn't a problem.*"

He raised an eyebrow and chuckled at her. "*I saw the car pull in. I'm impressed. But that was a curious choice of words. You must have an impressive friend if you think you could have done that.*"

"*Indeed.*" She smirked at him. "*But I wouldn't need him to do it. I just don't want that. Conquest is easy. Politics are harder.*"

He nodded, still eyeing her with curiosity, like she was a puzzle he was trying to piece together rather than a young woman and a terrifying witch. "*Indeed, they are,*" he said, giving pause as their food arrived. When the server left, Mister McDonough looked back at Ellyria, speaking in English once again. "It appears you like challenges, then." He took a bite of his parmesan crusted chicken. "I admire that."

She cut into her fish and ate as well. "So, you've learned an awful lot about me. Tell me, why do you think we might butt heads? What's your endgame?"

"The same as yours," he said. "However, we have different specialties. I'm a defense lawyer."

She nodded. "It shouldn't be a problem, then."

"Correct. In fact, I think it could be beneficial for both of us." He smiled. "I can help you gain that reputation you want, and you can help me with some of the more- troubling clients."

"Troubling clients?" She tilted her head to the side.

"To put it simply, other demons," he said, taking a bite of his meal. "We have a few people on our business team, but they are not the best. If you can become our lead for that, I would be thankful."

She smirked. "That shouldn't be a problem. I have a wonderful teacher."

"Good. We need the help," he said, but the smile on his face lightened the mood. "To be honest, I am trying to see if I can get out of mine, but time is kind of running out. The sooner you can get up to snuff, the better."

"Good luck getting out of that deal. You would be the first."

"That's what I'm hoping for. I have a feeling my demon tricked me, but I still can't figure out how. Legal writing isn't my specialty, so I would appreciate the help."

"I'm assuming you used the ritual and didn't just make a deal?"

He shook his head. "Not quite. I made a deal, but I needed help to do it. Just wasn't expecting the consequences to be so dramatic." He sighed.

She nodded. "Well, if you didn't use the ritual, you stand a chance. Did you see the contract? How was it worded?"

"I can do you one better. I have a copy," McDonough said. "Not with me, but I have one. They convoluted the wording, and I know that there is a loophole. I'm just not sure what I am looking for."

"Well, if there is one, I can find it. I might have magic, but my words are my weapons." Ellyria realized that she'd been so interested in the conversation that she'd hardly eaten and took another bite of food.

"Good." His tone rang out clear and decisive between them. "You're hired." He extended a hand.

Before she took his hand, she asked, "Are we shaking on the internship or an actual job offer contingent on passing the bar exam next year?"

"Both," he said without missing a beat. "If you are even half as good as your scores make you out to be, you will pass it with no issue."

"I have every confidence in that." She grinned, taking his hand. "Does your firm write employment contracts? Because I'll need to review it before I sign."

"We do, and that is fine." He smiled as she shook his hand. "I want to be a lawyer, not take souls."

Ellyria joked. "What's the point in going to Hell if you don't have the power to trap souls there with you for eternity?"

"To save the ones you love." Mister McDonough sighed. "Sometimes knowing you will be damned makes life a little better when you know someone else won't be."

She smiled, and her eyes got a little distant as she took another bite to eat. "I know what you mean."

"Was it worth it?" he asked. "Making the deal, I mean?"

She looked at him and felt thoughtful. "I cast the ritual. I didn't make a deal."

"Then you still have time to figure it out," he said with a nod. "Just don't regret your decisions." He finished his meal.

"I regret nothing. I don't want to get out of it, and I can't get out of it. Nobody's ever gotten out of a deal after using that ritual, and I know I won't try to be the first. I'm going to Hell." She shrugged once, as if to punctuate her statement.

He saw her resolution and gave a simple nod. "Good. At least you know what you're in for."

"Yes, I do." She nodded. She finished her last bite and looked up. "If you don't mind, I'm going to turn the volume back up now."

"I can do it. After all, I cast the spell to begin with," he said, waving a hand and Ellyria heard Zane's voice again.

Ellyria smiled. "Oh. You ruined my fun. I learned a new trick a while back and haven't run into people like me to try it out with."

"A new trick?" Mister McDonough asked.

"My family magic goes as far back as the crusades as far as I know. There's some interesting abilities that I have because of it."

He chuckled. "I have heard of your father, but never knew what he was capable of. So, it wouldn't surprise me to hear his heir would be just as strong." He chuckled, waving to the server for their check.

"Heard of?" she asked. "I didn't know about his reputation. We lived in the middle of nowhere."

"Us casters need to stick together, so we try to keep an ear out for one another." He smiled. "Sam was strong from what I heard before he ran off somewhere with someone. My guess is to that town of yours."

"Yeah, that sounds about right." She sighed. "I'll have to ask him more about it in October."

He raised a curious eyebrow at her response. "Apparently, he wanted to make sure whatever he was hiding was a secret, even from his own daughter." He tried not to sound that way, but he looked a little shocked.

"Let's just say that my coming of age was a bit jarring."

He made a face. "I'm sorry to hear that," he said as he stood up, leaving the money on the table for the check. "I hope you find the answers you're looking for. There are a few of us who are curious about what happened," he said, placing a hand on her shoulder. "Have a good night, Miss Grant. I look forward to working with you in the future." He smiled, taking his leave.

Ellyria felt a little baffled as he left her behind with nobody but Zane. She grabbed her purse and walked towards the car. "That was interesting," she said to the invisible demon, using silent communication.

"Indeed it was. He seemed to tell the truth, too."

"I agree. I didn't catch any falsehood coming from him." She nodded as she unlocked the car and hopped in.

Zane appeared in the passenger's seat next to her and looked at her. "I wasn't expecting another witch up here." He chuckled in shocked surprise.

She shook her head, working through a similar feeling. "We should expect more. The Puritans came here for freedom of religion. I bet there's a bunch of old Pagan and Wiccan families."

"That I was not expecting," he said. "We should be on the lookout then. It would be nice to have allies besides your future boss."

"I'll have to look at my book. I think I remember seeing a magic sensing spell," Ellyria said as she drove them towards the house.

He nodded, placing a hand on her thigh and smiling. "Congrats on getting the job."

"Thank you." She grinned. "I almost can't believe it."

"I'd pinch you, but I'd have to pinch me too."

Ellyria shook her head. "No, thank you." She looked over at him with a little sadness. "One more step closer to the dream."

"You are going to be great with or without me," he said. His voice was both soft and encouraging.

"I wish I had worded it different."

He massaged the place he was holding. "If ever there was someone to change the ritual, you would be the one to do it. This world is growing on me." His eyes looked towards the window, but focused their attention on Ellyria through the reflection.

She thought about his words. "I'll make it happen. Hell is about desires, after all."

He turned to look at her with a serious and impressed expression. It looked both doubtful and hopeful. "You would be the first person to change the terms," he said. "No one else has ever had the power to change them."

"You can start calling me Karen because I'm going to need to speak with your manager." She chuckled.

He laughed in kind. "Good luck. You will need it." He smiled, looking a little more hopeful for a brief second before it disappeared again.

"How do I summon the Dark Prince?"

"I have no clue."

She thought about his words and how she could speak to her father. Then she considered how she could summon Zangrunath. "I'll make a way."

He smirked. "If anyone can. It's you." The hand on her thigh squeezed. His thumb rubbed in little reassuring circles. "The most powerful witch I know."

She smiled. "If I have to, the seven seals won't stand a chance against me."

He looked at her and blinked. "If nothing else, we would see each other then, but I would refrain from doing that. The requirements are more like prophecies, and you would anger both sides if you did that," he said. "Please don't do that."

She took his hand and squeezed. A growl rumbled in her chest. "Mine."

He growled in kind, squeezing her hand. "Yours, and you are mine."

She parked in the driveway and stopped the car. Her body angled to look at him better in the cramped space. "I will do whatever it takes to keep you here with me. You are mine, and I am yours."

He leaned in and kissed her. "I will do whatever it takes to help you make that come true."

She got out of the car and strolled up to the house. "For now, let's celebrate."

He grinned a wide, toothy smile and followed her into the house. "Yes, I owe you." He shut the door behind him and turned into his demonic form.

Ellyria looked up at Zangrunath with trust in her eyes. "Please either go to my classes tomorrow or email my teachers about my absence," she said as they began an extended weekend of fun.

Friday, May 1, 2026

Zangrunath helped feed Ellyria the next morning. After he took care of her, he sat behind her on the couch while a duplicate Zangrunath hugged her from in front of her. The original behind her traced the seal on her back, and when he finished running his hands over it, she shook in his duplicate's arms. "What was that?" she whispered to him, sounding nervous. "It feels- different."

"I just unlocked the seal more," he said. "I wanted to feel closer to you."

She looked up at the copy in front of her, so she could look into his eyes. "It feels so," she shook her head, "exposed. Intimate."

"It is," he said to her as he caressed her arms. "I want to give you something that only people like us can share," he said to her as he looked into her eyes. "There is more to it if you are comfortable with that."

"Something between a witch and her demon?" she asked, leaning on the couch and finding the material scratchier than normal. "I don't understand. What does it do?"

"It makes you experience things as if you were in Hell. The experience is very intense. It can only happen between a caster and demon who are in love," he said while looking into her eyes.

Ellyria's eyes watered, and she nodded. "Oh." Surprised, happy tears fell. Her lips pulled into a smile. "That seal connects to- you want to touch my soul?"

Zangrunath nodded and turned her head to the side so he could kiss her. "I love you, Ellyria, and I want to be as close as possible to you." He smiled, wiping away her tears.

"I love you, too, Zangrunath," she said, nodding and looking into his eyes. "Please do it."

"Are you sure?" he asked before he started tracing the seal.

She nodded. "I trust you with everything that I am."

He kissed her, enjoying the rest of the weekend with his love.

# IV



After almost a full month of dropping off mail and delivering coffee, Ellyria got pulled into Mister McDonough's office. It was around lunchtime, so she guessed and brought her food in with her, knocking on his door before she let herself in. "Hello."

"Come in," Mister McDonough said from behind the door as he worked on a document.

"You asked for me, sir?" She smiled, closing the door behind her.

"Yes," he said, gesturing for her to take a seat. "I need you to look into something for me."

She nodded. "Of course, I'd be happy to help. What is it?"

"It is regarding one of our clients," he said as he laced his fingers together on the table. "I think they are a caster like us, but I am having trouble trying to track them down." His expression turned from conversational to one of annoyance.

"Do you have an address? I can go check for wards or spells on the place. Worst case, I douse them out."

He thought it over for a minute and nodded. "It would be great if you could do that, but you should know that they can get aggressive." He gave her an apologetic look.

"I am not concerned," she said without hesitation.

"You must be pretty confident in that demon of yours, then." Once again, he sounded impressed.

She leveled him with a gaze. "I'm disappointed you think I need him to protect myself, but in a word, yes. Zangrunath is a high-ranking demon. I have trusted him with my life for six years. Nothing will change that."

"I'm jealous. I don't have that kind of trust in mine." He sighed. "But you did the ritual, so it would make sense that it's different for you."

"Yes. There are things that the ritual does where a simple deal does not," she said, realizing she sounded like Zangrunath. "And you never showed me that contract."

"If you can find the client and make sure he is still alive and well, I will show it to you. Nothing against you or anything. I'm just nervous about letting people see it."

She nodded. "I understand. Just know that whatever I see is between me, you, and the Dark Prince. Oh, and the other two people in the room." She dispelled the volume control spell McDonough favored with a thought. "I wonder what they think of it?"

McDonough sighed as a female demon appeared next to him, leaning on his shoulder. "I think she is a lying little shit." The demon smirked.

A second later, Zangrunath appeared in front of Ellyria. "Be quiet, whelp," he said, looking down at the lesser demon.

"Why would I lie?" Ellyria asked. "If I were going to lie, why not go straight to the top?"

"Because you are a manipulative little bitch," the demon said with disdain in her voice.

Ellyria used her magic for a moment to keep the demoness's lips closed. "Okay. I see why you like that spell. Zangrunath is much calmer."

"Oh, I will make her quiet forever," Zangrunath said, glaring at the female demon with a look in his eyes that told them he was imagining stabbing the other demon and tearing her apart limb from limb.

"Yes, Astratoth is difficult to deal with at the best of times." McDonough sighed, glaring at the female demon before he looked at Zangrunath. "You, however, have much more self-control. That's good."

Ellyria gazed at Zangrunath. She was enjoying this moment more than she cared to admit and caught herself staring. "Do as you please, but no messes."

Zangrunath smiled and released a small growl. He walked up to the female demon and grabbed her by the back of the neck. "You and I are going to have a talk," he said before disappearing with Astratoth into a cloud of mist.

Ellyria looked at her boss, holding out a hand. "Address?"

He sighed and pulled out a sticky note, jotting down the address. "Here you go," he said, handing it to her. "Just stay safe and please don't let your demon kill mine. That hurts."

"Trust me, I know it." She rubbed her head where she remembered feeling being shot years before. "Trust me. If they're casters, I'll be fine."

He looked her over with a skeptical gaze and gave her a nod. "Okay. Just go make sure he is alive, and don't hurt him. We need him for the case we are working on."

"They'll be fine," she told him. "I'll go check on your witness. Real subtle there."

"The case is already causing enough problems. I didn't want to make it worse somehow."

She turned and left the office. "Time to go open Shelby up."

As Ellyria hopped into the car, she noticed her discarded planner in the passenger's seat. The little symbol next to the date reminded her that tonight was a full moon. She'd need to do cleansings tonight. After typing the address in the GPS and driving off, she could sense Zane's glee. She wasn't sure why. It was a first. Could he do this all along, or was this new? Or maybe he was just projecting the emotion like he would thoughts. Either way, she'd need to check sometime. She and Zane had an interesting relationship that had, to her knowledge, never happened before, or at the very least, happened with such infrequence that she wasn't sure any of those other couples were alive. She turned her attention to the road, following directions and getting there in record time thanks to turbo drive.

When she parked along the street in front of the house in question, Zane appeared in the passenger's seat, grinning like he had won the most sublime of battles. "So, this is the place?" he asked, looking it over. "It seems normal enough, but so does our house."

"Yeah. I'm not sensing strong magic, but that might be the point." She thought for a minute. "Can't douse it. Too obvious. I have the magic sensing spell, but that could be obvious too, depending on the type of magic folk."

He looked at the house and then at her. "So, we walk in?"

"Either that or I use my Mom's power to rip apart any magic there is in the place." She shrugged.

"I am fine with either option." He smiled at her. "I could always try to go scout the house out as well."

She thought for a minute. "Steve called them aggressive, so I vote for the option that keeps us off their property."

"Fine. We can do it the boring way." He sighed, making a face.

She rolled her eyes at him and concentrated in the back of her mind on taking magic away from the property. "What did you do to Narzgaloth or whatever her name was?"

"I gave Astratoth an ultimatum," he said, pronouncing each syllable of the name for her. "Stay quiet around you, or I rip her tongue out through her pancreas." His tone was lighthearted despite the threat coming from his lips.

She shivered. "That's barbaric." She sensed something in the house, grasping at the magic. "Prepare for a rather violent reaction in a minute," she said as she dismantled the magic from the domicile.

Zane watched as the glyphs and wards that were once invisible glowed and popped like magic confetti all throughout the yard. He smiled over at Ellyria and saw a man with shaggy blond hair marching out of the house. "I think he noticed us."

"I would hope so," she said, eyes closed in deep concentration. "I think I tore apart a summoning circle or something similar inside the house."

"What in the world were they summoning?" he asked as the man came up and banged on the window of the car.

"I don't know who you people are, but get the fuck off of my property!"

Ellyria turned to look at the man, rolling down the window. "We're parked on the street. This is public property." She looked at him with faux innocence. "Is there some sort of problem?" she asked as another sigil exploded like a firework.

The man looked back at the decimated wards, looking upset and scared. He knew they could see what was happening, running a hand through his hair. A nasty look overtook his face. "I know what you're doing! You're trying to get me to hurt more people. I won't do it!" He tried to grab Ellyria through the window.

Ellyria felt Zane take hold of her and move her out of the way. She lost concentration and found herself in the passenger's seat, looking at the back of his head. "What are you talking about?"

Zane grabbed the man by the neck. "Answer her question."

The man sputtered and coughed as Zane's hands gripped his throat. "Th- the wards p- protect me from the moon." He gasped, struggling for air.

"Son of a bitch," Ellyria said under her breath, getting out of the car and storming into the unsuspecting man's house. "I was a mythical creature before it was cool," she muttered like some sort of occult hipster.

Zane watched her get out of the car and followed her. His fist still holding, and now dragging, the man. "Show us." He let go of the man and pushed him towards the door.

Ellyria growled as she entered the living room to see an actual cage in the center with chains attached to the ceiling and walls. Beneath and around the cage, she saw a sigil carved into the ground- the one she'd torn all the magic from a moment before. "Lucifer be damned werewolves."

Zane followed them inside and released his grip on the man, pushing him into the room. He slammed the door closed behind them. His lips opened to let out a biting snarl of anger, but he got cut off.

"Now I have nothing to keep me safe for tonight." The man ran his hands through his hair as his throat rasped from the rough handling Zangrunath gave him moments before. His eyes looked from the now magicless circle to the young woman who had intruded in his home and destroyed his safety net. His eyes flashed with anger, and his nostrils flared. "Thanks for that." He sounded like he was about to let out a string of curses and oaths before Ellyria cut him off.

"No, you're not." She growled at him, sounding almost demonic for a moment. "Magic should come with warning stickers." She turned around, assessing the room and the area for the best course of action for a moment.

He gave the back of her head a dirty look. "I knew what I was doing. I was just trying to make it easier on everyone else!"

"No, you didn't." She reeled around and seethed at him, poking him in the chest as her eyes flashed with lightning. "Had you warded this place right, it would reek of danger so nobody with half of a sixth sense would come near it. Instead, you made it as unassuming as possible. *I* couldn't even tell there was magic here until it started going off like moist rock candy, and I'm one of the most magically gifted witches on the continent, if not the world!"

"I did what I had to do to live a normal life. You try explaining to your coworkers and loved ones why you have to call off every full moon."

She took a breath and shook her head. "You are so lucky that I'm a good witch." She conjured her wand and started casting proper wards this time. She wiped the old sigil away with a single swipe of her wand and redid the sigil at the center of the room. As she did so, she recreated the correct symbol from memory after many years of studying her grimoire. Midway through, she said, "Who all knows? Just us?"

"A lawyer, you two, and one other person." He sighed. "Not even my girlfriend knows."

"Which lawyer?" she asked as she infused the seal with her magic. She glanced over at Zane, looking emotional and dangerous.

"Steven McDonough," he said with a frown. "He has been helping me with a mess I made."

Zane chuckled and asked, "How bad was it?"

"I killed seven people. Woke up covered in their blood," he said in a broken sounding voice.

Ellyria looked at Zane as she cast the spells. She looked livid. "He sent me to you, knowing full well that it's a full moon tonight and knowing a good deal about what you were." The strokes that she was moving her wand in looked violent, like she was considering how she was going to slit the lawyer's throat with it after she got done with this.

"Sorry," the man said with a pained groan. "It's hard for me to deal with people because of all of this." He gestured to himself and around the house.

"Had he had an iota of respect, he would have warned me. He sent me here to test me." She finished with the sigil and moved out into the yard. "This will take a while."

Zane called out to Ellyria. "We are going to be home late." He sighed, deciding to help clean a bit in the meantime.

"We're staying the night. We're not going home," she said from just outside the door. "I need to make sure the magic worked."

"Really?" the man asked, glancing between the two strangers. "Why are you going through all of this trouble to help me?"

"Because I made a mistake, and I'm a decent person. Or, at least, I try to be most of the time." She looked over at him from where she was marking the front door with new runes. "You're not dangerous to me. Not in the same ways as a normal person."

Zane regarded the man and shrugged. "If you were an actual threat, we would have much bigger problems to worry about."

The man looked at the pair and nodded. "Thank you," he said. His expression looked overwhelmed and grateful. Zane noticed him wipe away a tear.

"Don't thank us yet." She stepped clockwise around the house as she made more runes. "Thank us tomorrow morning."

He nodded, moving to a closet to grab supplies to help Zane clean. "Okay."

Hours passed, and the sun was close to setting. "When's moonrise?" Ellyria asked as she finished infusing the wards with magic.

"Moonrise is 8:43, but the moon is full at 7:56. It is the moon being full that you need to worry about," he said, getting into the cage and locking the chains on his wrists and ankles.

Ellyria sat back on the old, beat-up couch, relaxing for a minute. "You won't require that. Had you warded this place the right way the first time, those seven people would've never been a problem."

Zane took a seat next to her, but pulled her close to his side in a protective gesture. "She fixed your failure of epic proportions. You can calm down now."

Ellyria looked at the clock. "Almost time." She assessed the man in the cage with a little annoyed eye roll. "What's your name, anyhow, werewolf?"

"Tom," he said before the transformation started and a pained howl ripped from his lips.

She watched as he doubled over, turning to look at Zane. "Are they wolves or are they more like half-people with hair? I only know they exist because of the spells in my book."

He shook his head. "It's neither. It is more like a spirit possessing him," he said as Tom's body changed.

"Aww, I thought he was going to turn into a cute puppy. That's no fun."

"If he worked on it, he could."

She watched with morbid interest as Tom gripped his head in pain. "So, he's just him, but feral?"

"More like trying to drive a car blindfolded while high as a kite."

She made a face. "So, like when you're possessing someone, but on steroids?"

"Well, kind of. He still has some control, but the other half is trying to take full control," he said as best he could.

She nodded. "Okay, so the Strange Case of Doctor Jekyll and Mister Hyde."

"That is accurate." He smiled; glad he could help her understand.

"Well, can he talk like that, or are we in for a lot of screaming and howling?"

"It depends on him and what his relationship with the spirit is," he said, watching Tom like a hawk. The other man was looking far more wolf-like. His frame becoming muscled and bulky.

Her head tilted as she watched. "So, he could turn me into one of them, or is that a myth?"

"Myth." He chuckled. "It is an inherited trait."

"That makes sense." She thought for a moment. "I'm willing to bet that his girlfriend has already figured it out. Any idiot who read that series of seven popular fiction novels about wizardry could make an educated guess."

Zane looked around the room and laughed. "You need to remember that people are idiots. She still might not know."

"She might not." She turned her attention back to the wolf boy as he was standing back up in an almost upright manner. "Better?"

Tom's body looked around the room and met the two sets of eyes that were watching him. A far more animalistic voice came out. "You two talk a lot," he said, stretching and flexing his supercharged muscles. "Yes, it is better." He looked at his hands and flexed them. He looked at himself, feeling impressed. It was the first time in his life he'd ever felt this way. He felt the freedom of the moment in his bones.

"So, you *can* talk like that. I expected snarling." She crossed her arms and got a haughty look about her. Pride swelled in her chest. "That's what proper wards are like. They don't just keep you in. They help you regulate and keep control."

Tom nodded and let out a sigh of relief. "I can't hear the other guy," he said, looking around the room with wonder. "Thank you. This is the first time I have had control."

"Just don't trust what you find on the internet again. I did, and I wound up with this big galoof." She gestured to Zane with a playful grin.

"You don't regret a second of it." Zane smiled down at her. His arm pulled her towards him, giving her a little squeeze.

"It's obvious it worked out for you two." Tom sighed. He shook his head at the strange and very intimate couple. "Just, please, don't talk about whatever you two are into."

Ellyria's lips pulled into a playful smirk. "Are you uncomfortable, bondage man?"

"I just don't want to hear about what a human and, I'm guessing since you look normal, a demon do behind closed doors," he said, shivering a bit as revulsion rolled through him.

Ellyria rolled her eyes. "If we were in Europe, you'd be more concerned about violence. America is all about Puritanical sexual stigma. It even shows in our literature."

Tom sat down on the floor and removed the cuffs from his wrists and ankles. "Well, of course, that would make sense. Puritans found the country seeking refuge away from a dictatorial king, so it only makes sense that it would bleed into modern day social life."

"Huh. A literal animal and well read." She smirked, looking at Zane. "I like him."

"We are not keeping him as a pet," Zane said with a serious expression on his face as he met her eyes. He looked ready to start an argument about it.

"Like Hell you will," Tom said from his place inside the cage.

Ellyria held up her hands. "Yikes. I didn't mean it like that." She held up two fingers. "I've got like two friends, including you." She pointed at Zangrunath. "At least I can be myself around him."

Zane gazed into her eyes for a moment longer before he released a sigh, nodding once. "Fine," he said, looking at Tom. "I know he won't do anything, anyway."

She glanced over at Tom and back to Zangrunath. "So, can we come visit once a month? The full moon is a restless night for me anyhow."

"That's fine," Tom said with a serious expression and a nod. His voice started strong and grew quieter as he spoke. "If you guys don't mind, of course. It would be nice to control him. He's caused too many problems. I don't want to live in fear of him anymore."

She looked at the runes on the ground and up from there to the cage and chains that hung limp inside of the miniscule prison. "Well, the first thing you'll want to do is move this mess out of your living room so your girlfriend can come visit."

"That's why I have a rug," he said, pointing towards the rolled-up area rug that was pushed flush against a wall. "It makes it easier that way."

"Alright then. Now tell me. What happens if she moves in and sweeps the floor?"

"I will say I like the design?" he asked with a lackadaisical shrug.

"You're missing the point. You need permanent accommodations if you want to rise above this." She gestured to all of him, letting out a long, weary sigh. "Rather than just living with it."

"It will happen in time. This is the first time I have been able to talk. Until now, I blacked out only to wake up in a destroyed room the next morning. I'm still trying to process this," he said, looking at them with a mix of ire and gratefulness that was hard to get a beat on. It seemed like his expression was changing from moment to moment based on fluctuating emotions. It became clear there was still at least a small fight for dominance happening inside of him they were no longer seeing on the outside.

Ellyria decided it was best to leave Tom be with his thoughts. She knew nothing about him. She couldn't even imagine what he felt right now. The best parallel she had was how fast her life changed for the better after Zangrunath came into her life. "You think the garage thing will work here like it worked at the old place in Oklahoma?"

"It's possible. It doesn't matter what the room is like as long as the runes are right."

She nodded, standing up. "I'm going to put my stones out to be cleansed. Then I'm going to go line the walls of your garage in lead. You're welcome."

Tom blinked with some surprise, but nodded. "That's fine. Thank you again."

Zane watched her walk away, admiring her form, before turning back to look at the werewolf. He gestured throughout the room. "So, how long has it been like this?"

Tom gazed about his room and shrugged again. "About a decade?" he said as more of a guess than anything. "It's hard to tell when it started. I was in college and liked to drink."

"So, you moved into the house ten years ago?" he asked. Tom didn't look that old.

"No," Tom said, shaking his head. "I moved here after the accident about a year ago. I've been scraping my life together, making ends meet. Trying to get by, you know? That is, until she showed up." He sighed right until the moment that he thought about Ellyria. A small smile graced his somewhat twisted features.

"If you even attempt to hit on her or give her any type of flirtatious look, I will rip you apart and mail the pieces across the United States." Zangrunath's eyes flared with a possessive fire that hadn't been there a moment before. After a moment, he took a breath, calming down. "But yes, she is strong."

Tom froze for a moment, realizing that Zane meant every part of his threat. "I wasn't planning on it. My girlfriend is amazing as it is," he said, averting his gaze from the demon.

"Good." Zane nodded. As he saw Ellyria come back into the room, he smiled.

She yawned as she laid down on the couch with her head in Zane's lap. "Well, I would stay up, but that always takes a lot out of me."

Zane nodded and sighed. "And you work tomorrow. You need to get some rest."

"I'm sure I will after that. I just feel rude since we're somebody's company."

"I know, but you still need rest. Get it while you can."

She closed her eyes and tried to relax. Instead of saying the words out loud, she used telepathy to speak into his head. "Night. Love you."

"Love you, too. Sleep well," he said as he stroked her scalp and hair as she fell asleep.

Tom looked at the two of them and smiled. "You two are adorable."

Zane glared, which made Tom retreat in his cage before turning around, laying down and falling asleep not long afterward.

Tuesday, June 30, 2026

After speeding home to get changed and picking up takeout, which Zangrunath was never happy about because it wasn't healthy, Ellyria stumbled her way into the law offices of Parker, McDonough, and Hannon. There were dark circles under her eyes as she approached Steve McDonough's office, knocked and heard a female voice through it.

"It's that tramp again," Astratoth said. "Don't show her that. She can't help you. Nobody can help you but me. Isn't that right?"

Steve looked over at the demon and shook his head. "I think she can. Come in!" His features held a victorious grin as he called to Ellyria.

Ellyria opened the door and walked in. She closed it with a little wave, letting a breeze close the door with a decisive click. She sat down, glaring daggers at the demon. "If you say anything further about me- in mine *or* Zangrunath's presence, I will make you suffer so much that you will beg for the fires of Hell."

Astratoth glared at Ellyria and saw the fire in the witch's eyes. She gulped. After that, she didn't speak another word before disappearing in a puff of smoke.

Ellyria looked at Steve. She was somewhere between exhausted, grumpy, and furious. Her expression was almost unreadable after such a large amount of magic use and lack of sleep. "Where were we?"

"Well, other than that impressive display, good job with Thomas. He told me you made him feel normal for the first time in ages." He smiled.

"I like him. After I stopped feeling blindsided and furious at the situation, I decided it was fun." She smiled, but it didn't reach her eyes. "We have plans to visit next month."

"I heard," he said, giving her a nod of approval. "You're going to see if he can get it under control, right?" he asked, leaning back in his chair a bit.

She waved a hand. "He was normal last night, but all that stuff needs to not be in the living room. Normal people don't have cages and chains right in the middle of sigils."

He chuckled at her description. "Normal is a very loose term with magic folk. For instance, how a person would think we were normal until they knew more than what they can see on the surface." He smirked, turning around and rummaging through his desk.

"I grew up normal until my sixteenth birthday," she said. "Then boom. Magic. Dad didn't have time to teach me anything before he passed."

"Then you know better than anyone why we need to work hard to hide what we are," he said, looking at her and placing a piece of parchment on the desk. "Now we can work together to deal with this as well."

She looked at the parchment. "And here I expected a scroll." She took out a legal pad and a red pen. "Bring it on."

He pushed his contract towards her. "As I promised, here it is. They were thorough, but I know that there is something there. I just can't figure out where it is." Steve furrowed his brow while gazing at the paper in front of him. "It's right under my nose."

She picked up the document and read. "So, it's been about three years since this started? And you asked to be an influential lawyer, yes?"

"Correct," he said with a nod.

Ellyria read for longer. She hummed as she stared at a clause. "This is odd."

"What part?" he asked, curiosity apparent in his voice.

"Article two, subsection C states the deal becomes sealed when you influence not just your current colleagues, but future generations as well. You hire the interns. By all rights, your deal should be done."

He raised an eyebrow and nodded. "True, but the next part states that it must also be by my hand. I don't always hire them. I oversee them, yes, but not always via direct means."

Ellyria glanced up at him with a look of concern. "You hired me."

"Yes, I did. This isn't that part I am worried about. I knew that would be a factor, regardless. What I am worried about is article six, subsection B."

"Let me get there," she said, reading on and taking a few notes as she did. She read over the article in question. "What's your worry in particular?"

"It says that upon completion, my soul will go to Hell. That I knew, but what it doesn't state is any of the ways for it to be completed. There was the hiring, yes, but it has no real factor for which I could say I'm done. And I just can't figure out a way around it." He sighed.

She read through the rest of the contract. There wasn't much left of it. A sigh escaped her. "This contract should both be done and shouldn't exist. Unclear terms are grounds for voiding a contract, which is my best guess why it hasn't terminated yet," she said.

Steve closed his eyes and sighed. "Of course, demons would have some weird issues with making a contract active and voided at the same time." He looked over at her. "So, what would you suggest in order to make it work out?"

Ellyria flipped the page on her legal pad and wrote out a clause, which he could add to the bottom of the contract. She ripped the page out and handed it over to him. "Find yourself an intern who doesn't already have a demon bound to them. Write this at the bottom of that document and have them sign it. Should fix your problem. This defines the terms of contract termination and constraints while also transferring it as you've requested."

He read over the document and nodded, letting out a long sigh of relief as he did so. "Thank you," he said. "It won't be hard to get the intern. There are only a handful of demons around here. I will figure it out and have it done soon enough."

"Alright." She yawned, covering her mouth with a hand. "I'll accept my fat bonus check whenever you've got that handled."

Steve sighed. "I will send the check via direct deposit," he said. His expression was serious and grateful, the relief palpable. "Now go home and get some rest. You look like a mess."

She sighed. "I'll take you up on that. Used a lot of magic yesterday."

"Good job again, by the way." He smiled. "That is the happiest I have heard him sound in a long time."

"Who knew that ripping apart his wards and replacing them with the correct ones would be the solution?" Her sarcasm hung in the room for a long moment.

"Go get rest, Ellyria." He chuckled, waving her off. "I will see you tomorrow."

"Thanks." She dragged herself to Shelby and got into the driver's seat before thinking better of it. She scooted over. "I shouldn't operate motor vehicles."

Zane appeared in the driver's seat in her place. "I will get you home. You just rest."

She laid down on the bench seat, resting her head on his thigh. "There was another loophole. I could've gotten him out without taking another soul, but," she paused, "I didn't think Hell would like me getting people out of deals."

He shook his head and stroked her hair. "No, they wouldn't. I can do many things down there, but saving you from the code is not one of them." He sighed before starting the car.

Her eyes closed. "When he transfers the contract, can we switch Astratoth out with someone tolerable?"

He thought for a moment. "That should be doable. There is nothing saying it can't be done."

"Transfer of contract should imply a reasonable change of terms," Elly said. "Night."

"Sleep well."

# V



Ellyria stretched out on the bed with her eyes still closed. She felt Zane there next to her and grabbed him, taking his arm. "Mine."

"Mine," he said, pulling her close and kissing her. "Happy birthday."

A smile pulled at her lips, and she opened her eyes. "Do I have to go to class today?"

"Not if you don't want to. Just say the word. I will take care of the rest for you."

"Can your copies go far from you? I want the real Zangrunath here with me," she asked, having never had a copy leave the house before now.

"They can go as far as you order them."

She nodded. "Send your duplicate to class in my place for the day, and from the original, may I please have breakfast?"

Zane nodded, making a copy of himself. It then changed to look like Ellyria. "Yes, and yes." He chuckled, going to go make her breakfast.

She crawled out of bed and shuffled out to the kitchen, where she sat in a pair of boy shorts and a tank top. "I want to wear nothing but pajamas today."

"I'm fine with that," he said, looking her over as he cooked. "You know me."

"Yes, I do." She grinned. "I don't have any plans for the day. Just didn't want to summon the energy to leave the house."

"Nothing out of the ordinary." He shrugged as he cracked some eggs into a pan. "Either way, I will do whatever you want to do."

She nodded. "I want to hang out with you, to be honest. We don't get many days like this."

"Well, we have options. I need to do a bit of work, but once that is done, I vote for games," he said as he plated the food.

She took the meal from him. "That sounds nice. I'll take a bath while you're working."

He nodded, moving to the computer. "If I get done early, I will join you."

She dug in. "I will let you get to it. Rob them blind."

"Will do," he said with a menacing grin as he went through spreadsheets and double checked sites.

Ellyria ate her bacon and eggs, savoring the flavors for several minutes before stealing a kiss from Zane's cheek as she retreated into the bathroom. She turned on the faucet and let the water get warm while she stripped down. Once it was a nice warm temperature, she stopped up the drain and slipped in. She sighed in content as the salts and bubbles rose in the tub. After it was full, she used a toe to turn the water off. Laying back, she closed her eyes for a bit. She could wash her hair in a few minutes. This was nice.

Zangrunath worked fast, not because it was Ellyria's birthday, but because he liked to get things done with quick efficiency. He bought controlling stock in a penny stock and then sold for triple the price when he saw it spike. As emails came rushing in, he smirked, but he ignored them. He wanted to spend time with Ellyria, so he stood up to join her in the bath.

Ellyria's eyes opened when she heard the door move. How long had it been? Hadn't she just gotten in the tub? She rubbed her eyes of sleep. "Zane?" she asked, looking over at him.

"Yeah, it's me." He smiled, turning into his demonic form before he joined her. "Relax. I will wash you." He grabbed a bath puff massaging and cleaning her back.

She sighed, leaning into the touch. "Thanks." The sudden irony of the situation hit her. She laughed. "So much for years ago when I said I wouldn't make you bathe me."

"You said nothing." He chuckled. "I wanted to do this. Mine."

She turned her head around to look up at him. "Yours."

He held her close, and once he finished with the soap and bath puff, he helped lower her head towards the water. "Hold your breath for a moment. I need to wash your hair."

She followed his direction and held her breath as he washed her hair and massaged her scalp. When it was all cleaned and rinsed, she turned to him. "Thank you," she said, kissing his cheek. "Let's play some games."

"Name the game." He smirked back at her.

"I'm thinking about a strategy game. I've got a feeling. Today is the day I beat you in world domination." She giggled.

"We shall see." He chuckled in kind. "Bring your A game."

She smiled. "Let me go grab a drink and snacks." She hopped out of the tub, grabbing her towel to dry off. She pulled on an enormous shirt and pajama pants. After that, she went to the kitchen, choosing a package of cheese crackers and a cola. "I know you love it when I drink soda." She giggled again as she booted up her PC.

He followed her lead and shook his head. "At least drink alcohol at that point. It will taste better." He sighed, starting up their favorite turn-based strategy game.

"I get it, but I think it tastes good." She booted up her game and joined the online lobby he started. "My only request is that you don't choose Germany."

"It is too sweet," he said as he chose Mongolia instead at her request. "It won't matter what I choose," he said, relaxing in his chair a bit and opening a card game up as his side game.

She picked the Aztecs before starting the game. She would try her damnedest to win, but regardless, she would enjoy her time with Zane. When round one started, she grinned at her spawn drop. "Good luck," she said, grabbing her head a bit as a headache built.

Zane rushed his troops to take out the surrounding barbarians. Then he started building his actual army. He rubbed his head as he felt her headache hit him. "You need to drink water."

She nodded and stood up, letting out a sigh. "You're right." She poured out her soda, grabbing water and a couple of pain pills. "Sorry." She took her turn and built up her defenses. There was only ever one way to get close to beating Zane at this game, and this was it. Several rounds passed until one of her scouts found his land on round forty-eight.

"Hello, pretty," he said, sending several squads to destroy the scout. "And goodbye." He chuckled as the unit got obliterated. "Your turn."

She rubbed her temples, drinking more water and closing her eyes for a moment. "I should've expected that. By the way, you know you get penalties when you declare a surprise war, right?"

"Yes, and?" he asked in return, looking at her with concern. "Are you alright?"

"Yeah. It's just a little headache. Nothing to worry about," she said, even though she closed her eyes against the pain for a minute. "It's the weather."

He looked out the window and saw that it was a nice sunny day. "Try to take it easy. If you need to, go lie down."

"I'm fine," she said, forgetting that he helped take away most of her pain. "Why do I need rest? I slept and took a nap. I'm good."

He gave her a critical look and nodded. "Fine. Just don't try too hard to beat me." If she was this insistent, then the ritual wouldn't let him do much about it. He went back to moving armies around to flank her.

She cursed, seeing his moves, but unable to do much to stop him. She bought another unit. "I don't think I stand much chance whether I hurt myself or not."

He checked his resource output and smirked as he found what he needed for his long game. "You can always throw in the towel. It won't cost you anything."

"What did you find?" she asked with a grumble and frustrated chuckle. A moment later, pain lanced through her forehead.

He turned, gazing at her with growing concern. "Okay. There is something wrong with you."

She winced, grabbing her head and massaging her temples. "Yeah."

Zane moved in front of her. He held her close, taking as much pain as he could. "What is wrong?" he asked.

"I don't know. My head just hurts." She shook her head. Tears streaked down her cheeks. "Something's wrong."

"I can tell," he said, wincing as he felt the pain. He carried her to the bedroom. "Did anything weird happen in the last few days?"

She tried to think. "Nothing. It was normal. Just my birthday."

"When was the last time you meditated?" he asked, guessing that this was something magical.

"Two nights ago on the full moon," she said, holding him tight and sobbing into him.

He held her close as the pain wracked through the two of them. Unsure of what else could be done, he gazed at her, taking more pain from her. He was nearing the limits of what he could help with, which made even the ancient demon concerned.

"It's been since Samhain at the leys," she said through broken sobs.

"Then let's get you there." He pulled her close against his chest. "I hope it will help."

She curled into him. "Are you okay with driving? I know you feel this."

"I'm not driving." He stretched his wings. "We won't get there quick enough." He made his way to the back door.

She nodded as she cuddled into his chest. "Is your copy okay?"

"He will be fine," he said, rubbing a thumb along her scalp in soothing circles. "Just focus on feeling better." He shrouded them in mist, and they took flight a moment later.

"Be quick." She tried to rest, but her mind spun with fear and possibilities. After some time, she asked, "Why is this happening?"

"I don't know." He kept his words honest, but strong and reassuring. He would take care of her and help fix this. She was his. She would be safe and alive if he had anything to say about it. He flew as fast as he could towards the ley line. "Just stay calm. I will protect you."

Elly nodded. "Okay." She took deep breaths, trying to remain calm, but the pain kept her from relaxing or meditating. "I love you," she said, fearing for the worst.

As his wings moved them as fast as they could, he rubbed her back as they got closer. "I love you, too." When they arrived, he landed harder than he cared for. He didn't want to jostle her.

She opened her eyes, squinting as she looked around the clearing. It made her head hurt to do even that, so she said, "Put me down in the center."

"Of course." He walked to the center of the clearing and placed her down.

She looked up at him as she felt the magic connect with hers. The pain was still there but somehow less, if only just a little. She reached up to stroke his cheek. "Mine."

"Yours." He smiled, seeing the pain in her expression soften a bit. He leaned down to give her a kiss.

"Sorry." She sighed, looking up at him. "I ruined our nice day."

"No, you didn't. Now we get to have a day out." He gestured to the field.

She closed her eyes. "I think I need to sleep this off now, but I'm scared."

"You sleep. I will watch over you." He sat down beside her and placed her head in his lap.

Her voice broke as some more tears escaped. "I don't want to die like this."

"You won't. I would die countless times before I let you die once." He sounded firm and possessive, the earnestness apparent in every urgent syllable.

She curled close to him and tried to focus on relaxing. Her eyes closed, and she breathed, using her meditation techniques to calm herself over a few minutes before she drifted off to sleep.

He held her close to him, wrapping his wings around her to give her some shade to rest in. He stroked her hair and thought hard. In all of his years, he had seen nothing like this before, and he needed answers. When she woke up, he was going to ask the only person he knew who might help- Steve McDonough.

A little over an hour later, Ellyria began speaking in her sleep. "Dad, help. Daddy. Something's- something's wrong." The words twisted and reordered but cycled on repeat.

Zane held Ellyria and nodded. "Yes, anything would help," he said to the open field. He would take any help they could get.

Ellyria opened her eyes. She wasn't lying outside. She was at her old house in Oklahoma. "Dad?" she asked, walking around and searching for him.

She walked around the house for several minutes. It was like she was walking through gelatin; her limbs were so heavy and slow. When she walked into her room, a voice called out from behind her. "Hey, sweetie. It's been a while since we last spoke." Her father smiled at her. He looked like he did when he was living, with a soft smile and kind, brown eyes identical to hers. His short black hair in the last haircut she remembered him having.

She turned in slow motion before a jarring sensation overtook her, and she could run up and hug him. The weights on her somehow lifted via magic. It felt like she could move like normal now. "It hurts."

"It will be okay, sweetie." Sam held her tight. His tone was quiet and reassuring. A hand rubbed her back.

"What is this?" she asked. "Our book says nothing about this birthday."

He pulled back and looked into her eyes. "I'm not sure what is going on. I never went through this."

She shook her head in confusion and pain lanced through her forehead, as powerful as it had when she was awake. Her vision blurred for a second as she rubbed her temples. "What? No-"

"This must have to do with your mother," he said, letting out a quiet sigh.

"I'm already strong enough. I don't need any other powers." She sobbed.

"I don't think it's about strength or power. It might be about lineage."

"I don't understand. What does that mean?" she asked. She didn't understand any of this. It made no sense.

He held her chin and looked into her eyes. "Remember when I said your Mom was an angel?"

"Yeah, you said she's dead. In Heaven, I guess."

"I never said she was dead. I said she was no longer around."

"Dad?" she asked. Pain was still at the forefront, but confusion and fear overtook that now. "What do you mean?"

"I mean that, when you were born, your Mom had to go back home- to Heaven." He kept his words simple, not mincing them.

She looked into her father's eyes as the pain and turmoil started to drag her into consciousness. Her vision went blurry again, and her father blinked from existence for a moment before reappearing a moment later. "No. No. I have more questions!" Her heart pounded as she screamed.

"I wish there was more time. We will talk again." Sam smiled. "He will keep you safe."

Elly blinked, and the scene changed. She opened her eyes and saw Zane above her where he was when she'd fallen asleep. "No. No-" Her voice became filled with the panic she'd felt moments before in the dream. Fear took hold, settling into her chest.

Zane held her close. "Everything will be alright," he said, trying to think of what the problem could be. He could still feel the agonizing pain she was in, and it wasn't improving.

She took his hand and said, "Eiael."

He looked at her with a curious expression. The name sounded familiar, but it didn't click right away. "What?"

"My Mom. It's my Mom."

He shook his head. Now he understood even less. "How? What thing is this?"

"I don't know." She grabbed her head and sobbed. "Woke up too soon. Dad- Dad said-" She sniffled, and her lip quivered.

"What did he say?" he asked, desperation kicking in.

She held him tighter. "She's an-" Ellyria looked up at him, tears still streaming down her face. Would he still love her if she spoke the words? Was this even real? "Angel." When she said it, it was like the other shoe dropped, making it real. She waited for him to disappear in fire and leave her.

Zane froze as she said the word. It was like the darkest of curses. He shook his head and released a growl before he picked her up, flying towards the nearest church that he knew of. He only knew its location because they passed it whenever he went to campus with her.

"Where are we going?"

"To the experts on those beings," he said, spitting the last two words. His body shifted from his demonic form into his human one.

She looked at him and nodded, trying to concentrate despite her pain. She wanted to give him the power he needed to help her get into the church.

He could feel himself growing stronger and looked down at her. "Focus on feeling better, not on me."

"You need it."

"No, I don't!" he said, flying faster as her borrowed magic spurred him on. "You need it more. I am expendable."

She shook her head and cried. "Not to me."

He let out a snarl of pain and frustration, seeing the consecrated grounds of the church in sight below them. He landed, pausing just before the fence that marked the entrance to the property. Taking a couple of deep breaths, he stormed in. "Somebody fix her!"

One priest and two other men dressed in seminary garb walked over with an urgency to their steps. The oldest man, wearing vestments, looked down at the young woman in the man's arms. He could see that the man was smoking as if being purified. Parts of his disguise faded to reveal patches of red skin before reforming back to that of his human Zane moniker. "What on Earth is wrong with her? Shouldn't you be bringing her to a hospital?"

Zane growled at the man. "Her mother is an angel," he said, spitting each word with disdain. He hated them, knowing them to be true. He had missed the signs. "Fix her."

The youngest and strongest looking clergyman took Ellyria from Zangrunath's arms. The fully ordained priest, who was the oldest of the small group of men, looked towards Zane without batting an eye. "Are you sure?"

Zane's eyes flared red. "Her mother's name is Eiael! Go to your books and fix her already!" He felt Ellyria's power fading from him. He felt pain now. A sigh that came out as a rumbling growl escaped him before he made his way towards the doors where the holy aura of the church could no longer hurt him. "I will wait," he said before stepping outside and leaning against the brick fence of the church building as his wounds now healed unimpeded.

Ellyria felt her magic coming back to her, but she also felt Zane getting further away. The pain got worse when he got too far. She reached and groped for him. "Zane! Zane! Zangrunath!" she said as impatient hands held her down and unfamiliar voices tried to soothe her. Why were they doing this? She needed him. Her Zangrunath. "Mine." She sobbed there on the floor with her eyes closed tight against the pain.

The three priests looked at each other, and without speaking, the youngest ran to grab a specific book. He returned, flipping pages. "Eiael," he said while he read. "It says he's male, not female. Rules over changes, longevity of life, and material things. Governs occult sciences." He looked at the older, more experienced holy men. "Why aren't you doing anything? Don't we join the clergy to help people?"

The eldest man knelt beside Ellyria, holding her head firm and still as she screamed in pain, writhing and kicking on the floor. She was shouting incoherent words and phrases in English and Latin. He looked at the youngest man. "She is nephilim, and Hellspawn brought her onto consecrated ground."

"So?" the youngest asked, gesturing to the woman who was in obvious agony. "This is no way to live. If you won't help her, I will."

The third man stood. "I will contact his holiness."

Ellyria snapped out of pain for long enough to shout, "No!" She dragged the priest back beside the others with her magic. Her eyes were open, but she wasn't seeing between the pain and panic she felt. "No. No. Don't call Section Seven. Please. They killed my father. I don't want to die." She gripped her forehead and screamed, "Zane!"

The one who got dragged recoiled, backing away from her. Shock and fear danced in his eyes. "Kill it. It's a danger to-"

The youngest priest pulled Ellyria away from the others. "No! She didn't hurt you. She's in pain, and you're talking about informing the authorities! What sort of men of God are we if we just let this keep happening?"

Hearing Ellyria's continued screams and feeling her pain growing instead of waning, Zane strode into the church with determination. Even though the pain was intense, he needed to be there for her. Like the priest, he knelt beside her and held her hand. "I'm here," he said with as much calm as he could before looking at the man across from him with dark fire in his eyes. "Let me make this clear. Help her or I will make sure that you meet your God much sooner than he intended."

The eldest priest looked at the demon, gave himself the sign of the cross and prayed. Without hesitation, the second man ran.

But the youngest shook his head at the other two. He pursed his lips and looked at the demon. "I'll try my best," he said, picking Ellyria up and bringing her into the back area where they gave baptisms to adults. He took a few deep breaths to prepare himself for any disturbing possibilities and walked straight in, muttering prayers under his breath. He prayed in silence, begging the cosmos for this to work. Otherwise, he feared the demon would end his life.

When Ellyria's body hit the water, it convulsed, and she gasped for breath as her head submerged. Her lungs found air again, coughing before the process repeated until she passed out, falling limp in the small baptismal pool in the stranger's arms.

Zane followed the man, watching to make sure no harm came to her. When she passed out, he looked at the priest that held her. "Is she going to be okay?" he asked.

"I think so, but I've never seen such a violent reaction to holy water." He saw the girl's chest rising and falling. "I can try frankincense as well," he said, climbing out of the oversized bathtub and handing her to Zane. "If nothing else, it gave her a break from the pain."

Zane winced as he felt the holy water touch him; it felt like acid. A growl escaped him. He didn't let go, however. He needed to make sure that she would get better. Part of it was the ritual, but he wanted it as well. "Try it. Do whatever it takes to fix this."

Ellyria didn't know where she was. Nothing looked familiar. There was nobody around. All she knew was pain. She walked until she couldn't take anymore, and she fell, crumpling onto the ground where she sobbed. "Zane. Zane. Help."

Several minutes passed before a hand touched the back of Ellyria's head and stroked her hair. The person didn't speak. It was a simple, gentle comfort. They pulled Ellyria into an embrace, holding her with tight protectiveness.

"Zane," she said as she cried in this new stranger's arms. She had no more strength or words. She feared to move or open her eyes, but the embrace was nice.

"I'm sorry," a soft, feminine voice said in a whisper. "It will be over soon. I promise."

Ellyria couldn't see straight, but she blinked up at this new person several times. She couldn't get a good look. It was a blur. "Who are you?" she asked between wracking sobs.

The arms pulled her tight. "You already know."

Tears stained Ellyria's cheeks. "What is this, M- mom?"

A sad smile crossed the other woman's face, not that Ellyria could see it. "*Destiny.*"

The response was clear and silent in her mind, whispered there almost like a thought as her eyes opened to find a censer of smoking incense swinging over her body. Zane held her hand while recoiling from the smoke. The pain in her head was gone. She didn't even have time to feel relief before she realized it was now replaced by Zangrunath's pain. She looked up at him with watery eyes. "Zane," she said, worried about how his flesh looked. His disguise fluctuated from intact to sloughing off in large chunks.

"Ellyria." He smiled. "Do you feel better?" he asked in a much more serious tone.

"A little."

"Good." He looked at the priest in training. "Good job," he said with a grateful smile.

The clergyman nodded. "Thanks. I'm not sure what I did to be honest."

"You made her feel better," Zane said, looking down at Elly. "That is all that matters."

Ellyria closed her eyes. "I want to go home."

"Then let's get you home." He nodded, picking her up and walking her out of the church.

She curled into Zangrunath's chest. "Zane."

"Elly." He rubbed her upper arm and shoulder to help comfort her. When they got outside, he shrouded them in mist and took flight.

"Thank you. You didn't have to hurt yourself for me."

He leaned in and gave her a gentle kiss. "It's fine. I wanted to make sure you were safe."

She kissed his chest, so she didn't have to move too much. "I feel different."

"Good different, or bad different?" he asked. His tone sounded too morbid.

She shook her head. "I don't know."

He sighed, giving her a squeeze. "It is fine. You will be okay. You are strong."

She grew quiet the rest of the way home, and once they were inside, he helped her down to rest on the bed. "Will you help me get comfortable? My clothes got soaked."

"Of course," he said, moving to get her out of the wet clothes. He walked around the corner to the bathroom. Grabbing her towel, he helped dry her off, being sure to be extra gentle, given all the pain she'd experienced today. "I am sorry your birthday was a bust." He sighed.

Once she was comfortable, she rolled over, laying down on her stomach. She hugged a pillow. After cuddling into the blankets and pillows, she said, "It's okay. I think I'll take tomorrow off too. Just to make sure I'm up to snuff." Sleep muddied her words. She was too tired to notice Zangrunath's reaction to seeing the new design on her back. The symbol there was familiar to anybody under the Dark Prince's rule. The symbol of the fallen. "Maybe you can go see if there's anything to learn back home."

"I think I know what the problem was." He sighed, moving to sit down next to her. His eyes gazed at the fresh symbol on her back without blinking or breaking away for a long moment. "You are a fallen angel," he said, tracing the new marking with a finger.

"I was already going to Hell. Didn't need the theatrics, big guy," she said to God as if he would hear.

"I think it means that you fell from grace or that they cut you off from your Mom," Zane said, trying his best to make a guess.

She shook her head. "I had no grace to begin with." She did a quick mental check. "I think I still have my powers. I don't get it."

"Maybe your Mom can't help you anymore."

"I never met her." She turned over to look at him. "I don't know how she helped me."

He shrugged. "She might have kept you out of His eyes, but I am not sure. He works way different from us. We are straightforward."

She opened her arms for him. "Just come over here and hold me. I want to sleep this off."

He nodded and laid down next to her, holding her in his arms. He wrapped one of his wings over her. "Of course. Get some sleep. You need it," he said, giving her a kiss.

She kissed him back and fell asleep too fast.

While Ellyria slept, the disguised Zangrunath that looked like Ellyria came home, and his memories rejoined the original. A man had followed her facsimile, starting after they'd left the church. The man himself wasn't familiar, but his disposition was. The clothing and wary glances almost gave him déjà vu from Ellyria's senior year. When he saw the van that followed him on the way home, it confirmed Zane's suspicions. Section Seven had found them.

Zane sighed at the news. Of course, they would find her after the mess from earlier. He thought about what he could do to try getting them out of this again, but he was drawing a blank. They had almost no scapegoats this time around. With Ellyria's schooling and the large amounts of money currently invested, they had even fewer ways to get away now. He needed to figure something out. She needed things to be as easy and normal as they had been for the past few years. He could tell that she wanted the end of law school to go smoothly. He just didn't have a clue how to fix it.

**Thursday, March 25, 2027**

Ellyria awoke in the morning sore all over from the debacle the previous day. Zangrunath was still holding her, and she kissed him. "Good morning," she said, but her voice sounded a little different. Even to her own ears, it was deep and sultry.

"Good morning. Are you feeling better today?" he asked as he kissed her in kind.

She sat up and shook her head. "I feel different," she said, looking at him with eyes that were closer to black than their usual chestnut brown. How could she describe her feelings when she couldn't pinpoint a single problem?

He turned her face to look into her eyes. "Your eyes are different."

She crawled out of bed and looked at herself in the bathroom mirror. "What's happening?" she asked, sounding seconds away from tears. "Would anybody know?"

"I don't know." He sighed, powerless to help her with this. "The only ones that might know are the church or your Mom. I am not sure who else."

She rubbed her temples to think, remembering his words from before falling asleep. "What about fallen angels? There have to be some."

He nodded. "Several. The Dark Prince was the first. The problem is finding them. They keep themselves hidden," he said, walking up to her and wrapping his arms around her middle. "We will figure this out."

She turned to him with fresh tears in her eyes. Panic was clear in her features. "Would he say? Would he tell you if I sent you and ordered it?"

He held her tight. "I don't know if he would say anything. And if you ordered me, that could take a long time."

Ellyria gulped. "I need to know what's happening to me." After a long moment of thinking, she sighed. "Call Steve. Ask him to cover for me at school. I need- I need-" She shook her head. "Take me to Stonehenge."

Zane's expression flashed from confusion, to understanding, to shock in an instant. Instead of arguing, he nodded. "Okay, let me get everything in order," he said, going to make a few phone calls to get everything sorted out for their spontaneous trip overseas.

She got dressed, noticing that her skin had a darker hue to it than before. Normally, she was pale. She lived in the northeast and wasn't active outdoors. Why did she look tan now? After another inspection, her hair was still near-black, so at least some things never changed. She walked past Zangrunath in the living room and grabbed an energy bar from the pantry. Even though she wanted a proper meal, she didn't have time right now. She needed results. She grew quiet and started planning. After a few moments, she scribbled hasty notes down on a paper. "I need the world's biggest ley convergence."

"I figured as much. That is why we are going to England," he said, finishing a call and dialing Steve. "We need you to cover for Ellyria for the next week." Zangrunath didn't bother greeting the lawyer when he answered. His words were the demanding orders of a general on a mission. "Something is wrong with her, and we are trying to figure it out."

"Is she alright?" Steve asked with concern in his voice.

"Yes and no. She is experiencing strange symptoms. We think it is magic related. We are heading out of town to get it fixed. I will keep you updated."

Steve took a moment to respond as he tried to think about any magical ailments he knew of. Coming up short, he sighed. "Let me know if there's anything else I can do. I'll see if I can find any information."

"Will do," the demon said before hanging up. He looked at Elly. "You ready? We have a plane to catch."

She took her notebook, pen, purse, and nothing else as she finished her energy bar. "Yeah." She sighed, trying to remain calm as she walked out to the car.

"Good," he said, turning into his human self before leaving the house. He got into the car and drove them to the airstrip. "I chartered a private plane in case anything else changes."

"Thank you," she said in her altered voice. She let out a frustrated growl, and it sounded like one of Zangrunath's. Her eyes closed. "Fuck."

He placed a hand on her leg as he drove. "We will figure this out."

"I'm scared," she said in a quiet voice.

"So am I." He gave a stalwart nod. "I want to help you so much more than I can, but this is beyond me."

"Thank you for being here." She gripped his hand tight. "I love you."

"I will always be by your side. I love you," he said, squeezing her hand in kind. Zane got them to the airport fast thanks to turbo drive. He pulled the car up to a security guard, flashed his ID, and wheeled into a parking lot. He parked as close to the hangar as possible and helped Ellyria out of the car.

She closed her eyes, waiting for them to get to the airport. When they arrived, she followed his lead to get to the private plane since she'd never been on one before. She kept focused on this one task, and the few small things that she could control. One of the first lessons of magical control was to calm your emotions, and she tried her best to do that now.

They walked through the large doors of the hangar to find a private jet with seating for eight waiting for them. Zane got them into the plane and sat Ellyria down in, making sure that she would be okay for a moment. After that, he moved to the cockpit to check on the flight plan with the pilot.

Ellyria looked up at Zane with a sad expression when he returned. She was at a loss for what to do or say. She was feeling so helpless.

He sat down next to her. "Don't worry. We will be in the air in a few minutes and arrive in about six hours." His tone was reassuring as he held her hand.

She leaned into him and closed her eyes. "What time will it be when we get there? Late would be good, but I don't care about low profiles right now."

"We should be there by midnight London time," he said, doing some quick math in his head. "Secrecy won't be a problem."

"Okay." She nodded. "I hope travel will be fast after landing."

"It will be. There will be a car waiting for us." He rubbed her shoulder in a reassuring gesture as she leaned on him.

"So much for a fun trip to Europe this summer." The plane taxied, and she grumbled a few oaths under her breath.

He sighed and looked out the window for a moment, letting her cool off for a moment. After takeoff, he looked back at her and gave her a kiss. "No matter what happens, I still love you. No physical transformation could change that."

Ellyria looked up at him. "I know. I just need to know what's happening. Simple as that."

"We will. If anyone can figure it out, I know you can." He smiled.

"Zangrunath?"

"Yes, Elly?"

"I can't believe I'm going to try this." She shook her head in bafflement after a long, serious look.

"Neither can I," he said, feeling just as shocked as her. "If you can pull this off, there is nothing you can't do."

She held him close. "I'm summoning the Prince of Darkness tonight."

He smirked. "That is the strangest and hottest thing I have ever heard you say."

"Am I going to be smote?"

He made a face. "I am not sure. If he casts spells, you should be fine, but if he attacks you, I will take the hit. Once," he said, trying not to groan when he imagined the pain.

Once the seatbelt light turned off, she stood up. "I need to get changed."

"Into what?" he asked. "You brought next to nothing and have all of your clothes on you."

"I can remake them. I just don't do it, like, ever." She shrugged.

"Oh," he said, trailing off for a moment. "I forget you can do that sometimes."

She nodded. "It's okay. I'd rather spend money than use magic on clothes most of the time." She moved into the small bathroom and remade her shirt into one with a bare back. She wanted to have an easy time showing her seal and the new sigil. When she returned, she sat beside Zangrunath.

He held her close when she sat down, looking her over. "You look good," he said. He glanced down at her back, seeing the sigil bare for all to see. "Let me guess, to prove to him you are one?"

"Whatever helps at this point." She smiled, but it didn't reach her eyes.

"You will be fine," he said, rubbing her arm and kissing her forehead. "I won't let anything happen to you."

"I know." She rested against him. "I'm going to sleep before we get there."

"Get some rest," he said, moving her head to rest in his lap. "I will let you know when we are landing."

Ellyria's eyes closed. Even though she hadn't been awake for long, sleep took her. While she rested, she dreamt of the summoning she needed to do, ways to improve her plans, and she felt like someone was guiding her, helping her make it right.

They made it over the Atlantic in a few hours. Zane kept a constant vigil, soothing Ellyria by rubbing her back. He watched her like a hawk in his worry and noticed that her skin had gotten even more tanned. She almost didn't look like herself. Her figure was the same, but the pallor of her skin made her look different. He saw his hand against hers and tilted his head to the side as morbid curiosity rolled through him. He let his disguise fall on just his hand and saw how much closer hers looked to his now. It was jarring. He made the disguise shimmer back into place and distracted his mind with the details of the next steps after they landed. When the time was right, he gave her a gentle shake. "Elly, we are going to land soon."

She hummed, still sounding tired, and grumbled a bit. After a moment, she opened her eyes and stretched. "Hi."

He looked into her eyes and saw that they were even darker than before. "Hey," he said, looking her over for any other changes.

"You look worried." She stared down at her hands. "What's wrong?"

"Your eyes are darker. Almost as dark as mine."

She sighed. "Okay. I'm- It's okay. We'll figure it out."

He held her close for a moment before gazing into her eyes. "I know we will."

"I'm becoming demonic," she said, more to herself than anything.

"I think it suits you well." He smiled with a bit of mischief in his eyes. "I will still love you, no matter what."

She kissed him. "Thanks. It's just confusing and concerning, and many other things. I expected this to happen after I died."

"You still look beautiful to me no matter what; now or after the deal is done."

She buckled up when the seatbelt light illuminated and held onto his hand as they waited for the plane to land. "I love you, Zane. Thank you. Even if you are excited that I'm- " She waved at all of her.

He squeezed her hand. "Anytime," he said. "Mine." The second word came out as a whisper.

Before she could respond, the plane's tires hit the tarmac. She sighed. "Never did like the landing."

He rubbed her thigh as the plane taxied around to the hangar. When they came to a stop, Zane stood up and held out his hand for Ellyria. "Let's go have a meeting."

She stood and took his hand. "I'm ready. I think." Her voice sounded as anxious as she felt.

He squeezed her hand once more. "Relax. He might be the ruler of Hell, but he doesn't *look* terrifying." He gave a soft, reassuring smile as he thought to himself, 'In his angelic form.'

"I'm more worried about the power I need to summon to get him here," she said as an unfamiliar sports car appeared in her vision. She squinted. "I don't know European vehicles."

He smiled and led her to the passenger seat on the opposite side of the car from what she was used to. He opened the door for her. "This is a supercar manufactured by a local company. They lend out their engines to vehicles that take part in some long-standing international racing championships," he said, since he knew she didn't really care much for motor sports. He walked around the vehicle and got into the driver's seat next to her. "I figured you would want to get there fast."

"I don't own this beast, do I?" she asked as she buckled herself up.

"No. I only rented it, but if you want one, I can arrange it," he said, stepping on the gas and rocketing them forward to the biggest ley line in the world.

"No, no." She laughed, gripping the seat a bit as he took off like a bat out of Hell. "I just know you and it wouldn't surprise me anymore."

He chuckled. "I buy things you will use. It would be silly to buy you a car that you would never drive."

She nodded. "That makes sense. So, I don't own the private jet either, right? I don't even know all the holdings I have anymore. Even though I try to keep up with what you do, you do a lot, and I get busy with school and the internship."

"No. Unless you take international jobs or work cross country, there is no reason to do that. As for your holdings, you have the same as you did before. I buy nothing unless you need it or ask for it first." He glanced at her before turning his attention back to the road.

"Well, thank you for being conservative." She grinned. "Still don't own the penthouse. Yet."

Zane laughed at that. "You can afford it now. Just tell me when and where you want. I will take care of it."

"I'm contracted at Steve's firm for three years after graduation, so hold off for now. Just keep growing what I have."

"Of course." He smiled. "I will make sure you can get whatever high end penthouse you want," he said as he pulled the car off the highway and took a round-about to get onto another road.

She tapped her toes in her impatience as she began to sense magic. "We're getting close."

He placed a hand on her leg. "Yes. Just breathe. I know you can do it," he said, believing in her ability to make this happen for the first time in history.

Ellyria nodded. "I will need you to make sure nobody gets into the circle while I'm forming it."

He looked out the window, seeing how dark it was as they left the city proper. Then he looked at her. "You should be fine, but I will make sure that no one stops you."

"Once it's started, it shouldn't be a problem. Then I want you with me."

He nodded, and a smirk curled his lips upwards. "I will follow you anywhere."

She looked at him with a serious expression. "Should I speak English or Latin?"

"Well, he speaks all of them, but Latin would be the best option," he said as he saw the old structure appear in the distance. "Just try to keep yourself contained. He is the most beautiful creature you will ever see." He released a sigh at the thought of Ellyria making an advance at the Devil.

"No, he's not," she said, looking at Zangrunath.

He smirked. "Remember when I showed you that beautiful man? He is far more impressive."

Ellyria nodded. "I understand, but he's not the demon I love. And to be honest, no. I was drunk."

He pulled the car into a parking spot and leaned over to kiss her. "Thank you. I love you."

"I love you," she said before stealing one last kiss and hopping out of the car. She felt a connection with the earth here, but she took off her shoes and socks, tossing them into the car all the same. She took in as much of the magic as possible and unconsciously floated towards the wonder.

Zane watched as Ellyria sparked with lightning as she moved towards the old structure. When he saw the electric current, he felt shocked, but figured it was because of the intense magical power here. He moved around the area, making sure there would be no intrusions to the ritual. He was a little nervous himself, but didn't show it. No mortal had ever made a deal with the *actual* Devil before. They made those stories up. He was excited to see history in the making.

Ellyria walked to the north side of the monument and started activating the near invisible ancient runes. Walls of force appeared, forming into a circle. When she finished, it became a dome as she walked in. Her feet were moving as if walking, but she still hovered a foot above the ground. Her hair stood on end as it had in years past. She summoned magical lines of electricity in the circle, and the power became thick and palpable. "Zane," she said before she closed her eyes to concentrate on the casting.

As he watched the impressive magic, Zangrunath noticed a few guards approaching. The man knocked them out, growling low as he protected his witch. He would have killed them, but he didn't want to make the ritual go haywire by adding human sacrifice to the equation. He turned back towards Elly when he thought he heard her call him, but he saw she was busy working on the last few parts of the ritual. So he hung back, continuing to keep her safe.

Ellyria felt something huge was about to happen. She pushed her own magic into the summoning without realizing that she was also draining Zane because of their connection. She felt a surge of energy and somebody or something circling her. Before she could stabilize the magic, she still needed to concentrate for a moment. Then she could open her eyes.

Zane continued to guard the area. As he did so, he felt weaker. It was subtle at first, but now that the magic flowed faster and stronger, he felt his movements become more sluggish. He shrugged it off initially and then needed to turn into his demonic self in order to keep moving. He looked back at Ellyria and saw the spectral form of two wings sprouting from her back. It was an incredible sight to see. He felt his movements slow down, and he gritted his teeth through it. He knew she was determined to see this through to the end.

Ellyria opened her eyes to find what she could only describe as an angel, but with altered features. Before her stood a man in stature, and like Zangrunath had described, more beautiful than any she had seen before. His hair was the darkest of black. His eyes were two obsidian orbs to match. On his back were six wings; all of them were upside down, looking like they would move the wrong way. Their color was the same shade of black as his hair, but they had an aura of divinity that was almost too much to bear. The fallen seraphim looked around the area before he turned his gaze to Ellyria. "What is this?" he asked with a voice that commanded authority while sounding confused and intrigued by his predicament.

"*My name is Ellyria Grant.*" She stood tall, hovering in the air and looking back at him. "*I summoned Zangrunath to me seven years ago. My father was a human, and my mother an angel,*" she said in perfect Latin before turning and showing her bare back with the new symbol upon it. She didn't notice the spectral wings there. "*Something happened yesterday, and I need to know what's happening to me. What is this?*"

Lucifer gazed at her with a perplexed expression. He raised an eyebrow, noticing the all too familiar seal on her back before he glanced over to see one of his generals moving closer. He smirked at the two of them before landing on the ground. "*To put it into the simplest of terms, they cut you off from divinity.*" His head tilted to the side, and he walked a slow arch around her. "*Your body isn't used to your powers without their help yet. It will take some time before you can control it,*" he said, leaning down and inspecting her sigil.

Zangrunath tensed up as he watched his King circle his witch and inspect her. He got as close as he dared. He wouldn't hazard touching the man who ruled all of Hell. "How long will that take?" he asked, not looking directly at the Dark Prince.

Lucifer turned to look at his general and smirked. "Well, Zangrunath, that could take a few days, a few months, maybe even a few years." He chuckled at the demon before he turned towards Ellyria, leaning down to meet her gaze. He searched deep into her eyes and even her soul. "*You, however, Miss Grant, are strong. Strong enough to summon me here.*" He hummed before a confident chuckle escaped him.

Ellyria gulped, but didn't have the mental capacity to feel fear at the moment. She had a lot more questions she doubted she'd get the chance to ask, so it was time to cut to the chase. Her eyes darted towards Zangrunath, and she licked her lips before she spoke again as she pulled a document out of her pocket, which contained hasty scribbles written in the airplane bathroom where Zane wouldn't see. "*I'd like to make an addendum to my ritual contract while you're here.*"

A curious look crossed the ruler of Hell's expression. He moved one of his wings over the contract in her hand, and it appeared in his hands. He read it over. "*And what addendum would that be?*" he asked as his eyes scanned across the page.

"*I want Zangrunath by my side for the rest of my natural life. I'm prepared,*" she looked at Zangrunath with a little smile and a significant look, "*for a soul binding.*" She remembered looking at one part of her grimoire that was next to the demon code Zangrunath didn't care for. "*In return, you can have my copy of the demon code.*"

"Ellyria!" Zangrunath called out to her before his whole body was stopped by a gesture from Lucifer.

"*This is between me and her, general, not you.*" The Dark Prince smirked at the demon before he gazed at Ellyria. He thought it over for a moment, closing his eyes in thought. When dark eyes opened, he gave her a serious look. "*To spend the rest of your natural life with a demon, I find to be a little less than my services,*" he said, pausing for almost too long. "*But having a copy of the code back in its rightful place is quite tempting, and one such as yourself amongst my ranks will be useful in what is to come.*" He paused, and he extended his hand for her. "*You have a deal.*" His eyes glowed like smoldering embers now.

She looked at him with a serious expression. "*Let me see that the contract hasn't changed first.*"

He released a sigh and waved a hand, summoning her contract to his hand. "*When the deal becomes solidified, the changes will take place,*" he said, showing her the document.

She nodded, looking at Zangrunath for a moment before she took Lucifer's hand. "Are you okay with this deal?"

Zangrunath felt his body relax a bit, and he looked at her and his King. "I want to be with you," he said. "I will follow you anywhere." His lips curled into a smile just for her.

Lucifer raised an eyebrow at the display, and he laughed at the pair. He chuckled for several long moments; this was the most hilarious entertainment he'd had in quite some time. A moment later, he quieted himself, wiping away merry tears from his eyes. "A half angel and a demon fall in love and talk with the Devil to stay together. It sounds ludicrous. Yet here it is." His piercing gaze shifted between the pair.

"*If nothing else, we will be an eternity of entertainment for you,*" Ellyria said as the corners of her lips tilted upwards. She knew the words would intrigue Zangrunath in years previous. "*He is mine. I am his. We are one.*" She took his hand and couldn't see the power glowing in her eyes. "*Make it happen.*"

There was a visible pause when she said that. "*Fine.*" He smirked as flames enveloped her and Zangrunath. The seal on Ellyria's back burned and shifted, becoming more intricate as a sigil burned itself into place on Zangrunath's back as well.

Lucifer smirked at the couple, and the contract in his hand changed, adding the new addendum she requested. He let go of her hand, taking a step back. "*There. It is done. You two are now bound mind, body, and soul.*" He gazed around, becoming a little bored now. "*Is there anything else that needs to be done?*" he asked. "*I am a busy man.*"

Ellyria looked up at Lucifer in pain, confusion, and maybe the first bit of fear. Her words, however, didn't show any of that. She chose them with care, calculating each syllable and breath like a demon might. "*Nothing now, but I can already tell that things will be fun when I join you down there.*"

He waved her off and made his way back to the center of the circle. "*You will be busy while down there, so enjoy your fun while you can.*" His expression became a mixture of knowing, mischievous, and sinister. "*Enjoy,*" Lucifer singsonged in a low baritone before he spread his wings, vanishing from sight in a blinding light that seemed to outshine the sun for the briefest of seconds. Moments later, the magic settled and the dark stillness of night returned to the area.

Ellyria turned to look at Zangrunath before the massive use of magic rebounded, hitting her full force. Seconds later, she fell in a heap on the ground, unconscious.

Zangrunath took a knee as the magic subsided. He looked at where his King was moments before. Then he walked over to pick up Ellyria with gentle care. She was out cold, and he knew she would be for quite some time. He walked back to the car, and as he set her in the seat, he saw the seal on her back, making a face. He sighed, seeing that Lucifer had changed her seal. The soul binding worked into the annihilation ritual now. Anything either of them felt from now on would be on a soul deep level. He shut the door and changed back into his human form. "We are going to need some time to figure this out," he said, getting into the car and driving her back to the airport so that they could fly back home.

## Friday, March 26, 2027

Ellyria awoke with a pounding, magical hangover. She was lying down on a small bed and looked at the unfamiliar surroundings before she realized she was back on the private jet. The sheets slid across her skin, and she groaned at how sensitive it was. "Turn it off, turn it off, turn it off."

Zane stepped into the small room and leaned down next to her. He looked into her eyes, sighing. He wished he could help. "I can't," he said, a frown taking his features.

"W- what? I didn't ask for this." She closed her eyes tight as she tried to remember the now somewhat blurry conversation and her request, which was a terrible idea since it also made her focus on how her body was feeling. She was a live wire right now.

He nodded. "That is why I called out. What I feel all the time, you feel all the time." He wanted to soothe her, but knew that it wouldn't help her while she adjusted. "That is soul binding."

Ellyria nodded. "Okay. I guess I didn't understand this part." She gripped the bed sheets tight in order to distract herself. "So, you have this headache, too."

"Yeah," he said with a frown. "It sucks." He sighed, going to get her some water.

"Did I mess up too bad?" she asked.

He came back into the room and handed her the glass. "No, it was just bad timing, I guess. Drink this, but go slow."

"Is there something in it?" she asked as she followed his instructions, trusting him regardless of his answer.

"It is water with lemon. You will just take a while to get used to this."

"I have goosebumps all over right now."

He smirked. "I figured as much," he said, seeing the telltale bumps on her arms. "It will take some getting used to. I'm sorry in advance."

"Yeah. The car ride will not be fun." She frowned. "I'm sorry I screwed this up."

"You did not." Even though he smiled at her, his voice was firm. He wanted to be reassuring and give her a kiss, but that would cause more problems than it was worth. "Things will just be different for a while."

She handed him the glass of water and laid down. "Mine."

"And you are mine," he said in return. "I will let you know before we land. Try to get some rest if you can." He knew it was going to be difficult.

"Body, mind, and soul," she said, thinking about the Devil's words. "What else changed?"

"Well, I know I don't have to follow your orders verbatim now," he said, already halfway out of the small bedroom door into the cabin. "I realized that when I was driving back to the jet."

Ellyria sat up, realizing the bed sheets weren't doing her any favors. "How so?"

"Well, when I am driving you somewhere, I am focused on getting you to that place. Nothing else. When we drove back, my mind wandered, trying to process what you had done," he said, shaking his head a bit. "You made a deal with Lucifer." He chuckled at the words; they sounded ludicrous.

She crawled out of the bed and pulled him into a hug despite herself. "I'm glad that you've got more freedom."

He wrapped his arms around her. "Thank you." He rubbed her back out of habit. "It will be nice to do more and be autonomous."

She tensed at the feeling of his hands on her, but grit her teeth through it. This was normal now. She didn't have a choice. "And in Hell, we can be together. I think."

He pulled away when he felt her grow tense. "Sorry," he said, gazing into her eyes. "Yes. We will be together. Some rituals are permanent, and this one stands among that group."

"He looked at me strangely," she said after trying to relax for several moments. She looked up at him, pulling away and holding his hands. "I don't know what to think of it."

"I think it was because he knew what all of this was going to be like for you now. Why do you think he said, enjoy?" He sighed.

She rubbed her temples. "I thought it was more like, enjoy your mortal trifles because I'm going to work you like a dog when you get to Hell."

"That too." Out of the corner of his eye, he noticed he was seeing land out of the plane's window. "We will be on the ground soon."

She nodded, taking a seat and buckling up. "I'll prepare for the landing to be a rough one."

He nodded and sat down next to her, offering his hand. "Don't worry. I will be right here." He kept his tone was calm and reassuring.

She took his hand and sighed when she noticed the odd hue of her skin. "I'm hoping this is only a couple more days. Much more and I'll look like you."

"A few days. A week or two, at most." He nodded. "You are strong. You will have this under control in no time."

"How am I supposed to go to school like this?" she asked.

"You did well when we opened the seal the first time. You can do this."

"Any suggestions to help with this?" She leaned her head back on the headrest and looking at the ceiling while stifling a groan.

He nodded. "You will want something to counteract it, perhaps a pin in your shoe or something," he said. "It isn't a perfect fix, but it will help."

"We'll figure it out. At least you'll be there to help." She sighed yet again.

"Of course." He smiled at her, squeezing her hand. "Always. Now and forever," he said as the plane landed. He watched Ellyria with worry. He didn't enjoy seeing her like this. "I will try to get you home as fast as possible."

She nodded several times. "Thank you."

## Sunday, March 28, 2027

Ellyria sprawled and stretched out on the bed. Her skin was a normal color, but her eyes were still darkest of obsidian. Content and happiness washed through her. Happiness filled her as she got control of the changes. She was several decades away from being comfortable looking like a demon. She gazed over at Zangrunath. "Can we talk?" she asked.

"Are you not doing that right now?" He chuckled.

She swatted at him. "Oh, eff off. Can you tell me more about this soul binding thing? I don't think I really understand it all yet."

Zane nodded. "Of course." He moved his fingers to his thigh and pinched until it stung. "It is like the deal but much more powerful."

She winced. "Ouch."

"I am sorry," he said. "I am proving a point."

"Okay, so it's just that? That's it?" she asked, rolling over a bit to look at him better. "Given the name, I thought there was more."

He hummed. "It binds two souls together. When our deal ends, we will still be able to do the mental talk. My constitution will still aid yours. You will be healthier and live longer."

She tilted her head. "It sounds like the annihilation ritual for people who never cast it."

He nodded. "The ritual is based on soul binding, yes."

"But are there differences?" Ellyria asked. "I know souls get lost to Hell when the Annihilation ritual gets cast."

He shrugged. "Not much. It's subtle things that aren't necessary. You won't notice them. Better eyesight and senses, but nothing nearing what I can do. The sterilization thing I never understood the reasoning behind-"

She sat up so fast that her head spun. "The what?!"

Zangrunath blinked, surprised by her quick and violent reaction. "Soul binding sterilizes the two bound souls. I thought you knew that when you suggested it. You've never mentioned that you wanted children, and we've always been careful about that. So, I thought you were fine with that end."

"No, no, no-" she said, shaking her head and placing a hand on her chest as her breathing hitched. Tears pooled in her eyes. "Zane, you never thought that, maybe, I was waiting to be done with school before being ready to think about children? I don't know what I want, but I wanted options. You're a master tactician. How could you be so-" She caught herself before she blurted something stupid that resulted in an argument.

"Despite our connection, I cannot hear your thoughts," he said with a low growl before releasing a sigh. He sat up and pulled her against his chest. A hand moved up to stroke her hair and upper back. "I'm sorry," he said in a soft voice. He tried not to sound begrudging, knowing that this would not be fun for him.

The tears streaked down Ellyria's face. She sobbed into him. "Fuck!" Her fists balled up, and she pounded his chest in frustration, making herself grunt in pain. "How could I be so stupid?"

"You're not stupid. You do things without thinking them through or without knowing all the details first."

She pulled away, looking up at him. Her face was puffy and red, but not in the demonic way. "I might've wanted to be a mom. Now we'll never know." Her voice cracked.

Zangrunath sighed. "You can still be. Just not like that."

She gulped and nodded. Her throat was thick with emotion. "I just wanted-" She looked down at herself for a moment. The foggy dreams she had of their future together were destroyed before it could even solidify in her mind. She sniffled and pushed away. "I'm sorry," she said as she climbed out of bed. "I need a minute."

He looked at her and sighed. Sometimes, Ellyria's greed was a pain in the ass. The door to the warded spare bedroom slammed shut as he watched her. He thought he heard a muffled scream. He stood up and went about cleaning the house, sending a duplicate to make a dessert for her. If there was one thing he knew for certain after seven years, she liked her sweets after crying herself dry.

# VI



When Ellyria got dressed, she ignored her professional clothing and outfits. Instead, she chose a comfortable shirt and a hoodie with jeans and sneakers. The bar exam was long, and she expected a cold room. Zangrunath, as usual, had her breakfast ready. "I don't want you to take this for me, but," she said between bites, "I need a favor."

He looked back with a curious expression, leaning on the counter. "What's that?" he asked, tilting his head to the side.

"I want you to watch my answers. If I go below the passing rate, I want you to tell me which questions to try again." She sighed. "This is just for insurance. Otherwise, don't interfere."

He nodded. "Will do." He smiled. "All you ever have to do is ask."

"I know." She smiled in return. "It feels like cheating, but I want this."

"You will get it."

She finished her meal and kissed him. She groaned, realizing her mistake. Mornings were still rough on her with the change to the seal. Sleeping was a battle for three weeks but became somewhat normal after they'd purchased a sixth pair of soft sheets, which she deemed soft enough. Zane didn't mess around and purchased ten more sets of the sheets and controlling stock in the company. "Calm down," she said to herself with closed eyes as she focused her mind on other things.

Zangrunath chuckled at her. He knew she was having some difficulty with this transition still, but it was in his nature to enjoy other people's suffering. "Do you want me to drive you so you don't have to take longer to get there?"

"No." She shook her head. "I'm never going to get used to it that way." She took a breath. "This is normal now. I'm still just getting used to it."

"You are doing a great job," he said with an encouraging smile. "I knew you were going to push yourself to overcome this, and I am impressed by how well you are doing. I'm proud of you."

She pulled him into a hug. "I love you," she said before grabbing her keys, purse, and lunch. "Today's going to suck." She groaned while trying to sound positive. "Let's do this thing!" She locked the door and walked to the car. When she noticed the unmarked Section Seven van at the end of the street, she paused, walking over to him. She knocked on his window. "Hey, Larry," she said with an apologetic smile. "I'm taking the bar today. You don't have to follow me. It won't be exciting."

Larry sighed and shook his head. "Sorry, Elly. It's my job. I will stay in the parking lot."

"I would hope so." She laughed. "All of this over casting a couple of minor spells in high school." She shook her head, straightening back up. "Sorry in advance for the boring day."

"It is what it is," he said, waving her back towards her car away from his surveillance van. "Good luck today."

"Thanks." She smiled, walking back to her car and hopping in. The car looked empty, but she spoke to the open air, knowing that Zane was inside and invisible. "He still has no clue, right?"

"Could not have any more of a clue if we spelled it out for him," Zane said with a dark chuckle.

She smirked, taking a breath to steel herself before starting the car. "I will get used to this."

"You're doing great," he said, trying not to mock her misfortunes too much. He liked to tease her, but knew not to anger the woman who could rearrange his atoms.

"Thanks, Lucy, buddy ol' pal," she said, throwing the car into reverse and heading towards the school.

"You like it when you get home," Zane said, whispering the words into her ear.

Goosebumps raised up on her arms at his words, and she shivered. "Oh, it has its benefits, but the drawbacks outnumber them at the beginning. I'll stop calling him Lucy. Don't look at me in that tone of voice," she joked while releasing a sigh.

The invisibility covered up his smirk. "I would appreciate it if you would refrain from angering the Prince of Darkness. It will work out better for us in the future."

"I get it," she said as she parked. She eyed Larry parking a respectful distance away and sighed. "At least, it's just the one. Like Corbin. Should've expected it after the fireworks at the church."

"Yeah, I didn't help with that either," he said with a sigh of his own.

She grabbed her things. "Alright. Mental talk only. Can't have them think I'm cheating."

"Of course. I will try to stay quiet for the entirety of it. I know how much you like interruptions while working."

She looked at her phone and saw a couple of text messages. One was from Steve and the other was from Tom; both wished her luck on her test. She tossed the phone on the seat and locked the door. "I will bend this test to my will." She grinned as she walked towards the building to take her exams.

"You've got this," Zane said through telepathy as she walked into the building. As Ellyria went through security to get into the exam room, Zane checked on the exam itself. He scanned the pages. No one could see the invisible demon. When he finished reading, he smiled to himself. He wouldn't need to tell her anything. She had this in the bag, and he knew it. So, he would still double check her answers like she asked, but he knew he wouldn't have to say a word to her. Everyone else, well, he would enjoy watching the worry and panic on their faces as they struggled.

At the door, Ellyria showed her photo ID and took off her hoodie for them to check it and her arms before she pulled the garment back on. Even though she knew this was serious business, she never realized just how much. She saw a few of her classmates in the room with her, along with a few unfamiliar faces from other schools. She smiled at those she knew and ignored the ones she didn't. At nine, she got her exam. She wiggled and adjusted in the uncomfortable seat, looking at the clock. This was going to be a long day, and after six hours today, she would still have to return for another grueling six hours tomorrow. On the proctor's go, she opened the booklet and got started.

Several hours later, Ellyria ate dinner like a wild animal at home. "How'd I do for day one?"

"You did just fine." He smiled at her. "I didn't think you would need help to begin with."

"Me either, but I still was worried." She sighed, almost inhaling another bite. She forced herself to slow down.

"Calm down. There is plenty of food, and you are not going anywhere. You don't have to inhale your meal."

She nodded. "Sorry. Didn't realize how hungry all of that testing made me." She took a sip of water and looked up at him. "If you don't mind, I'm going to relax in the tub for a bit and pass out for the night. I'm exhausted."

"Have fun." He gave her a knowing smirk as he cleaned the kitchen. "And sleep well," he said, moving to give her a kiss. "Love you."

"Love you," she said before heading off to bed. "I require cuddles later, though."

"I will hold you close as you drift off to sleep."


**Thursday, May 20, 2027**

Ellyria almost overslept. She'd forgotten to set her alarm the previous night, but lucky her, Zane was there. Her eyes peeked open to see his black ones. "Hey," she said as she felt their bond for the day. Her skin crawled just feeling his hand on her shoulder, but she leaned into it instead of recoiling. This needed to become normal again.

"Morning." He gave her a kiss before giving her some space. "Come on. You need to get ready for school."

She growled before forcing herself out of bed as she saw the clock. "Ugh. I slept in."

"I know. That's why I woke you up," he said as he got up to make her a light breakfast. "You just have a little longer before this is all done."

"Waiting on my scores will be the hardest part, but we are going to Europe. So, it'll make it tolerable."

"Oh yes, it will." He smirked while working on her food. "I will get to show you all the sights."

She came out of the bedroom in an outfit similar to the previous day, seeing his look. "I'm not even dressed pretty right now."

"And I would still wreck you like Diana." He chuckled. "I don't care what you wear. I always want you," he said, putting a plate of fruit in front of her.

She covered her mouth in horror. "You can't just say that!"

"Why?" he asked.

"Well, there's respect for the dead." She blushed, covering her face. She grabbed some fruit and ate. "Okay. I was hungry."

"I know. I could tell," he said, leaning on the counter as he watched her eat. "Also, you love it." He smirked.

She nodded and smiled. "Seven years together will do that."

"It has been a fun seven years." He nodded in kind. "I wouldn't change it."

"It has." She smiled, raising an eyebrow as a thought occurred to her for the first time. "Wait a second. What's the soul binding mean regarding marriage and that whole token?"

"Well, thanks to the binding, our souls connect, so I guess you could say we are married," he said, thinking it over. "Even if we aren't, I don't care. I am glad to be with you."

"I just wish I knew about one choice I was giving up." She sighed, looking at the wall with a thousand-yard stare.

He looked back into her eyes with a soft, sympathetic look. He wished he could give her everything she desired, but this one thing, he couldn't. Not anymore. "Sorry, but that is beyond the both of us now."

"I know. I hadn't even thought hard enough on whether I wanted kids to know if I should feel cheated or not. Everything took a backseat as I focused on school, but might've wanted a family."

He reached across the counter and held her hand. "I would rather just have you."

"I would've died trying anyway, or so say, all horror movies." She laughed.

"Not too far off, but not right, either." He shrugged, looking at the clock. "Alright. Enough baby talk. You've got to finish your exam. We have a plane to catch later."

She looked over at the clock. "Shoot. Sorry." She shoveled the last bit of food into her mouth, put the dish in the dishwasher, and grabbed everything she needed before rushing to the car. She looked at her watch and over at Larry in his van. "Great." She jogged over to his van. "I'm running late, so I'm going to be speeding," she said through the window. "See you after my vacation."

He gave her a nod. "Drive safe. Have fun!" He smirked as he started the surveillance vehicle, so he could try keeping up with the muscle car.

Ellyria took off down the street, peeling out. "I can't believe I screwed up my schedule today."

"Calm down," Zane said, using their mental speech. "You will be fine. Just get there and the rest will take care of itself."

"I swear, I'm going to teach myself to ley walk one of these days." She continued to mutter oaths under her breath as she weaved between vehicles.

"When you do that, I might not keep up with you," he said, thinking about his ability to move between sigils and minor teleportation over short distances. "Stupid limits."

She shook her head as she pulled into the parking lot, finding only the furthest spots available. "I can take you with me, according to my grimoire."

"I have never done that," he said as she walked towards the school. "I don't understand the specifics."

"My understanding is that it's watered-down teleportation for normal witches, but since my family can tap the leys anywhere" She arrived at the door to the testing room with about two minutes to spare, leaving her sentence hanging as she went through the same process as the previous day's screening. Then she walked into the testing area, sitting down as the clock struck nine.

"You could teleport anywhere," he said, sounding impressed. "That would save a fortune."

She gave a mental nod. "Only problem is, I'm not sure how discreet it is."

He hummed as he thought. He agreed with her assessment. "It might raise some concerns. It's okay. We will worry about that later. For now, ace this thing so we can go to Europe." He smirked as she got her testing booklet for the day. "We have a club to join."

Ellyria adjusted in her seat, and with the movement, her focus shifted for the next several hours. When she turned in her documents, the proctor reminded the group about the results being mailed to them in about ten business days. A few groans filled the room, but celebration was the general feeling all around as the group shuffled out of the testing area. Ellyria hopped into the Shelby a few minutes later, waving at Larry before heading towards the airport. "Well, three years of school didn't go to waste. You didn't stop me at all."

"You didn't need it." Zane smiled, appearing next to her in the passenger's seat. "You had it in the bag."

"You already know my score, don't you?" She giggled, knowing Zangrunath well by now.

"Of course." A dark chuckle rumbled in his chest.

She looked at him with growing impatience and grumbled. "For the love of Lucifer, Zangrunath."

"You can wait like everyone else." He smirked. "Besides, I plan on distracting you once we get to Europe. You won't have time to worry about the score."

Ellyria sighed, but nodded. "And when we get back, I'm a lawyer."

"With a job already lined up," he said. "No need to worry."

"Yeah. Parker wasn't happy about my contract, but McDonough and Hannon overruled him," she reminded him yet again.

He nodded, having heard it several times before, but he was proud of her. "And I didn't help with any of that. It was all you."

She got irritated at the thought of Mister Parker. "That standard contract was a joke, and he knows it. Besides, after three years, New York calls."

He sighed a bit, knowing she was getting herself worked up for no reason. "I meant that most of it didn't need my help. That was you having your own connections." He reached over, placing a hand on her thigh. He looked at her with a serious gaze and said, "When New York calls, I will make sure your penthouse is ready for you."

"I've got my eyes on a new development I noticed from our last visit." She smirked.

"Really? Which one is that?" he asked.

She shook her head. "Can't remember the name, but I have the website saved on my phone." She pulled it out of her hoodie pocket. "It's going to be open for buyers next year. All the companies seem kosher, and the prices are going to start at twenty million, so I'm assuming the penthouse will be somewhere in the thirties or forties, given the current market."

He took her phone from her as she drove and began scrolling through it. He looked it over and gave a few nods of approval. "If you want it, I will get it. Shouldn't be difficult. I will make sure we have enough money to outbid any other takers." He placed the phone back into her hoodie pocket.

"Oh, we're making this happen." She smiled. "The concept art has me excited."

"Then I will get it." He grinned. Her smile and excitement were intoxicating. "I want to make sure I see that smile on your face."

She showed her identification to a security guard at the airport and pulled into the parking lot next to the hangar. "I'm going to miss you, Shelby baby." She rubbed the steering wheel.

"Don't worry. She will be here when we get back. And if she isn't, I will kill everyone here to find out where she is." An evil grin took his face as he got out of the car.

"There are several movies with similar plots. None of them end well."

"Well, I am a demon, so I think I might have an edge on those human vigilantes," he said, looking proud of his strength and prowess.

She fanned herself and winked at him. "I know it's a bunch of movies, but damn me again, that would be a fight."

He smiled and gave her a kiss. "You just have to tell me to win."

She hopped out of the car, locking it up. She saw Zangrunath had their luggage in tow as they walked to the plane. "This feels like the beginning of a new adventure," she said as she climbed up the steps into the cabin.

He put their luggage away before he sat down next to her and pulled her close. "If I am beside you, I will go anywhere."

"To Hell and back," she said, thinking about those words. She gave him a curious gaze. "Would I get summoned with you now?"

He paused and thought it over for a moment. "I think you would." He didn't know for sure, so he guessed as best he could. "Even if you didn't, we would work hard to get back to one another."

She leaned into him. "Regardless, I'll always be with you." Her hand rested on his chest.

He leaned against her, wrapping his arm around her waist. "And I, with you," he said, giving her a loving kiss.

Their kiss lingered for a minute as the pilot walked by and into the cockpit, laughing at the young couple. As things were closed off and the plane took flight, Ellyria pulled Zangrunath out of his seat. "Let's see about that club." She winked.

Zangrunath followed her and closed the door behind them. "Yes, let's see what the fun is about."

**Saturday, July 17, 2027**

Ellyria dashed around the house, grabbing gemstones and herbs. She shoved those into her overnight bag. She checked herself in the bathroom mirror, making sure that her outfit was perfect. After deciding she looked good, she joined Zangrunath in the kitchen, packing up the dessert for tonight's dinner in a to-go container. She turned to him with a wide smile gracing her features. Excitement overtook her. "Are you ready?"

Zane smirked, holding back a chuckle at her expense. "Of course, I've been waiting for you."

She shook her head at him and gave him a playful push. "Let me just grab one of these delicious brownies and give it to Larry."

"Alright. I'll get everything loaded up in the car for the night," he said, giving her a kiss. His human disguise shimmered into place as he pulled away, grabbing her bag and the food as he strolled out the door.

Grabbing some tinfoil, she wrapped up a brownie and followed Zane out the door, trusting that he had locked up the house well in hand. She strolled towards Larry's van with purpose. She was glad to wear comfy, stylish sneakers instead of heels. Most mornings when she brought items out to him, she wore work clothes and heels, but tonight was just a dinner date. She stopped on the passenger's side of Larry's van and knocked on the window.

He wasn't in the driver's seat like usual. Then again, he was here or following her for at least sixteen hours every day. It was unrealistic to think that he never moved or left the vehicle. She heard some muttering coming from the back. One voice sounded like Larry's, and the other was lower. She guessed it was another somebody coming from Section Seven to check on the agent's assignment, but it didn't matter. She tolerated the guy to keep the Lucifer damned organization off their backs. Larry was ignorant, and that was good for her. The vehicle shook, and a black curtain moved between the back and the front cabin. She waved. "Hey, I brought dessert," she said, loud enough to be heard through the closed window.

Larry popped out into the cabin. He noticed a flash of orange flame come from behind him and winced, hoping that Ellyria was in too much of a hurry to notice. He sat in the passenger's seat and rolled down the window. "Thanks," he said, taking the treat. "Full moon tonight."

"Yep. I've got my visit with Tom. We're having a double date with his girlfriend, Michelle." She smiled. "Anyway, try to get some rest. It's going to be a boring night, as usual."

Larry smiled, nodding as he saw her take a step away. "Will do. Thank you, Elly. Have a wonderful night."

"Thanks." She nodded in kind and headed towards the car. She hopped into the passenger's seat and buckled up. "Alright. Let's head to dinner."

Zane leaned over and stole a kiss from her cheek. "Let's go see Tom and figure out how this date is going to go." He chuckled, curious about how tonight's events would play out.

"Well, it's either going to go well, or Michelle's memory will get erased. If that happens, we'll have to console an upset werewolf." She sighed.

"Then I am glad we are not bringing copious amounts of chocolate cake," he said while driving them towards Tom's new apartment. "That would just be torturous on the guy."

She looked over at him. "Was that a backhanded dog joke?"

Zangrunath looked her dead in the eyes and didn't hesitate. "Yes, it was," he said, focusing his gaze back on the road.

She looked back at him for a long moment before a snicker escaped her lips. "Damn demons." She shook her head and squeezed his thigh. "You're the worst."

He saw the apartment complex come into view and maneuvered them to the correct building before parking the car. He leaned over and gave her a kiss. "You love me despite it all." He smirked, squeezing her hand once as he hopped out of the car.

She got out and went into the back to get her bag, watching as Zane grabbed the dessert. She eyed him for a moment. "I love you," she said just for him as they walked up to Tom's place. "Let's do this."

He held the dessert in one hand as he held her hand with his free one. "We've got this," he said as she knocked on the door.

A moment passed before Tom answered the door with a smile. "Elly, Zane! Hi, welcome. Please come in." He gestured them inside the apartment as a woman stood up from the nearby couch. He let out a small sigh of relief. "Elly, Zane, this is Michelle. Michelle, Elly and Zane."

Michelle walked up and hugged Ellyria first, followed by Zangrunath. "Hello, you two. I have heard so much about you. All good. Sorry. I would apologize for being a hugger, but that's just how I am."

"Nice to meet you." Ellyria giggled, accepting a one-armed hug. "Tom is always talking about how amazing you are."

Zane nodded, getting a hug from the woman and tentatively hugging her back as he moved over to set the dessert on the counter. "He won't stop talking our ears off about you." He chuckled. "Much to our dismay. He can get annoying."

"Oh, be nice," Elly said with a little tut, putting her bag down near the door. "Good to see you, Tom. Glad to hear that your job didn't give you a hard time with taking today off."

Tom blushed, but nodded. "You as well, Elly. They didn't mind too much. I had some time accrued, so I thought it would be nice to have a proper weekend off." His eyes drifted over to Michelle for a moment. He looked anxious.

"They work you too hard there. Just say the word and I'll sue them for violating labor laws," she said, glancing over to Michelle as she took a seat at the table. "I work for a law firm." She flipped some hair over her shoulder. "And they don't have me doing anything."

Tom shook his head. "That would be overkill in way more ways than one." He shuttered. "Pretty sure things will pick up for you soon," he said, sitting next to Michelle on the couch.

"They are just a bunch of jerks." She sighed, glancing back over at Zane. "Sorry. This job has just not started out how I imagined it."

"I'm with you on jobs that pay the rent. I hope it gets better for you. You're Tom's friend, which makes you my friend, and you deserve the best."

Zane leaned in and gave Ellyria a kiss on the cheek. "It will get better. It will just take some time, is all," he said, glancing over at Michelle. "So, what do you do for work?"

Michelle waved a hand. "Retail. It's Hell, but it is what it is."

Zane let out a small chuckle. "Oh, I beg to differ, but I won't try to argue it. People are idiots." He glanced at both Tom and Elly with a significant look on his face.

"Alright, so what do you do that is worse than retail?" Michelle giggled in return.

"I trade on the stock market," he said with a growing smirk. "It is rather high stakes and keeps me thinking several steps ahead."

"And he puts up with me." Ellyria giggled.

Tom laughed at that. "I don't know which is worse, putting up with you or dealing with Wall Street. Either way, he has a full plate."

"It's putting up with me, for sure." She laughed, kissing Zane. "I'm a pain in the ass."

Tom smiled and squeezed Michelle's hand before he looked at the time and stood up. "Well, let's get the dinner started, shall we?" he asked, heading to the kitchen to get the food going.

Michelle stood and followed him. "Of course. Where are our manners? We didn't even make hors d'oeuvres."

Zane stood up, walking over to the kitchen. He gestured for Michelle to sit down. "We've got this. You ladies can relax while the guys slave away," he said, moving to wash his hands.

Ellyria rolled her eyes at Zane, but also knew that the ritual did some weird things to him sometimes, like making him want to check her food for poison, which was annoying and hilarious. "Don't mind him. He basically waits on me hand and foot. I don't even know how to function without him."

Michelle sat down at the table across from Elly. "I would say that I'm jealous, but I don't know how I would handle that. I like my independence."

"I'm plenty independent. Just treated like a princess." She smirked. "I assume it's like Tom treats you. He is always fawning over you, and I can see why. You're super sweet."

"A compliment that I don't deserve." The other woman blushed.

Tom smiled over at her. "Not true. You deserve that and more if I have my way," he said as he filleted some fish to be grilled.

Michelle chuckled. "I just want what every girl wants. Competitive cuddling and chocolate."

"Hear, hear!" Ellyria said.

Zane shook his head and chuckled as he cleaned the vegetables, eyeing Tom as he made the food. He leaned in towards the man and asked, "Do you have any plan on how to tell her, or are you just playing it by ear at this point?" He couldn't help but notice a lack of magic and the supernatural being brought up.

"I don't know how to do this. Just kinda winging it," Tom said. An anxious sound escaped him as he sprinkled some lemon juice into the pan.

Zane paused as he heard that, giving Ellyria a look that screamed, 'you have got to be kidding me'. He shook his head. He started slicing into the veggies as decisive chopping sounds filled the space and sighed. "We will take care of it," he said, trying to think of a way to start this conversation.

Ellyria noticed the look on Zangrunath's face. Nothing quite like seeing an angry demon on the weekend to liven it up. She flipped some hair over her shoulder again, guessing what was going on by appearances alone. "So, what do you do for fun? Movies, games, books?"

Michelle hummed for a moment while she thought. "I don't get as much free time as I'd like, so I tend towards television and movies. Ways to unwind after a long day at work."

"What do you like to watch?" she asked, hoping for a positive response. The last thing she needed to hear was horror movies.

"I'm a sucker for soap operas and romantic comedies, but I will watch just about anything as long as it's good. I don't care about bad television. It's not worth my time."

Elly nodded. Almost as bad as horror, but she could spin this. "I always hate those parts of soap operas where a character reveals a deep part of themselves and the significant other dumps them. Like, what about them changed?"

Michelle sighed as she mulled over the description. "I kind of get that. It depends on what it is. Like, a serial killer is a whole lot of nope, but if it's more like a secret identity or a power, that would be fine. I think I could live with that if all that stuff existed." She giggled.

Elly smirked. Now this was where she wanted it to go. "If all of that was real, it would have to excel at hiding in plain sight." She glanced over at Tom and Zane.

"Who knows what you would have living next to you, then." Zane chuckled. "You could live next door to a dragon and never know it."

"I'm pretty sure that I would notice if there was a dragon next door." Michelle laughed, glancing over her shoulder into the kitchen.

Tom smiled. "I think they would surprise you." He chuckled. "If magic were to exist, I don't see why creatures like that couldn't just change their appearance to blend in," he said while plating up the food as he glanced at Ellyria and Zangrunath.

"And there are plenty of creatures that wouldn't need much to blend in. Witches and werewolves, for instance."

Tom brought over the food and set the plates down at the small dining table. "The only actual issue some of those would have would be during full moons," he said, looking at everyone before digging in. "Enjoy."

"Oh. Thank you, dear," Michelle said, grabbing her utensils. "I'm kind of glad werewolves don't exist. That sounds terrifying."

Tom ate slower as he heard her words. "Why would you be terrified of them? They didn't choose to be that way."

"But they become rabid and attack people."

"Given enough time, I think they could control it," he said, releasing a nervous laugh. "Besides, wouldn't they have magic to help calm them?"

"If they had magic, maybe it could work." Her words hung in the air while she ate. She glanced at Ellyria and Zane. "Are you not hungry?"

"Oh, sorry. Just interested in your opinions," Elly said, before taking a few bites of her own meal.

Zane looked at his food and nibbled on it. "I kind of had a big lunch, so I'm not super hungry. I will try to at least get some of it down. As for the whole magic thing, I think it would be fun. So many possibilities," he said, knowing all too well what it could do.

Ellyria nodded. "Imagine if you could go halfway across the continent in a blink."

Michelle let out a small sigh as she finished her meal. "Traffic would be so much easier to deal with."

Tom chuckled, eyeing Ellyria for a second. "I didn't know you could do that."

"I can't," Ellyria said without thinking, "yet."

Zane released a sigh as he glanced between the pair and saw the confused look on Michelle's face. "As subtle as a porcupine acupuncturist, guys," he said, shaking his head.

"What?" Michelle's mouth opened wide open in shock.

Tom winced as he realized the mistake. He gazed at Michelle and took her hand. "There is more to me and us than I led you to believe," he said, gesturing to Zane and Elly.

"Um, okay? How so?" Her hand shook in his.

He squeezed her hand, hoping to reassure her. He took a deep breath and checked the clock before turning back to look into her eyes. "You know how I was talking about werewolves earlier? A lot of what I said comes from experience."

She nodded. "So, you don't eat people?"

He shook his head. "No. I work hard to make sure there's no chance of me hurting people. I work my schedule around the moon, so it doesn't happen."

"I- isn't tonight a full moon?"

"It is." He nodded, taking a breath as he rubbed her hand with his thumb. "I wanted you to see me for who I am and to prove to you I have it under control."

"And they know about this?" she asked as she caught up on what was happening. One of her fingers pointed towards Elly and Zane, who she wasn't looking at.

"We're the werewolf busters. He can't get past us."

"They helped me get better control." Tom smiled. "Now it's a lot easier to relax on full moons as my other self. It's been a year, and it still feels weird."

Michelle did a double take between Tom and his friends. "Do you become an actual wolf?"

"Yes, and no. I have heard stories of other people like me being able to do that, but I don't have that type of control yet. For now, it's more like the movies, but much less angry," he said, looking at Elly and Zane for help as he gathered the empty dinner plates, bringing them into the kitchen.

"He can talk. It just sounds different. And there's a bit of a physical transformation."

"He is also taller," Zane said, sitting back in the chair and relaxing.

Michelle stared at Tom. "Uh, thanks for trusting me."

Tom plugged up the sink, letting the water run for a moment and setting the dishes inside to soak. He added a good bit of dish soap before turning off the water and walking back to the kitchen table. He stole a kiss from Michelle. "I love you. Why wouldn't I trust you?"

"Because I'm normal and might go running and screaming at any moment?"

He nodded again. "I know. You could." He sighed. "You are worth the risk." Feeling the change taking place, he took several steps back.

Ellyria looked around. "Where'd you put the sigil in your new place?"

He chuckled and pointed beneath them, gesturing to the area rug. "Lucky me, I can hide it well."

"Ugh. I told you not to do that," she said, crossing her arms and leaning into Zane. "Normies can find it way too easy."

Tom shook his head and gestured for her to look more closely. "No, it's the rug," he said, grimacing as he changed. "I talked to a guy-" A grunt escaped his lips as his limbs elongated, and the hair on his extremities grew at an expedited pace until it became a coat of patchy fur in places. He took a breath, looking far more composed after the worst of the transformation. Then he felt well enough to finish the sentence. "And I had the sigil stitched into the rug."

Michelle watched Tom's body contort in fascinated horror. She took several steps back into the wall, making her wonder when she'd even stood up. The only thing keeping her from darting out the door now was the fact that the other couple were much closer to Tom and looked relaxed around the werewolf. "That looks painful."

Tom stood up straight, stretching his body as he adjusted to this new form. He looked into her eyes with his soft brown ones, except now a deep purple hue ringed around them. "It is, but it gets better. What do you think?" he asked.

"Uh, I'm still processing."

"Take all the time you need. I just want you to know that I promise not to bite," he said, trying to liven up the quiet room.

"Yeah. He's pretty chill. It's me or Zane you have to worry about. I'm going to cleanse my stones on your balcony. Do you want me to smudge your apartment?"

Tom thought it over for a moment. "If you don't mind." He smiled at Elly before he made his way to the fridge to grab a couple of beers. "Kind of hard to do things looking like this." He walked up to Michelle with slow, measured steps and offered her one of her favorite local brews of a pineapple passionfruit German ale.

Michelle never felt more grateful to receive alcohol in her life. She drank the beer down to the label before wiping her mouth. "You're doing who, with the what?"

Ellyria rifled through her overnight bag. "I'm clearing dangerous energy from my magic stones with the moon, and I'm going to go do a ritual to make sure ghosts and other unwanted things can't get in or get the Hell out if need be."

"To put it in as simple terms as possible. She is going to make sure the magical security system is functioning right," Tom said.

Zane shrugged and leaned back in his seat. "I suppose that is a proper explanation. Though not what I would have gone with."

"How would you explain it?" Michelle sighed, trying to calm down and failing.

"She is going to have a magical bubble bath to calm the magic down and then pour salt to keep out the ghosts." He shrugged, debating having a drink of his own.

Michelle groaned. "I'm sorry I asked. This is just confusing. Weird is out the window."

"I hate to say it, but weird is pretty normal around me." He eyed her with a curious gaze, unsure of her thought process or reactions still. "It gets easier."

She looked at him and away again, trying to rectify the man and beast together in her mind. "I hope so," she said, drinking more.

Tom nodded and took a step back from her. He wanted to give her some space to process things however she needed. As he moved to the couch to sit down, he sighed. He turned on the television for background noise, but wasn't watching. "Anyone interested in dessert?" he asked, trying to lighten the mood.

Ellyria called out from the balcony. "Yes! I had to smell those brownies for way too long today."

Tom nodded and went into the kitchen. He washed his hands, flicking a finger and extending a claw to cut the treats. After placing them on some paper plates, he handed one to Michelle. He popped outside and left the second on the small balcony table for Elly.

Michelle sat back down and nibbled on the brownie. "Thank you. This is good."

"You're welcome." Zane glanced between the couple, reading the room for all but a second before standing up. "It's not difficult. Just a recipe I found online." He shrugged, moving outside to give them some space.

Ellyria turned to Zane when he came outside. She'd just finished putting out her gemstones. She glanced at the door. "Well, I don't hear running and screaming."

"She is calm. It is possible our calm demeanor rubbed off on her." He shrugged. "Who knows? Maybe she is into it, he said, glancing inside as the couple sat in the room without looking at each other.

"I was." She giggled, stepping over and raising onto her tiptoes to kiss him. "Eventually."

He smirked. "You love every second." He wrapped an arm around her. "And I'm glad you did. It made everything easier for both of us."

She leaned into his form. "And now you're stuck with a crazy witch that doesn't think before she acts."

He smirked and kissed the top of her head. "I wouldn't have it any other way," he said to her.

"Thank you, Zane," she said, grabbing the plate that Tom left and digging in. "We'll give them another couple of minutes."

Zane nodded. "Yeah. I hope they will talk this out and be alright in the end," he said, looking in to see the two still sitting on opposite ends of the couch.

"Maybe she'll lighten up by the end of the night. She was much more fun earlier." She smiled.

He chuckled and nodded. "Which is why I am going to just stay like this all night." He gestured to his human disguise. "I'm pretty sure she would be gone if she found out about the other stuff."

Ellyria hummed in appreciation of the tasty dessert. "I don't blame you. Sorry you can't be yourself."

He shrugged. "Don't worry about it. I will make up for it at home."

She shook her head at him. "I'm hearing, 'I'm not only going to be demonic, but I'm going to turn my arms into foam dart guns and shoot you'."

"Something like that," he said, kissing her cheek. He planned on wrapping her up in his wings for cuddling.

She smiled. "Alright. I'm going to smudge this place."

He smiled and nodded. "Alright. Go all magicky and get this place up to snuff."

She giggled and grabbed a bundle of sage. She opened the door back into the living room. Stopping for a moment, she raised a finger to the end of the herbs and lit them on fire, letting the smoke rise for a moment before blowing it out. She chanted, walking around the place and waving the smoke all around the outer edges of the room. "Don't mind me."

"You're fine." Tom watched her walk around the room. His nose flared, and he closed his eyes. He paused for a long moment before sneezing. "Sorry," he said, moving to blow his nose with a tissue. "Haven't gotten used to smelling that while like this."

"Just be grateful it's not wolfsbane." She headed down the small hallway to the bathroom and bedroom.

"Oh, yeah. That's what I need- a severe asthma attack," he said, shaking his head and taking a long draught of his beer.

"Does wolfsbane hurt you?" Michelle asked.

Tom shrugged. "It's kind of like an allergy," he said, trying to think of the right words. "I can touch it and be fine. If I eat it or smell it, I will have trouble breathing for a while. Eating it will make me sick. Found that out the hard way."

"I'm sorry. I'm glad you're okay."

He smiled. "Thank you. It took some time, but just like any allergy, you get used to it after a while."

She took a deep breath. "Thanks for trusting me. Wish you would've broken it to me a little different, though."

"Sorry." He winced. "I was thinking it over for a long time and every way just didn't seem to work. No matter how I spun the idea around in my head, you left me at the end. I figured that having other people around would make it less weird and more believable."

She sighed. "Other people helped, but seeing you change like that after just being told magic is real is more than a little jarring."

"Again, sorry," he said, moving a hand closer to her. "I'm not the smartest cookie in the lightbulb drawer."

"I don't know how many idioms you just combined into a weird malaphor." She giggled.

"Neither do I, but I'm glad that you smiled." His lips quirked up into a wolfy grin.

"It's easy to smile when you're being a dumbass."

He chuckled. "Well, that's easy. That's my M. O." His hand stole hers, and he stroked the back of it with his thumb. "If you have questions, I will answer them. I am an open book."

She shook her head. "I'm still kind of in shock, so you might have to wait."

"That's fine. Take all the time you need. I'm just glad you're staying around."

"I'm not running and screaming, but only because breaking in a new boyfriend is exhausting." She chuckled, scooting closer.

He smiled. "Thank you. I know it's a lot to take in, but I promise to help you in whatever way you need," he said. "On the plus side, I am warm and soft in the winter."

"Do you change on command or just full moons?" she asked.

"Mostly full moons, but I can change if need be. It just takes a lot of focus."

She bit her lip. "Is it something you can bite and give to other people?"

He chuckled. "No, that's a movie thing. It's passed down. It's a family thing. So, nothing to worry about there."

"Okay." She sighed in relief, looking exhausted.

He wrapped an arm around her. "Yeah, it's not as bad as you think. You can go lie down. By the time you wake up, I will be back to normal, and we can talk about it more in the morning."

She nodded, seeing the other woman walk back into the room, looking just as tired. "Yeah. I think it's about that time."

He nodded. "Go get some rest. Sleep well." He smiled, standing up and helping her to her feet. "I will clean up around here."

She held his hand for longer than necessary and moved in for a kiss. "Goodnight."

He squeezed her hand and leaned in to kiss her, being gentle. "Goodnight. I will see you in the morning. Love you."

She smiled, yawning and heading into the bedroom to get some sleep. "I love you," she said as she closed the door behind her.

Tom watched Michelle head into the bedroom before he turned to look at Elly and Zane. "Thanks for coming over, guys. It helped a lot." He released a sigh of relief. "I don't think I could have done it without you."

Ellyria nodded a couple of times, covering her mouth as she yawned. "Welcome," she said, grabbing her overnight bag and carrying it to the bathroom. "I think it's about that time for me, too."

"Get some rest. I still have stuff to clean up." He went into the kitchen to continue cleaning up. "Sleep well."

Elly got changed and wandered back out to the living room, laying down on the couch. "Zane?" she asked, wanting him close as always.

Zane glanced at Tom and sat down on the couch. He rested Elly's head on his lap. "Yes?"

She smiled, closing her eyes. "I love you. Play nice with Tom."

He leaned down and gave her a kiss on the temple. "I will. I won't do anything too drastic." He chuckled, stroking her hair as he waited for her to fall asleep. "Love you. Sleep well."

Hearing his reassuring words, she relaxed. It was a little bright and noisy in the living room, but within a few minutes, she was sound asleep, using him as her pillow. Light snores escaped her, filling the room with the rhythmic sound.

# VII



Zangrunath rested in bed as Ellyria slept in his arms. He thought about the last couple of months with Elly working at the law firm. He knew she was happy to have a demon on her side, making things go smoothly. It wasn't as perfect as she envisioned it, but he knew it could only improve. He smiled down at her and gave her a kiss.

Ellyria awoke and grumbled something unintelligible. "Don't make me go."

"Sorry, but you have to," he said. "Come on. I will get breakfast started." He climbed out of bed and headed towards the kitchen.

She growled. "But Parker treats me like a glorified intern. It's like-" She sighed. "What's the point?" She got out of bed and got dressed.

"Yes. He is a jerk, but he will get what is coming to him," he said before leaving the room to get the food going. "Worst-case scenario, scare him a bit. He will either stop or I will kill him. Really, no in between."

"Three years at worst," she said to pep herself up more than anything. She came around the corner into the kitchen. "At least I'm helping the fun clients. When they give me clients."

"You will get there," he said, looking up from the stove. "I am still bound to help you."

She pulled on her heels and sat down at the bar stool at the kitchen island. "I know. You're stuck with me."

"Do you hear me complaining?" He smirked as he slid a plate of bacon and eggs in front of her.

She ate, but she made herself go as slow as possible. Dread filled her as the time she needed to leave for work approached. "Nope."

"Good. I know you aren't either." He leaned on the counter to watch her.

She took several bites before speaking. "Given that I made the deal, you can bet that's right."

He leaned in and gave her a kiss on the cheek. "I love you."

She smiled, knowing she didn't have to say it back. "And I you." She took time to finish her meal and cleaned up. "Now off to the second layer of Hell."

He laughed and shook his head. "Not by a long shot. You goof."

"Sure feels like it right now."

"This is nothing compared to Hell," he said. He gave her a nudge.

"At least in Hell, you'd be at my side and not making sarcastic comments into my ear while invisible." She sighed, grabbing her things and a muffin for Larry in his van. "Let's get going."

"This is true." He disappeared with a dark chuckle. "Lead the way, my lady."

She walked out the door and tossed her things into the car before walking over to Larry's van. She knocked on his window. "Hey, man," she said, plastering on a big, fake smile.

"Mornin'." Larry returned the smile, looking distant. "On your way to work?" He chuckled, already knowing the answer.

"Ugh. Yeah." She handed him the muffin through the window. "I believe you said lemon poppyseed was your preferred poison."

He took the pastry with a grin. "Yes. Thank you. It's been a while since I last had this."

"Well, I live to please." She waved. "Off to go deal with the patriarchy."

"Give 'em Hell," he said as she walked away, eyeing her like a hawk while she got in her car to head off for the day.

Ellyria sauntered away, heels clicking all the way back to Shelby. "Still clueless." She giggled as she hopped into the car.

"Ignorance is bliss. Just leave him be. It is better this way."

"It's difficult pretending to be just magical enough for him to need to watch me, but not magical enough for him to report any strange occurrences," she said as they pulled out of the driveway.

"Thank goodness you created enough wards and runes around the house to make him think all is normal. That helps more than you know."

She nodded. "I get it. It's just silly that he gets thrown off hovering a grocery bag into the house when my hands are full every once in a while."

He chuckled. "The look on his face is priceless."

"Someone sent him to check in on my potential misuse of magic. I don't know why he gets surprised when I use it." She shook her head.

"My guess is because he doesn't see it often. Section Seven isn't so much about *using* magic as keeping demons and witchcraft in check."

"Oh, I know. Lesson learned." She sighed. "I hope Larry will still be the guy when we move. He's easy enough to deal with."

"If not, you could always sway him with your charms." He smirked into her head.

She rolled her eyes. "You said charms. I heard breasts."

"And?" he asked, sounding confused, which she couldn't see thanks to the invisibility. "If it works, it works."

She grumbled. "I don't like showing my chest off to get what I want."

"I know. Just remember that I have no issues with you using whatever means necessary to get what you want, so long as no one touches the merchandise."

She barked a laugh at that and pulled into the firm's parking lot. When she got to her reserved space, she growled. Somebody took her spot. Again. "I'm going to cut these interns."

"Would you like me to have their car towed?"

She shook her head, switching over to their mental chat. "No, I'm not that spiteful. I doubt they can afford to get it out if I do that." She wrote the license plate number down and parked in a different spot. "I'm going to find out whose car it is and have a conversation."

"I can't wait to hear that conversation." He chuckled.

"It will sound like underhanded threats and a contract to sign afterwards," she said, imagining the scene in her mind's eye. She grabbed her purse and made her way inside.

"I would expect nothing less from greatness." There was a smile almost visible in his voice, despite his current invisibility. As she walked inside, he grew quiet so she could work without interruption.

Ellyria stopped at the receptionist's desk and gave her the plate information. "Julie, do I need to see you or security to find out whose car this is?"

She looked at the paper and nodded. "I can take care of it. That guy has been doing this way too often." She sighed, opening a document, and looking for the car's owner.

"Thanks, Jul. How was your weekend? Do anything fun?" she asked.

She shrugged as she typed on the computer. "Not much. I just stayed home and caught up on my murder stories." She chuckled. "How about you? Anything interesting in your life?"

"About the same as you." She smiled. "Except I don't bring work home by watching murder stories."

"I just work at the desk." Julie chuckled as she handed her the paper with the man's name. "There you go Elly. Enjoy."

"Oh, I'm going to enjoy this one." She smirked, looking at the name and rubbing her temple. "Dammit, Jeremy."

"Don't give him too much trouble. He's new."

She shook her head. "I'm just going to scare him a bit. I paid my dues as an intern. He can do the same."

"Agreed, and he's kinda cute." She smirked.

Ellyria giggled. "Oh, I see. I'll go easy on him." She winked before strolling over to her miniscule office.

Julie nodded, giving Elly a little wave as she walked away. "Thank you."

"So, what are you going to do to him?" Zane asked, excitement in his voice.

"I'm going to ask for coffee, have him sit down and tell him off. If it happens again, I'll tow the car."

He let out a small sigh. "I would have just towed it, but you are in charge."

"I'm doing Julie a solid. The receptionist is always a good friend to have," she said.

He thought it over and gave her a mental nod.

She sat down and booted up her outdated desktop. It was taking forever to load. "Oh, joy."

"I know. Ours are much faster." He chuckled.

"I'm going to throw this thing." She sighed as she typed in her password. "They could at least give me a computer from this decade."

"Yeah. Twenty seventeen wasn't that great for computers." He sighed, trying to lighten things up as best he could.

"This operating system is ancient," Ellyria said as she opened the company's instant message system and sent a message to Jeremy. "Well, coffee inbound."

"I will sit back and watch the show."

She nodded, checking her emails as she waited. "I'll try to make it good."

"Thank you. It's almost like watching television. You are my entertainment."

She rolled her eyes, firing off a couple of responses before Jeremy walked in with her coffee. She looked up from her work before smiling. "Thanks for bringing that in, Jeremy." She gestured to the seat across from her. "Please sit."

"Um, okay." He nodded, sitting across from Ellyria and looking at her in confusion. "Is everything alright?"

"Yes, and no. I need you to do something important for me, though." She waited for him to respond.

"What is that?" he asked, nerves clear in his tone. He shifted in his seat in sudden discomfort.

She gave him a no-nonsense gaze. "Go out to the parking lot and look at where you parked this morning."

"Uh, what?" He looked like he wanted to say more, but stood up anyway.

"You heard me. Go look. Then come back."

Jeremy seemed somewhere between shaken and confused. He walked out of the office, leaving for several long minutes before he walked back into the room with a sheepish expression. "I- um, I'm sorry."

She sighed, looking over at him. "It happens. It's obvious you were in a hurry, but you're not earning any brownie points or favors from me at the moment."

"It won't happen again," he said with a nod. "I will go move my car now."

"No." She waved a hand. "I'm busy and won't move Shelby for something so silly. It's yours for the day, but if it happens again, I'm towing it."

"Yes, Miss Grant," he said, hanging his head in defeat. "It won't happen again. Will that be all?"

"No." Ellyria smirked. "Julie likes three creams and one sugar in her coffee."

He raised an eyebrow, but nodded. "Okay. I will go get that for her now."

"Thanks." She smiled, waving him off and going back to work. "Now, to pretend they've given me anything to do with my law degree."

Zane mentally smiled. "You've got this. Just a few more hours, and you can head home."

"I'm always home when you're around," she said in a corny voice.

He sighed as he noticed Steve McDonough walking up to her office. "Incoming."

She nodded, looking up to see Steve at her door. "Hello, sir."

"Good morning, Ellyria." He smiled as he let himself in. "How are you doing today?" he asked, shutting the door behind him.

"I'm doing well," she said, smiling despite herself. "Please tell me you have something? A business deal? Hell, I'd take a prenup at this point."

"I have something for you, something that I know you can handle," he said before placing a folder on her desk. "I have a case that needs a certain discretion. The client is a caster like us. They're trying to charge him for a crime he didn't commit."

She looked at the documents. "A defense case. Not my specialty, but if they're like us, I'll take care of it."

"That is where it gets interesting." His smile grew. "The guy who did it has a demon."

"Do we know which one?" she asked.

"No clue." He shrugged. "My guess is that it is a deal, but if it is a ritual, you are the best person we've got."

She smirked. At least he gave her something *interesting*. "I would be the expert after March."

"Yes, you are." He chuckled at her as he walked back out the door. "This is yours. Give 'em Hell."

She stood up and moved around the table to take her new client's hand. "Good to meet you." Ellyria gestured to a chair. "Please make yourself comfortable."

"Thank you," he said, sitting down in the offered seat. "I'm Michael. Mike to my friends."

She waved a hand and closed the door behind him. "And I'm Ellyria Grant."

Mike released a sigh of relief as she shut the door with magic. "I'm glad that you won't think I'm crazy then. I hate normal people. They're so boring."

She looked over her shoulder at the blank space. "Zane?" she asked.

Zane appeared next to her and smiled at the man. "Yes, Ellyria?"

She smirked. "Thanks. Just needed to prove a point for that one." She turned back to Mike. "You can tell me anything, and I will believe it."

Mike nodded, eyeing Zane as he disappeared again. He looked back at Ellyria before he sighed with relief once again. "Thank you. That makes me feel better."

She used some magic to flip open his file, glancing through it. "So, what's going on?"

"About a month ago, I was coming back from a ley line. Just needed to meditate, ya know? On my way back home, I was driving across a bridge when I see this car come speeding across the way. I thought I was going to get hit and reacted naturally. Instead of swerving, I put up a wall of force, but the other car veered off before it hit and careened into a bus." He stopped short of finishing his story, trying to shake the memory from his head. "The bus went up in flames. A couple of people got injured, and an elderly woman died. I saw a demon come out before sprinting away," he said, shaking a bit. "Mine was the only other car on the road, and the police thought I caused the accident. I did nothing wrong."

She nodded. "Well, the good news is that it looks like there are some excellent witnesses to use to corroborate that. The bad news is, if it is a demon, we're going to need to get to them before it does." She paused for a minute. "If it ran away, it sounds like he was some low-level scum. Zane would've turned to mist before leaving."

"I hope it works out that way. I really don't want to be blamed for the damage that was done. It feels like I can still hear the screaming," he said, holding his head and trying to block out the memories.

She reached across the table and took his hand. "It's okay. After this is all over, we can erase the memory."

He looked at her. "Maybe. I don't like the idea of messing with people's heads. Even if it is hard to remember."

"It's always up to you. Now it looks like you have an excellent case. I want you to go home, ward the ever-living Hell out of your house and keep a low profile. I'll take care of the rest."

He nodded. "I already warded my house, so I will just keep lying low until you say otherwise."

She shook her head, taking out a piece of paper and drawing a couple of simple, linear runes. "With these?"

"No," he said, taking the paper from her and drawing far more intricate runes with large sweeping curves and swirls. "These."

She looked them over. "You need to add these." She drew another rune, which was based on the thick, scratching strokes of the demonic language. "With these, if you amp the power up over a few days, even Zangrunath wouldn't be able to get in. Maybe." She gave a cheeky grin. "Regardless, low-level demons would struggle against it."

He looked the sigil over and nodded. "Thank you." He stood up. "I will go home and add those right away."

She tossed him a charged piece of malachite. "You can borrow that one. I know warding can take a lot out of us."

He caught the gemstone and smiled, taking a few steps back. He pulled out a piece of opalite. "Thanks. I will give it back the next time I see you."

"You're welcome." She waved. "Have a good day."

"You, too," he said, tracing sigils into the air before vanishing into a wisp of smoke.

"Nice exit strategy. Not ley walking, though." She turned around to look at the space she best guessed Zangrunath would be in. "If there's a demon involved, I'm worried about the witnesses."

"Yes. It would mean he either earned the demon's ire or it didn't kill its mark. Then it would try to clean up its mess." He appeared, giving a decisive nod as he best explained the demon's reasoning.

She sighed. "I don't like either of those options."

"Well, lesser demons have little control. They throw themselves at the job until they get it done."

"So, we also need to figure out who or what is behind this. Otherwise, it will keep happening."

"Yeah." Zane sighed. "If we cut the head off, the demon ceases to exist on this plane."

She nodded. "Well then, I'll go make sure the witnesses are as safe as I can make them while we wait for this court date, and you go find out who this demon is and eliminate its master. We'll get some fun for you after all."

He smirked and gave her a kiss. "Thank you. I have missed going and extracting information the fun way."

"If you go down below, say hi to the boss man for me." She chuckled.

He shook his head at her. "I won't do that unless I have to. For now, I will do this the old-fashioned way. Torture."

Ellyria kissed him, shivering a little at the thought of what he was looking forward to. "Enjoy," she said, as if she was telling him to have a fun night out with the boys at the bar.

She grabbed her keys and purse before she marched across the office to see McDonough for a moment. "I'm going to go speak with our witnesses. I'm worried about their wellbeing."

Steve nodded. "That is why I let you take it rather than doing it myself. You have a better relationship with Zane. He listens to you."

Ellyria nodded. "You need to transfer that thing," she said.

"I'm working on it." He sighed. "You make sure they are safe." He waved her off.

"You get this court date moved up, and they will be."

He nodded. "I will see what I can do."

Ellyria walked out to her car and plugged in the first address on her GPS, following the instructions before she made it to a gated retirement community. She sighed, but explained the situation to the irate security guard before he let her through. The house was a little run down, but still nice. She parked and cast a heavy non-detection spell on herself as she warded the house against demons. Before she knocked on the front door, she went to go talk to Larry, who was still following her in his surveillance van as usual. She knocked and got into the van with him, letting the spell fade so that he could see her. She sighed. "You're going to see weird shit today."

Larry jumped and looked startled as the passenger door opened of its own accord. In the back of the van, a body moved and shifted before quieting down again. He glared into the dark space. "Weird how?" he asked as the witch sat down in Section Seven's van.

"Look, I know you are at least familiar with what I am and what I do, but I know you don't always know what I'm *doing*." She covered her face and groaned for a moment. When she took her hands away, she glanced around the vehicle. A lot had changed about the religious sect's vehicles since she had last stolen documents from one. There was a lot less identifying information in the van that indicated the owner of the vehicle. Her eyes settled on Larry's hip to notice that he didn't have one of the nasty holy magic imbued guns at his side. Ignoring it with a little shrug, she started talking as she'd intended to do. "Under normal circumstances, I wouldn't do this at stranger's houses, but I just got a client that has a demon after him."

A look of startled surprise washed over Larry's face. "Oh. Well, I mean- I can't stop you. You are helping someone. I just need to report anything out of the ordinary. Maybe I can let this one slide."

She sighed. "Don't get in trouble for me. I just wanted you to know. It's sad, but I'm used to Section Seven being around in my life. Thanks to my Mom, I had a bunch of agents at my house when I was younger. I thought they were DEA for several months. I don't want to live like that again. At least it's just you," she said, glancing into the back where she'd heard somebody moving a moment before. "Most of the time."

He did a double take, looking from her into the back. He couldn't see the other occupants of the vehicle, so he waved it off. "Thanks. We aren't bad guys. We are trying to keep the balance. That's all. Some might see us that way, but people shouldn't be able to do the things you do. It's just- wrong. You know?"

"I try not to do anything world altering." She nodded, letting out a sigh. It was accurate enough. She had used mind blowing magic, but it hadn't changed the world, mostly just her own. "I know there's some of us who don't give a damn about that." She gazed at the house. "Protecting is worth all the energy it takes, though."

"That we can agree on." He smirked, gesturing for her to step out. "You go do what you need to do. I will tell them what they need to hear."

She nodded, heading back towards the house. She knocked on the door, and an elderly woman in a pink wig with big, oversized glasses that dominated her face opened it about two minutes later. "Hello, Missus Hayworth." She offered her hand. "I'm Miss Grant, a lawyer representing the gentleman about the incident on the bridge about a week ago."

Missus Hayworth thought about Ellyria's explanation for a moment. "Oh yes. Mike was his name. Good lad. He was a bit shaken up. Is everything alright?"

Ellyria smiled at the woman's concern. "He's well for the time being, but it's my job to make him the best case possible. So, I was wondering if I could borrow some of your time to take a statement? I want to make sure that I understand everything that happened."

"Of course," Missus Hayworth said, letting Ellyria into her house. "Can I get you something to drink?"

"Just water please," Ellyria said, sitting at the dining room table. She took out a tape recorder and a legal pad and pen. Her eyes darted around the room to check for any signs of current or former demonic presence. "You have a beautiful home."

"Thank you. I work hard to keep it that way." She chuckled, coming back with the water. "So, what would you like to hear?"

Ellyria smiled. "Would you mind if I record this?"

"Go ahead. I don't mind." The older woman smiled.

Ellyria started the tape recorder. "Today is Monday, August second at," she checked her watch, "ten fifty-eight a.m. Location is at Missus Darlene Hayworth's residence. My name is Ellyria Grant. Missus Hayworth, could you please state your name for the record?"

"Darlene Hayworth."

"Thank you, ma'am. As you know, this is regarding the accident at the Western Avenue bridge. Could you please describe what you witnessed in your own words?"

"Yes. I was walking our dog Lucy at Riverside Park near the bridge when it happened. I honestly don't think I would have noticed if Lucy hadn't barked. When I turned around, I saw the driver of the other vehicle hit the bus. Then the bus caught fire." She paused for a moment, trying to think of the right words. "Then, an animal ran away from the fire. Maybe it was a dog or a raccoon? I am not sure, but it was bigger than normal and ran like it had an injury of some sort. As for Mike, it looked like he avoided being hit himself. He didn't hurt anybody. It was all whoever was in that other vehicle."

Ellyria nodded. "Thank you, Missus Hayworth. I'll save my questions for the courtroom. I know you've already written a statement for the police report, but if there's anything you'd like to add before the time comes, please let me know." Ellyria fished out one of her business cards and handed it to the other woman.

Darlene thought for a moment. "I don't know if it will help, but I think the driver had a tattoo on his arm. It was big and looked like the Roman number for one." She gestured to her arm to show the size.

"Let the record show that Missus Hayworth gestured from just below her shoulder down to her elbow," Ellyria said for the recording.

She nodded and thought for a moment. "That is all I can remember."

"Thank you, Missus Hayworth. Recording end time eleven fourteen a.m." She clicked the stop button on the machine.

"No problem, Miss Grant. I am glad I could help." Darlene smiled.

Ellyria packed up her things and reached across the table to shake hands before showing herself out. "Thank you so much for your time, ma'am. I look forward to seeing you again."

"No problem. It was nice having the company. Have a wonderful day, Miss." Darlene stood up, showing Ellyria to the door.

Ellyria walked out to Shelby and took the tape out of her recording machine, replacing it with a new one before putting a label on the old one and placing it inside of her lead-lined briefcase for good measure. "With magic involved, it's my best bet." She rested her head on the back of the seat for a second before starting her car. She had more witnesses to see. "I hope you're having more fun than me, Zangrunath," she said via their mental speech.

Zangrunath was at the scene of the crime when Ellyria spoke to him. "So far, just more questions," he said as he surveyed the area and pieced together where the demon came from and ran to. There was just one problem. The paths didn't add up. He shook his head; something wasn't right. The car crashed the way it did, but there should have been no way for the bus to catch fire. He closed his eyes and sniffed around for demons. He froze. There wasn't one demon; he smelled two here. "We have a problem."

"I only accept bad news on the third Thursday of each month between the hours of one and two after I've eaten ice cream," she said as her mental voice oozed sarcasm.

"Well, that is a problem for a different day, because there wasn't one demon here. There were two."

"Great!" She punched the gas, and a growl rumbled in her chest.

"I know. I am just as confused as you." He sighed and followed the trail of the closest scent. "I will see what I can find out."

She smiled. "If you catch anybody, destroy them with prejudice."

"With pleasure." He smirked, and his nostrils flared as he did his best to follow the old scent.

Ellyria spent the afternoon with home visits to as many witnesses as she could. Over and over, it seemed to be the same story. Mike didn't cause the problem. The demon did. So, why was Mike arrested? That piece of the puzzle made little sense to her, but she hoped to figure it out soon. She arrived at the apartment complex of the last witness around three thirty, and as she was getting out of the car, the sound of gunshots rang out around the area. She ducked back into the car and screamed for Zane.

Zane appeared next to her in a puff of brimstone, covering her body with his own. "What is going on?" he asked with a snarl, searching for the source of the gunshots.

"I was going to see another witness. Then there were gunshots out of nowhere," she said as her body shook with adrenaline and panic.

"Stay down," he said as he blinked away and searched for the source of danger. He wound through the building before finding a door that was wide open. He approached the entrance with cautious steps, looking inside to find a man lying against the back wall of the apartment. The bullets tore the man's body to pieces with bullet wounds. He released a growl before searching for the shooter. Not finding any enemies nearby, he checked the nameplate on the door and sighed. "Elly, what was the witness's name?" he asked out of morbid curiosity.

"Elijah Montgomery."

Zane sighed. "Well, he's dead," he said. "They shot him all to Hell."

"Demons?"

"Demons don't use automatic weapons," he said, seeing the number of shells on the ground.

"This just got complicated." She grabbed her phone and hit Steve's contact info. It rang three agonizing times before he answered.

"Hey, Elly. What's up?" Steve asked.

"I'm lying on the floor of my car after hearing one of our witnesses get murdered maybe fifty feet away from me," she said. "I need a better court date."

Steve audibly deflated over the phone. "I will work faster." The line disconnected soon after.

Ellyria sat up in her car, looking all around the complex for anything suspicious. She saw nothing, so she tried concentrating on magic. She was getting a ping nearby, turning her head to see a flash of a figure before it disappeared. Another groan escaped her. "The danger's gone for now."

Zane growled and appeared next to her. "What is this case?" he asked her, sounding pissed beyond reason.

"Someone trying to frame a magical person to get them into prison, I guess?" She shrugged. "Regardless, I'm done for the day. Gunshots are where I draw the line."

"We are heading home." He nodded in agreement, gazing back at the apartment and shaking his head.

She held his hand for a second before letting go. "I love you." Starting up the car, she took off towards their place, revving the engine a bit.

He squeezed her hand in a gentle, reassuring manner. "I love you, too."

They sat in companionable silence for the drive. When they got home, Ellyria locked the door and started walking to the back door instead. "I'm getting in the hot tub. I need to relax."

Zangrunath nodded. "You do that. I am going to keep an eye out around the house," he said. Ever vigilant, he gazed out the front window.

"Should I strengthen the wards?" she asked, pausing halfway out the back door as she was kicking her shoes off.

He looked for a moment, shaking his head. The only thing he saw out front was Larry and his van. "No. Between a witch, a demon, and Section Seven outside, we should be fine."

"With you around, I could never worry." She smiled.

He eyed her and smirked. "I know. Now I just need to be more careful than ever before, is all. I can't be as reckless as I was in the past."

She shuddered, finding it hard to imagine Zangrunath being afraid of anything. "What happens now? If-"

"Everything gets amplified," he said. "The good *and* the bad. If I get hurt, it will feel excruciating for you."

"Thank you for worrying about me." She walked back inside and kissed him, stepping out back again to get into the hot tub.

"I will always worry about you," he said, following her out into the backyard and stealing a kiss. "We are one. We need to watch each other's backs."

She nodded, touching the crystal around his neck and charging it with magic. "We do."

"Thank you." He smiled, stealing another kiss. "You make me far stronger than I have any right to be."

"I could say the same about you. I summoned the Devil because of your help."

He shook his head. "You did that by yourself. I was just there."

She tossed her suit jacket over a lawn chair, giving him a deadpan stare. "I felt how tired you were afterwards. Don't lie to me."

"You know I can't." His voice rumbled deep in his chest as he growled in a flirtatious manner. "It was you alone who summoned him. I couldn't muster that kind of power if I tried."

"I used yours, though," she said. "I felt it."

"You drew some of my power, yes." He sighed, stepping into her space. His face loomed over hers as if he were about to steal her lips for a fiery kiss. His fingers trailed down her side softly. "In the end, you were still the one who did it."

She sighed, dropping the argument in favor of enjoying his attention. She giggled at him. It was so easy for her to get him to flip that switch between raging in anger and love or adoration. She started unbuttoning her blouse. "Prepare for a back massage. Today has been Hellish."

He pressed the electronic panel a couple of times for her to get the jets going. "Just be sure to start out slow on the settings."

Ellyria gave him a playful swat as he stalked off, shaking her head at him. It had been five months since the soul binding. The change wasn't so bad anymore, and she only had moments of difficulty now. She followed his suggestion, though, and soon found herself fast asleep in the hot tub.

Zangrunath finished making her dinner, stepping outside to check on Elly. He smirked as he saw her sleeping soundly in the tub, lifting her out to bring her into the bedroom. He wrapped her up in a towel to dry her off. Placing her on the bed, he let her rest a moment as he packaged up the meal that he made for her. It could be her lunch for tomorrow. Then he went back to join her in the bedroom. He laid down next to her, holding her close to him to help keep her safe. He wanted to keep her protected. She was his, after all.

Tuesday, August 3, 2027

Ellyria's phone rang, waking her up at two thirty in the morning. She saw the caller and groaned. "Hey, Steve," she said in a tired voice.

Steve didn't hesitate to dive right into the conversation, sounding as tired as she felt. "They killed another witness."

"Is there magical witness protection?" she asked.

"Not to my knowledge." He sighed. "Besides, we couldn't do it to people who don't use magic. That would anger Section Seven."

She growled under her breath. "What about warding their houses when I go to visit them?"

"No. That shouldn't piss them off as long as the people in question don't know that magic exists."

She sighed in relief. "What do you need from me, boss?" Ellyria asked with closed eyes and growing sarcasm. "Just called to give me the fantastic news?"

"Don't bother coming in today. Focus on figuring out what is going on. I will compensate you for the time. This can't keep happening," he said, yawning as he spoke.

"Consider it done. Whoever is coming after Mike just made this personal."

"Good," he said, sounding vengeful as he hung up the phone.

Ellyria sat up. Now she was wide awake. "Alright. I'm up. Who's dying?"

"Just give me a name and I will mount their head above the mantle," Zane said with an evil grin.

"I don't know, but we're going to find out. What do you need?"

"If we can get a demon, we can get a name," he said with a decisive nod.

She brushed her hair out of her face while thinking. "To Missus Hayworth's house."

"Get dressed and lead the way." His leg bounced in anticipation, already prepared for battle.

She hopped out of bed and got into street clothes. "We can't get into her community at night, so we're flying."

"So be it." He nodded. "Just point me in the right direction."

She jumped into his arms. "Head towards the office. It's close."

He smiled down at her and stepped outside. His thumb lightly rubbed reassuring circles on her shoulder. He shrouded the two of them in mist, spread his wings and took off towards the office.

Ellyria kissed his cheek. "Thank you."

"You're welcome." Zane smiled and gave her a kiss on the temple.

"Who would've known when we met that I'd feel this bloodthirsty?" She wondered when she became a magical bounty hunter or whatever, rather than a lawyer.

"I wouldn't have believed it." He chuckled. "It would have made this far more interesting if you were like that when you were younger."

She shivered. "I would be a literal psychopath now."

"Then I would have fallen for you in another way." He smirked.

Ellyria leaned into him. "You're insane."

"Of course, you don't go to Hell and come out a better person." He chuckled as they flew through the night sky.

"I'm going to Hell, and I feel pretty good about it." She giggled.

"I give it a century or two before you snap," he surmised. "Either way, I will be there to see the blood."

She shook her head. "I think my dark side and yours are just a tad different."

"Complimentary dark sides." He chuckled.

"You can be murderous, and I'll be manipulative."

"That is fine by me." He nodded, holding her a little closer.

"Yours."

"Mine," he said, giving her a little squeeze.

She pointed down to the buildings they needed. "It's down in there somewhere."

He nodded and flew closer to the ground. "Just tell me where to land," he said, glancing from house to house with his superior night vision.

Ellyria squinted, trying to find the right house in the darkness, eventually finding it by sensing her own magic guarding the house. She was about to point it out when a flash of light lit up the wards. "Not good."

Zane swooped to the ground and set her down a suitable distance away from the house. "Stay here. I will go find out what the problem is," he told her as he disappeared, making a beeline for the house.

Ellyria bit her lip before running towards the house. She needed to be there to help, but she was so focused on what was ahead of her that she didn't notice what was looming nearby in the shadows.

A set of demonic eyes trained on Ellyria, and as she ran to help Zane, the low-ranking demon growled, sprinting after her. It wanted to get a snack. It caught up to her fast, and in a swift strike, razor sharp nails sliced into her leg. When she toppled to the ground, it circled her like a shark.

Ellyria tumbled to the ground in a heap. She screamed at the pain, and her entire body jerked with a convulsion. She hadn't gotten injured since the soul binding. The worst instances were the few times she'd stubbed her toe or bumped her head. This felt akin to being stabbed twenty times. She righted herself, looking around in a panic. When she saw the glowing eyes of her attacker, her hand moved to cover the injury, and she threw out a hasty wall of force to keep the unknown demon away.

As the wall of force wrapped around Ellyria, an enormous wall of fire erupted around the demon. Zangrunath appeared between them, seething in anger. He glanced at Ellyria. "Are you alright?" he asked with a bloodthirsty growl.

"I'm fine! Do what you need to do."

"My pleasure," he said, glowering at the demon that was trying to escape the circle of fire. He chuckled darkly as it tried and failed to run away. Lesser demons were pathetically weak. It was laughable. He walked through the flames unaffected and ripped the legs off the demon. He smirked as the whelp in front of him recoiled in pain. The squelching sounded like music to his ears. It clawed at the ground, trying to get away. Black, ichory blood spilled all over the circle. Zangrunath picked up the demon by its hair and held it up to look into its eyes. "Tell me who your master is," he demanded, grabbing part of the demon's exposed bone and twisting it slowly.

The demon released an ear piercing howl and tried to slash at Zangrunath, to no avail. The superior demon kept it at arm's length. By the sheer force of Zane's strength and will, it couldn't get any good licks in despite its best efforts.

Zane growled and ripped out the bone that was in his hand, tossing it to the side. "Tell me or I keep doing this until you are a breathing torso," he threatened. His nails dug deeply into the other demon's flesh. Pin pricks of black blood oozed from the wounds.

The demon screeched and wailed as Zangrunath tore it apart bit by bit. It raised a hand to its throat. There were several garish white scars marked the red skin. The markings formed into a rough, but visible, rune that functioned as a way of silencing overly talkative demons. It was a punishment from Hell itself, or the demon's master didn't care for its opinions. Regardless, it revealed that the whelp couldn't speak.

"Fuck!" Zane said, ripping off the demon's arm and tossing it to the side. "This was a waste of time."

As Zane turned to walk back to Ellyria, the demon that was bleeding out released a call that echoed through the night. Zane turned to glare at the demon with wide eyes before three more demons leapt through the fire, attacking Zane all at once. In perfect sync, they jumped and clawed at him in an attempt at rending flesh from bone as they landed on him.

Zangrunath let out a scream of pain. When he had a moment to recover, however, he grabbed one of the three demons by its tail. His grip was vice-like as he swung the weakling around like a rag doll, using its body as a weapon against the other two. He crushed two of the heads together. The second demon fell to the ground in a daze momentarily. With a wrenching motion, Zane removed the tail and spine from the one he was swinging around in one fell swoop. He took the gory and sinewy bone, wrapped it around the third demon, and used it to strangle the last demon that had attacked him. He held the demon as he watched the life fade from its eyes and crushed the head of the second. A moment later, he looked at the one who had unleashed the call and found that it was dead as well. He snarled and turned back around to help Ellyria. He knew she would be in pain.

Ellyria let the wall of force fall and grabbed onto Zangrunath, tears in her eyes. She had felt every blow the same as him. She didn't even attempt to get up. It hurt far too much to try. When he knelt, she leaned into his shoulder and sobbed. "Ouch."

"I know," he said as his body regenerated. "I'm sorry. Neither of us expected anything like that," he said as he picked her up. "What sort of sick bastard makes a horde pact?!"

Ellyria concentrated through both of their searing pain for a moment before the injury on her leg healed with magic. She clung to him as she grunted at the sensation of the forced expeditious healing. She did her best at ignoring the associated itching that went along with it. "What is a horde pact?"

Zangrunath shook his head and looked down at her with concern in his eyes. "In layman's terms, it is as close to summoning me as one can get, but instead of one, you get six. They can go farther, attack individual targets and work as a unit if need be. And everything they see, their master sees. It is like a hive mind."

"How can we find their master?" she asked, wiping away her tears.

"It works differently from our deal. The person would need a large amount of magic to sustain it, so they would probably be at a ley line right now," he said, wiping a stray tear from her face.

Ellyria looked at him and took a calming breath. "Hang on." She closed her eyes, reaching out magically and feeling the leys. The magic came to her beck and call. She opened her eyes. It looked like lightning wreathed her irises, and instead of brown, there were black orbs staring back. It was like a miniaturized, controlled version of the demonic transformation she experienced after being marked fallen. "I think I found them."

"Show me." The phrase sounded like an order but also a statement of tantamount trust.

She thought for a moment, remembering the passages of her grimoire. She understood the concepts of what she wanted to do, but she had never tried before. Part of her had been waiting to test it out in a more controlled setting when she had spare time in case something went wrong, but desperate times called for desperate measures. She was exhausted, in pain, and just wanted the threat of a group of demons attacking to be in the past. She pulled magic around them. Her eyes firmly closed as she focused on latching onto the ley line. Keeping concentration and focus, she visualized what she wanted. A gut churning sensation washed over her, and had her eyes been open, she would've seen night turn into day before they appeared at the center of the active ley she'd found. Her eyes opened, and her head spun. "Woah," she said, feeling off kilter from using the new magic.

Zane felt dizzy as well, recovering fast and taking a knee to set Ellyria down. He looked around the area and saw a van sitting not too far away. Zane took a few steps forward before he paused. The van looked familiar. "What the Hell?" he asked in confusion.

She bent over and put her head between her legs. "What?" The recovery from what she'd just done held most of her attention now.

"Isn't that Larry's van?" he asked, making sure he wasn't seeing things.

She glanced up. "I see the shape, but your night vision is better than mine."

Zane nodded. He'd forgotten about that detail, sending her the visual with telepathy. As he did so, he watched the pocket door slide open. A second later, two demons darted from the van, charging at them as snarls and howls released from their throats instead of words.

Ellyria heard the door of the van open and the vehicle's engine start. She reached deep into herself and added weight to the barely visible vehicle. A scream of frustration and the buckle of the vehicle's chassis filled the air. She tried to stand, but the magic she'd used the day before and just now had been too much. She fell.

Zangrunath growled and turned his arms into blades as he charged the two demons. After dodging their pathetic attacks, he sliced them into minced meat. He glared at the van, storming towards it, and changed his arms back. He wrenched open the door, ripping it from the vehicle with a metallic screeching. Reaching in, he dragged the driver from the vehicle and threw them towards the center of the field closer to Ellyria, who nearly passed out. He had time now to look at the driver. It was Larry, and he looked terrified to see a demon far larger and more intimidating than what he had summoned.

"Zane," Ellyria said in exhaustion. She wanted to sleep, but knew it was way too dangerous. She tapped the ley to regain her strength in a more expeditious manner.

Zane strode forward and picked up Larry by the collar of his shirt. "So much for playing the fool," he thundered. Where Ellyria had unconsciously borrowed his power before, he was doing the same now. The clearing they were in rumbled, and the surveillance van tipped onto its side, crashing into the trees beside it, thrown like a child's toy by the wave of powerful magic.

Larry looked between Zangrunath and Ellyria. His eyes widened. He tried to wiggle out of the demon's grip, but exhaustion from the pain of losing his demons, getting thrown a hundred feet, and the magic from all the executions he'd orchestrated hindered him. "Fuck you both!" He spat into Zangrunath's face. "You are what's wrong with this world. A half angel that does literally nothing good for people who are suffering. I'm glad that you went to that church. I hope the Vatican hunts you for the rest of your life. You deserve to live in fear, just like everybody that you terrify with that unnatural power of yours!"

"You framed the innocent. You killed people for speaking the truth. The Vatican observes, keeps the order. What sort of end justifies the means?" Zangrunath asked, shaking Larry and hearing a satisfying pop.

"He was just going to use his power to mess with more people," Larry said. He coughed as he struggled with the pain of being made a demon's rag doll. When would his literally damned summons make it back? He needed some backup here. "And those people were just as bad. They wanted to protect that monster. They could have helped that bus, but they stood there and watched as people died!" He coughed again and blood came out, splattering on his face. He grew pale, processing that this was the end. His head turned towards Ellyria. His eyes were dull and cold. "No witch I observed ever helped anybody other than themselves. Rot in Hell, bitch."

"I trusted you. Murderer!" Ellyria screamed the accusation, pointing at him. Magic formed as she lost her temper and a pointed spire of earth shot from the ground near her hand, extending and careening towards him in an instant. The clearing was silent for but a moment before a loud squelching echoed throughout as the makeshift, natural spear pierced Larry through the heart. She hyperventilated, realizing what she'd done, and the magical stalagmite crumbled to the ground, reforming with the earth. Blood sprayed everywhere, covering both Zane and Ellyria.

Quick on his feet, Zane sidestepped Ellyria's attack, holding the Section Seven agent in place. He glared into Larry's eyes, watching the light fade and knowing where his blackened soul would go. He dropped the shish kabobbed body before he walked over to Ellyria, holding her close. "It's okay. He's dead."

She gripped him tight and sobbed. "That doesn't get easier."

He nodded and rubbed her back. "I know. That is why I try to distance myself from everyone."

Ellyria held him tighter. "No. You don't. Not from me."

"Everyone but you. You are the only one who matters to me."

"Mine." She nuzzled into his shoulder.

"And you are mine," he said. His wings wrapped around her. After a moment, he shrouded them in mist and picked her up, taking flight towards their house. "Let's go home."

She fumbled with her phone as they flew, sending a text message to Steve. 'Threat neutralized. I'll be in tomorrow.'

"I'm off today," she said, pocketing her phone.

"Get some rest. You used a lot of magic, and we both got hurt." He stroked her hair. "I will make sure we get home safe."

She nodded and closed her eyes. "I love you," she said as she drifted off.

"And I you," he said, giving her a kiss on the cheek. Zane made it home in record time and set her down on the bed. He grabbed a washcloth in the bathroom and dampened it, wringing it out well. He wiped the blood from her face, getting any spots he could find and helped her out of her gore covered clothing. After he tucked her in, he climbed in next to her. He gave her another kiss and fell asleep at her side. It had been a long day, and he needed rest too.

Ellyria awoke before Zangrunath. Light filtered through the windows, and she saw her demon sleeping beside her. Resting peacefully. She smiled, running her fingers down the side of his face all the way to his hip. Her fingers ran back up, and she saw his eyes open. "Good morning. I didn't know you could sleep." She smiled as she met his black gaze.

He smirked at her and stole her hand to kiss. His lips meeting the inside of her wrist. "I don't need to. Doesn't mean I can't do it if I want to," he said, running a hand down her side like she did to him.

She shivered at his touch. "I just want to be close to you right now."

He nodded and put his wing over her. His tail wrapped around her waist, holding her close to him. "That is fine."

"Let's make this my first and only defense case," she said as she rested on his chest.

"Agreed." He sighed with relief. "That sucked."

"It did." She wiggled her leg. "I never want to get hurt again."

He made a face and kissed her. "I'm sorry that I let that happen to you. I should have been there to protect you." His tone was sincere and apologetic.

She shook her head. "I should've paid better attention. It's my fault."

"I ran ahead without making sure that there was nothing that could hurt you. The fault is mine." A hand ran up and down her back. "I have superior senses to you, millennia of experience in tactics, and could have created a duplicate for protection. I failed you."

"We can argue this all day." She shook her head. "I'd rather not. I'd rather be grateful that it wasn't worse."

He nodded and sighed, squeezing her a bit as he did so. "Let's just relax," he said, brushing her hair from her face.

She laid there for a minute before her stomach growled, ruining the moment. "Stupid human body."

Zangrunath sighed and sat up. "I will make you food," he said as he picked her up, bringing her with him. "But I still want you close to me."

She sat on the counter where he put her down. "No eggs, please. Just not feeling it."

"Toast and bacon then. Maybe some jam on the toast," he said as he started moving around the kitchen to make her breakfast.

"Thank you." She smiled at him, watching him as he worked.

He smirked and turned to look at her. "You are very welcome."

She chuckled at the look in his eyes, deciding that changing the subject was best before breakfast got delayed. "I want to use my specialty at work so much." She sighed. "Instead, I get to play a magical detective."

He nodded as he put the strips of bacon in the pan. "At least you are doing something. It's better than sitting behind a desk all day pretending to work and hating everything."

"I kind of do hate everything, to be honest." She frowned.

"There are moments, yes." He looked over at her for a moment, reaching over to the loaf of bread and popping two pieces into the toaster. "You are going to use your skills soon enough. Once this case is over, I know you will get something."

"I would take anything at this point. I just want to sink my teeth into a contract and tear it to shreds, figuratively speaking." She blushed.

He laughed at her description. "Depending on the contract, you might get to do that literally." He spread strawberry jam on the toast and plated up everything for her.

She licked her lips. "This smells great."

"Well, eat and see if it tastes just as good." He smiled, placing the plate in her hands.

She took the plate and dug in. "You always take such good care of me."

"I try my best." He watched her for a moment, leaning up against the counter.

She pulled the piece of toast from her lips and looked at him with some emotion as she chewed. "I dread the day you have to take care of me as an old lady. So not sexy future demoness."

"You will always look the same in my eyes," he said, going to the sink to clean up the small mess he made.

She took another bite. "I don't want to imagine it. The idea of it freaks me out. I hate it. I don't know why I brought it up."

He shook his head at her. "You will be a sexy demoness. Hell makes sure you are at your absolute peak performance.

Stop worrying about all of that. You are powerful in your own right, and that is what I see."

Hopping off the counter, she chuckled at him. She took her plate into the living room. She hit the power button on the computer. "I'm going to play some games. Maybe something with tower defense."

He smiled and followed her into the living room. He turned on his computer. "You do that. I'm going to destroy the world by playing strategy games."

She grinned at him. "Enjoy."

# VIII



The room was empty besides Zane, who was always there. "It's a Monday sort of Tuesday," Ellyria said with a groan as she sat at her desk, looking over her emails.

"At least, it is a four-day week. It will be shorter than normal."

She sighed, looking at her messages and growing still. "Excuse me a moment. We may have finally struck pay dirt." She stood up and fought to walk, not run, to Steve's office. "Is it true? Are we brokering a merger with the W's?"

Steve glanced up at her and smiled. "We are working on something, yes. Nothing has been finalized yet, but so far, things are looking good."

Ellyria turned her head as Parker came up behind her and touched her shoulder. It made her shudder with revulsion. "Good morning, you two. We're having a meeting with the law team starting in ten minutes. Be ready to talk deals."

"Thank you, Parker. I'm aware," Steve said with a sigh, standing up and grabbing a few items from his desk.

"I'll be there with bells on," Ellyria said with a wide smile, going to her office to grab everything she needed. "By Lucifer's blackened throne, yes."

"Congratulations." Zane sent her a mental smirk. "I know you will get this deal solidified."

She made her way into the conference room with the confidence of somebody who owned the place. "You bet I am."

Ellyria sat beside McDonough and clicked her favorite red pen to be ready. Her trusty legal pad in front of her as Parker loaded up a presentation on the projector. She read the contract that was posted on the screen, frowning more the further along she got.

"This is awful," Zane said. It sounded more like a sneer than anything. "This is them buying out the company."

"The company with the highest net revenue becomes the chief controlling entity," she said in return. "Of course, they make more money. There's two of them."

"Then fix it. You did study for this, right?" he asked rhetorically.

Ellyria snapped out of the conversation to find Parker looking at her with surprising intensity. "Miss Grant, good of you to join us. Now, as I was saying, I'm quite pleased with this deal. Would you care to share your- expertise?" he asked, but he couldn't hide his clear disdain for the young woman as he spoke.

Ellyria put her pen down and leveled him with a murderous gaze. "I think that, if you'd like White and Whitaker to be your boss, you should sign that atrocity post haste."

"What?"

"Article four subsection B. Controlling stake goes to the company with the highest net revenue," she said. "That's my biggest concern. The second being that this requires us to move to Worcester."

He shook his head and shrugged. "Okay. Moving isn't a problem. We can get everything transferred over within a year."

"This document gives us sixty days and may I remind you, voids my contract, sir," she said. He must think that it was a bonus to get her out of this place.

McDonough spoke up before Parker could chime in and smiled at Ellyria. He knew that she, of all people, would get this shored up. "Then what would you recommend, Miss Grant?"

"I would recommend that the section about controlling parties change to most resolved cases within the past five calendar years, and if you believe we can move in a year, I suggest changing it to two years to leave room for error. Since I remember you reviewing and signing the lease on this building for another year last month, I would shoot to finish moving by the end of that term to avoid paying month to month," she said with confidence.

McDonough spoke again. "Why is there a move involved?" he asked. "Why can't we have the same company with two separate branches? Wouldn't that help increase the number of clients we can take in? You know, accessibility."

"I agree." Ellyria nodded, gazing at the dumbfounded Parker. She thought for a moment and turned back to look at the contract, directing Julie to scroll down for her. The final article had her seething. She turned to speak to McDonough and Hannon. "The future company in Worcester is to be dubbed Parker, White, and Whitaker. This writes both of you out of partnership."

McDonough glared at Parker. He turned bright red as anger overtook him. "What did you do?"

Parker stretched his collar as the sweat was rolling down his face. He couldn't meet Steve's eyes. "It was a lot of money."

"You already signed this, didn't you?" Ellyria asked.

"What type of idiot turns down a one hundred thousand dollar raise!?"

Ellyria stood up. "Show me McDonough and Hannon's partnership contracts."

"I don't know how that will help." Parker shrugged, snapping and pointing at Julie to get the documents for her. "I already finished this deal."

"Show. Me. Their. Contracts," she said, leaning forward on the conference room table like she was preparing to jump over it just to strangle him. A low growl rumbled in her chest.

Julie ran into the room, looking down and away to avoid having the anger of the room directed at her. She handed Parker the file folders.

"Fine," he said, tossing the folders across the table. They landed just short, sliding the rest of the way before bumping into her hand. "Good luck," Parker said, as he walked out of the room. The look of victory was clear on his face even as he ogled her.

Ellyria looked to McDonough and Hannon. "I'm going to need overtime," she said with a grumble before storming towards her office. "And get me Parker's *current* contract."

"Granted. Give me five minutes," Steve said as he left the office, going to fish out his former partner's contract from their file storage room.

"There has to be verbiage in here that voids the new one," she said to Zane as she slammed her office door and dug into McDonough's documents.

Zane gave her a mental nod. "Of course, there has to be. No contract would ever be that one sided."

"If this deal goes through, my employment contract is void. I wrote my contingencies with the completion of the penthouse in mind, and Lucifer damn it to Hell, they still need to finish building it."

"I promise you will get that penthouse," he said. "If need be, we can pay double."

"Sorry, but I need to focus," she said as she read and made highlights. She sent an instant message and coffee appeared a few minutes later, along with Parker's contract. She sighed. This was going to take a while.

**Wednesday, September 8, 2027**
The office was dark. The only illumination coming from Ellyria's computer screen and a small desk lamp. She smiled and giggled. She was so far gone that she'd hit slap happy. "I found it." She jumped up out of her seat, almost toppling the office chair over. "I found it!"

Zane spoke for the first time in hours, clearing his throat before he did. "What did you find?"

"Parker's contract. The old one states he needs approval from all partners to sell, trade, or otherwise dissolve the firm. There's some old verbiage that has changed since the old partners retired, but the intent is there. And," she laughed like a lunatic for a moment, "he voided his own partnership by going over their heads."

Zane appeared next to her and smirked. "That is hilarious."

"McDonough, Hannon, and Grant has quite the ring to it."

"Yes, it does." He chuckled, giving her a kiss. "Good job. I knew you could do it."

She picked up all the documents and looked at the clock. "Oh, Hell. I've got to be back here in six hours."

He glanced from the clock over to her. "Will you be okay to drive?"

"No," she said without hesitation as she packed up. "I need you to drive."

He nodded and turned into his human self. "Let's get you home."

"I want a shower. I feel gross," she complained as they walked out to the car.

Zane walked behind her, stopping when he noticed that something was amiss. He placed a hand on Ellyria's shoulder. "I don't think we are driving home." He growled as he noticed the damage to the car.

Ellyria noticed the vandalism, and her chest tightened as she tried hard not to cry. A whimper escaped her lips. "Parker is going to pay," she said instead of giving in to the heartbreaking feeling of despair that overwhelmed her.

"If you want me to cut his brake lines, I will."

She shook her head. "No. He's about to see his world burn." Exhaustion hit her, and secrecy be damned, they were getting home. She tapped the leys and knitted together the tires, repairing the damage to the classic vehicle. "Nobody messes with this car."

"I love it when you get angry." Zane smirked, opening the door for her.

"I'm going to write him out of law on the east coast," she said as she grew more irritated. Tired, hungry, and frustrated were not a good combination for her at all. She huffed, crossing her arms as she flopped into her seat.

He got into the car and placed a hand on her thigh. "Calm down. You are too tired."

Ellyria looked out the windshield with bleary eyes. "I never liked that touchy misogynist, and I'm going to make him pay."

He started Shelby, and she roared to life, sounding angry. "I think she agrees with you."

"I want to see him watch his world fall apart in front of him." She sighed.

"I know you will." He smirked, giving her a kiss. "Close your eyes, and I will get us home fast."

She closed her eyes and sighed. "Sorry. I've been exhausted and hangry for hours."

"I will make sure you get a big breakfast in the morning."

Ellyria yawned. "Let me sleep in more than normal, please. I'll get in right at nine instead of early."

"Will do." Even though he knew she wouldn't see it, he nodded. He got them home in record time, and by the time they arrived, Ellyria was out cold. He lifted her up and put her to bed, holding her while she slept.

Zangrunath's wake up call was the only reason Ellyria stirred. She yawned and looked at him with a groggy expression that spoke volumes. "I'm up," she said, sitting up. She knew she didn't have all the time she usually did. "I'm going to go take that shower."

He smiled and pulled away. "Go enjoy it. I will have breakfast ready when you get out," he said, hopping out of bed and making his way to the kitchen.

She got cleaned up and put on one of her nicest outfits before strolling out into the living room with her heels in hand. "I am as ready as I'm going to get today."

"You look dressed to kill," he said as he placed an enormous breakfast in front of her. "Enjoy. If you want more, I made extra just in case."

"Take me now," she deadpanned as she eyed the food with a different kind of lust altogether. She dug into her meal and didn't stop to even look at him until her plate was clean. Ellyria glanced at the clock. "Ack! We've gotta go."

Zane nodded and disappeared before talking into her head. "Lead the way. I will follow you anywhere."

"Parker's going to be pissed that my car is intact."

"He will never figure it out." He chuckled.

She shook her head, still feeling beyond frustrated with the man who would become her former employer soon. "If he ever does, it'll be because I killed him."

"If that happens, I will bring the popcorn. You are going to ruin that man's entire career."

"Oh yes, I am," she said. She grew quiet as she drove to work, smiling to herself. When she pulled into her parking spot, she noticed that someone tagged the sign overnight. "Oh, it keeps getting better."

He chuckled. "Well, it's his funeral. Never start a fight with a nephilim."

"I made a deal with the actual Devil. I am coming out on top of this thing," she said with telepathy as she strode out of the car with her head held high. She pulled her briefcase to her with magic and locked Shelby. "Let's go destroy a career."

"I can't wait to see this." Zane's grin was palpable in her head as she strode into the office with confidence and on a mission.

She walked into the office, reached over Julie's desk as she sat on the counter and dialed the number to speak to the office. "This is miss Ellyria Grant. I'm calling a partner's meeting in five minutes. Thank you." She turned to Julie. "Have Jeremy brew a fresh pot of coffee. We're going to need it, and please have security ready." She slid off the counter and walked into the conference room, winking at Steve.

Julie nodded and got to work, getting everything ready. As Ellyria walked in, McDonough looked at her curiously. "Please tell me you found something?" he asked, sounding hopeful.

"Bow down to me in my glory," she said in a stage whisper, giving a little curtsey.

He released a tremendous sigh of relief and sat down in a chair. "Thank you! I didn't get any sleep last night after that incident." He smiled. "I will get some rest tonight."

She sat down and crossed her legs. "You're going to be paying me a lot of overtime. I left at three a.m. Also, Parker tried to mess with my car."

He sighed, but nodded. "It's fine. If I know you like I think I do, you saved this company."

"Oh, and so much more." She grinned, watching Daniel Hannon and Joseph Parker file in.

Parker looked at her and smirked. "Good morning, Miss Grant. Did you have a pleasant drive into work this morning?"

"Yes. I did, sir." She smiled with false sweetness. "I might have been *tired*, but it was better than driving *smashed* after a night out."

Parker raised an eyebrow at that and shook his head. "So, what is this meeting about?" he asked with obvious impatience. "I need to head to Worcester soon." He glanced at his watch.

She leaned over across the table and looked deeply into his eyes. "Why is that? You're no longer a partner here. The new contract is void."

He paused and looked at her with a surprised and critical gaze. "What are you talking about? I have my name on this company."

"You do now, but when you became partner, you signed a contract that makes your partnership null and void if you do anything without the consent of the other partners. It seems the old bosses didn't trust you." She smirked.

Parker's eyes went wide. He looked at her in shock. "No, no, no. That contract was over when these two took their places. That doesn't work in this situation."

She looked down at the documents. "I don't see an end date on here."

He walked over and took the paper from her hand, hastily reading it over. "There has to be an end date." His expression turned from one of confidence to visible frustration.

"So, we're done here, right?" she asked.

"You bitch!" he said, pulling a fist back before McDonough caught it.

"I wouldn't do that if I were you. Unless you want to be fed that arm," he said to Parker, knowing that it wouldn't be him doing the feeding.

Parker seethed in rage now. "No! This company is mine. I own you," he said as he marched towards the door. "I am going to bankrupt all of you and wipe my ass with your savings accounts!" His scream echoed in the conference room as he slammed the door, shattering the window in the door with the force.

Steve sighed and looked at Elly. "Thank you, Ellyria. You saved the company," he said, offering his hand to shake.

"I just did my job."

"And you did a good job at that." He smiled at her before a car alarm went off outside.

"I'm going to go kill him now," she said, marching out the door and running on her heels into the parking lot. "Zane, can I borrow some strength for a second?"

"Take as much as you need," Zane said, lending her his power as requested.

Ellyria ran up to Parker as he was bashing into Shelby with a baseball bat and decked him as hard as possible in the face, knocking him over the side of the car with the force.

Parker fell onto the ground and slid on the asphalt. He stood up on wobbling legs and spit out a bloody tooth. He growled, standing up and charging at her. "You ruined me!"

Ellyria didn't know what to do, so she ducked, feeling Parker's momentum throw him over her. He fell back onto the ground. She stood up straight and stomped with all her might onto his chest. "You ruined yourself, and you will not mess with that car, dirtbag."

He groaned in pain as he felt and heard cracking in his chest. He rolled to the side and gasped for air.

She turned around, walking away as she heard the security guard calling out from across the parking lot. She didn't see him reach for her until she was already on the ground.

"I'll kill you!" Parker said as he tried to pull her towards him, and his hands went for her throat.

Ellyria's eyes went dark black, and her skin changed before his eyes. "I will destroy you." She kicked him in the groin with her heels.

Parker grew pale as a ghost, falling over in pain. He fell to the side and tried to crawl away. He glanced back at the beginnings of Ellyria's demonic looking transformation and shuddered. His body was in agony. He tried to get away faster, but stopped, cowering in fear when he saw her looming over him.

Ellyria stood up and kicked his side, making him roll over again. "If you ever touch me or my car again, I will make your life a Hell so miserable that you will beg me just to end it."

He whimpered and nodded. "I won't do it again." He shivered as he looked up at her. "I'm sorry!" He sobbed, curling up as he prepared to be beaten more.

Ellyria glanced over at the approaching group of onlookers and looked at Steve McDonough. Her eyes were still the darkest of obsidian. "I'm going to go write a restraining order," she said, pretending to cry and covering up her face so others didn't see the physical changes of the half-demonic transformation on her face. "Let me know if you need anything."

Steve looked a little shocked, but nodded. "If I do, you will be the first to know."

She ducked into her office, using random bits of the errant magic she'd picked up, trying to make the changes clear up. "Dammit," she said as the adrenaline and Zangrunath's power faded from her.

"Calm down," Zane said in a soothing tone.

"Trying." She sighed. "I just assaulted a guy."

"No, you didn't. It was self-defense. You did nothing wrong."

She rubbed her temples. "I broke laws."

"If it ever comes to that, there are people who will back you up," he said while trying his best to reason with her. "Besides, he won't press charges."

"I'm okay." She took a breath, muttering the phrase over and over.

Zane sent her calming thoughts and murmured into her head, "You are fine. He attacked you, destroyed your property and tried to sell out a company he had no right to sell. He has more pressing matters to worry about, like embezzlement and fraud."

"I'm sorry." She pulled up a restraining order form on her computer. "He's not coming near me again."

"He would have to get through me first. Mine."

She felt the mental caress of the single word. "Just don't forget whose you are," Ellyria said before yawning widely.

Zane sent her a mental smile and let her continue her work. "Just let me know when you are ready. I will take you home."

"He smashed Shelby again." She sighed.

"I know." He sighed. "You need to have it towed back to the house so you can fix it."

She waved a hand. "Would you mind calling? I just want to get this one thing done right now."

"Of course." He smiled, appearing next to her in his human form, looking sharp and attractive in a business suit. He picked up her office phone and got to work making the arrangements she asked for.

Ellyria grew quiet. She focused on getting the task at hand done, and once she finished, she brought the printed document to Julie at the front. "I need this to be approved at the courts." Can we have Jeremy messenger it over, please?"

Julie nodded and took the pages from her. "Yes. I will have him get it there as soon as possible."

"Thank you," Ellyria said, through exhaustion, making her way to McDonough's office. She yawned again. "Do you need anything? I'm tired. Only got a couple hours of sleep."

He shook his head. "No. Go home and get some rest. In fact, take the rest of the week off. You helped us keep this place and got assaulted because of it. You deserve it."

"Paid leave, I hope." She winked.

"Yes. Now go rest." He waved her off. "I will take care of everything here."

"Thank you." She smiled. "See you soon. Let me know if there's anything you need."

"Will do." Steve told her, going back to his work at the computer.

As Ellyria walked out of the building, she could see Shelby being loaded onto a tow truck and Zane walking over to her.

"You ready to go?" he asked her, already knowing the answer when he saw the exhaustion in her eyes.

"Yeah," she said with a small voice as she took his hand.

"Alright." He led her away from the building, making sure that any prying eyes were long gone. Once they got out of sight, Zangrunath turned into his normal self and picked Ellyria up. He shrouded them in mist and flew them towards the house.

She leaned into him and tears fell down her cheeks. "Not my car."

"I know," he said, rubbing her shoulder. "We had to make it look believable. She will be home in an hour at most, and I will have her in the garage. You can fix her whenever you are ready."

Ellyria sniffled. "It's not what it is, but what it means. I made a promise."

"I know. I know what it means to you, and I won't let you break that promise."

She nodded. "Thank you."

"No problem." Zane kissed her on the cheek and pulled away with a smile on his face. He landed in the backyard before bringing her inside and placing her on the bed. "Sleep well."

"I'm gonna mess up my sleep schedule."

"Then stay awake until a normal time," he said, knowing she was too tired to try at this point.

Ellyria sat up and the room spun. "Dammit."

"I figured as much." He chuckled, tucking her in. "Just sleep. We have four days to fix it, after all."

"Fine." She growled in her crankiness.

He gave her a kiss. "Sleep well. Love you."

She curled up, cuddling into a pillow. "Night love."

# IX



Standing in her backyard, Ellyria bundled up in a coat and blankets for the cold weather. She didn't think she needed the power of the leys to keep her dad around for the night. She set up the ritual, and in no time at all, her father's specter was in front of her. "Hey, dad." She smiled. "Thanks for showing up a few months ago."

"No problem, sweetie." Samuel smiled in return. "It was the least I could do. You needed help."

"Yeah." She sighed. "It was a rough day."

He made a face. "I'm sorry."

She rubbed her head unconsciously at the thought. "So much has happened this past year. I don't even know where to start."

"Well, how is school coming?"

"I passed the bar in May with a 280." She smiled. "Then I started working at a law firm at the end of June."

"I'm glad." He looked a little teary-eyed. "Just wish I could have seen all that."

She shook her head, trying not to cry as well. "I didn't walk. It would've been too bittersweet."

"I still would have liked to see it. I miss a lot like this." He gestured to himself.

"You get to see Mom sometimes, though." She smiled at the thought.

He chuckled and shook his head. "No, I don't. She's busy being herself."

"I'm sorry." She frowned. "That sucks."

He smiled. "It's fine. She is busy. When I see her, I know it will be well worth the wait."

Ellyria stared at her father as she tried to remain calm. "I did world altering magic this year too." She changed the subject. "Stuff that mom might be angry about."

"Like what?" he asked. "Can you bring people back from the dead?"

"I don't think that would be so difficult, but I think I might get smote for trying." She paused. "I summoned the Devil himself."

Her father froze, blinking several times. "What?" There was no way that he'd heard that right.

"He's also a fallen angel. I needed to know what was happening to me, so," she shrugged, "I asked the only source I knew of for sure."

He sighed. "Well, at least, you got out of it scot-free. Right?"

"We changed my deal while he was here." She waved a hand with surprising flippancy, but her expression grew smug. "It's kind of too much information, but Zangrunath will always be around to take care of me."

He nodded. "At least you're happy."

"I am," she said, looking down at the ground. "I'm so close to getting what I want. It's like I can almost taste it."

"Did you enjoy the journey?"

"It was a lot of hard work, but I enjoy what I do. And I'm great at it," she said, trying to be honest. After a long pause, she decided it was time to say what she'd been waiting for. "I asked Zangrunath to stay inside for tonight. I wanted," she trailed off. After a moment, Ellyria sighed and looked up at the sky, holding back tears. "I'm so screwed up, daddy."

He looked at her broken expression, wishing there was some way that he could help his baby girl. "No, you're not, sweetie," he said. "You are unique. I know you might think that you are something beyond reason, but I can assure you, you are not the first nephilim."

"I've killed people. I did it brutally, and for things that could have been much worse. And what's worse is-" She took a breath, wiping away a tear from her eye. "I can never have kids. That's my biggest mistake. I didn't realize what I was doing. What I was giving up."

Her father grew quiet for a moment as he processed her words. He nodded. The gesture looked sad and final, yet understanding. "I killed people too, so I understand that. I do." He paused, trying to think of what to say in response to her other news. "I- you might not have kids of your own, but you can still be a mom." A sad smile took his lips. "If you do, I know that you'll be great at it."

"They won't be magical, though. I kind of ended our family line by accident." She waved a hand, and their grimoire appeared in her hands. "Nobody will use this again after me."

He frowned. "Somebody will use it. As much as I dislike the idea, I would rather have someone use it than have the knowledge in there get lost to time."

"I gave away the pages of demon code to save myself."

"Who did you give it to?" he asked, letting out a deep sigh and rubbing his temples.

"Good ol' Lucifer himself." She gulped with a bitter chuckle. "That was terrifying."

He groaned when she said that before looking into her eyes with a forced smile. "I guess that's better than it falling into Section Seven's hands. Had that happened, it would have caused a war."

She wiped her face and shook her head. "I won't start the next holy war."

"It wouldn't be a war so much as an extermination. You gave it to the right being." He smiled at her. "I know he will make sure it's kept out of the wrong hands."

She reached out to touch him, and her hand went through his. "Dammit." She sighed, glaring at her hand. After a minute, she looked up at him. "I'm sorry. It can't be too much longer. I have an important meeting tomorrow."

He nodded in understanding. "It's fine. I know you are a busy person now. Just try to stay out of trouble. Alright?"

"I always do." She smiled. "I might be a partner at the firm when I talk to you next year."

"I look forward to finding out." He smiled.

"I love you, Dad."

"I love you too, sweetie." His smile was bright for her as he fought away the sadness of knowing they would be apart for another year. "Take care."

Ellyria watched her father fade away and stood up to head inside, where Zane was at his computer desk playing games. "Thanks," she said to him, coming up behind him and hugging him around his shoulders.

Zane smiled and turned his head to give her a kiss. "It's fine. I know you like to have private talks with him. It is no big deal," he said while sending hordes of minions at an enemy he was fighting against.

She sniffled. "This year made me miss him a lot." She stood up and walked down the hallway to get ready for bed.

He saved his game and followed her to the bedroom. "At least you can still talk to him. There are people who don't get that option." He sat down on the bed, watching her go about her routine.

"I know," she said, while cleaning her face in the bathroom mirror. She kept her voice at a whisper in order to avoid having him hearing the emotions there.

"You know you can always talk to me about anything. Right?" he asked.

She nodded. "I do, but you hate it when I cry. I don't like seeing you in pain like that."

"I would much rather be in pain than have you feel you need to hide or suppress things," he said. "You know I can take it. I am pretty durable." He chuckled.

She finished what she was doing in the bathroom, turned around and climbed into his arms. "It's just me rehashing the same shit on a different day."

He held her close and gave her a gentle kiss. "You like to make up things in your head. Just take a calming breath next time you think something is going to go wrong and watch as it doesn't. Okay?"

"I will try," she said as she laid down next to him. "Now get over here and cuddle me."

He smiled and laid down, pulling her close to him like she asked. He gave her a squeeze. "Better?"

"Much." She smiled. "Goodnight, Zangrunath."

"I love you, Ellyria," he said, giving her a kiss. "Sleep well." He stroked her hair as she laid in his arms.

Monday, November 1, 2027

Ellyria pulled into her parking spot at the firm and hopped out of Shelby. She had a big smile on her face as she walked into the conference room. "Hello, McDonough. Hannon. How are you this morning?" she asked.

"Doing well," Steve McDonough said with a smile of his own. "How about yourself? Have a good weekend?" he asked before the meeting got started.

"Oh, you know. Got to see some distant relatives." She smirked.

A knowing smile pulled at his lips, and he nodded. "Good to hear."

"I hate to skip the formalities and get straight to the brass tacks, but I have a client coming in an hour. You wanted to see me?"

Steve nodded again and looked at Daniel Hannon. "Yes. We wanted you to look over this new contract we are working on and get your thoughts on it." He slid the folder to her with a serious expression.

She opened the file folder and looked it over. After about a minute, she looked up. "You really want me to be your partner?" She predicted this, but she didn't expect it so soon.

Daniel smiled. "Well, yeah. After you helped us keep the place, it's the least we can do. You know what you're doing, and we're both glad to have you be our partner."

She beamed at them. "Of course, I'll have to read this over. How do you feel about a branch in New York? I have my eye on a penthouse that I can bid on next year."

The two looked at each other and nodded. They looked back at her. "That is fine by us," Steve said.

"Thank you!" She grinned.

"You're welcome, but before any new branch gets made, we still have work to do. So, go make sure our clients get taken care of." He chuckled, waving her out the door.

"Of course." She grinned, standing up and heading to her new office. She closed the door and locked it behind her for a moment. "Zane," she whispered.

"Congratulations." Even his mental speech sounded enthused for her. "I knew you would get it."

"Get out here and hug me," she said. It came out as an order thanks to the ritual.

He chuckled and appeared next to her, lifting her and spinning her into an embrace. "There. A big hug for the big new position you got."

She stole a kiss from him. "Thank you."

"You are very welcome." He stole one more kiss, knowing she had work to do and clients to see.

She unlocked her door. "It's all falling into place."

"Just a little while longer and the deal will be done. Then it will just be the two of us with no magic forcing my hand." He smiled before disappearing.

"You, me, and a New York penthouse." She smirked, getting to work for the day.

"I look forward to that day," he said before growing quiet so she could work in peace.

# X



Ellyria paced back and forth like a lioness in the living room as she stood behind Zangrunath's computer screen. "I can't believe that they're starting the bidding at midnight," she said. "They're killing me."

Zane shook his head and pulled her to his side. "Calm down and relax," he said, giving her a kiss. "You want this, and I will get it for you. I am not worried about the price. We have the money."

She looked at the current account balances on the documents strewn across the table. "I know. I'm just anxious. This is new to me."

"I can tell." He chuckled. "You haven't stayed still for over thirty minutes. Your legs are going to give out before the bidding ends."

"It's only two minutes to midnight. I'm fine."

"Then prove it to me by sitting down and trying to calm down," he said, patting his lap for her to sit in.

She sighed and took a seat as she was told. "There. Happy?" she asked, checking the clock as her leg bounced.

"That is better." He wrapped his tail around her waist, focusing on the screen. "You are still a nervous wreck." He glanced down at her.

"I just know what I want." She sighed as anxiety tightened in her chest.

"I know, and you will get it," he said, kissing her cheek and placing a hand on her leg to help calm her. "Trust me."

Saturday, July 1, 2028

She watched as the site ticked over to a new screen, refreshing as Zangrunath's fingers got to work on the keyboard. She shut her eyes. "Oh, I can't watch."

"Relax," he said as he put in a small starting bid. "None of these other people have a clue what they are dealing with." He chuckled as he saw several other bids come in. He shot the price up a bit. A few more bids came in, raising the bid to fifteen million. He laughed as he doubled the price in one go, making several other bidders leave in short order. "Play hard, live harder."

"I know we have it." She gulped. "And I know it's going higher, but that's a lot of money."

"Nothing that I can't get back." He shrugged as fewer buyers continued to bid as the price skyrocketed up. "Just close your eyes and focus on the image of us relaxing on the balcony."

She sighed. "We're going to have to buy all new everything."

He shook his head. "No, we don't. Just because we have the penthouse doesn't mean everything needs to get more expensive. We can still bring a good bit with us." He placed another bid, raising the price to over thirty-five million.

"Are we selling this place, then? I've kind of grown attached to it." She frowned as nostalgia overtook her.

"Only if you want to. We could always rent the place out."

Ellyria thought about that. "We would make a killing."

"Extra money, yes." Zane chuckled. Several bidders left, leaving one other person. He raised the bid again. "If you wanted a killing, I would suggest video games."

She chuckled and nudged him. "Oh, hilarious. Time to throw in the towel, mister millionaire. You ain't winning this."

He cracked his knuckles and sent the price up to forty million. "There. Either they stop or I put it to fifty."

"I really don't want to imagine spending that much." She whined in distress at the thought.

"Imagine it as pennies," he said as he waited for a moment with nothing changing. "It is silly when you think of it that way."

She giggled. "Like the greedy cartoon duck with the top hat and monocle."

"Give me some time and I could make that real." He smirked as the other person left, leaving them the last remaining bidder. A few moments passed, and the screen changed, informing them that they were the winner. "Now the place is ours."

She pulled him in for a tight hug. "Oh sweet, merciful Lucifer, yes!"

He gave her a kiss. "Feel better now?" he asked, already knowing the answer.

Relief washed through her. "Yeah. Thank you. My devilishly handsome hero."

"You are very welcome. Now go get yourself a celebratory drink while I take care of the paperwork." He chuckled, chatting with the seller.

She stood up and moved to the kitchen where she grabbed a cola and whiskey, filling an oversized glass with double the whiskey over the soda. "Your favorite drink for me to have."

He smirked as he saw the beverage. "Well, that will do the trick," he said as he completed the paperwork, focusing for a few minutes until he got finished. After a moment, he leaned back a bit and turned to her. "We will have the keys by the end of the week."

"Really?!" She bounced a bit in excitement.

He nodded and smiled. "Yeah. The last inspections were completed a couple of weeks ago."

She lifted her glass. "I'll drink to that. Woo-hoo!"

He smiled and walked up to her. "As will I." He stole a sip from her glass.

"I haven't gotten drunk in forever." She smiled. "Good thing we've got a four-day weekend ahead of us."

He gave her a kiss. "Then let me help you with that." He moved to the kitchen, grabbing a bottle of whiskey so she could get drunk. He walked up to her and raised the bottle up. "Cheers! To the penthouse."

"To the penthouse!" She took a large swig of alcohol before sauntering over to the television. "Let's watch campy horror movies and make a drinking game out of it."

He took a large swig from the bottle and smiled. "Alright, and anything that they get right about Hell is a double."

"Ha! I love it." She chuckled. "After I'm good and not sober, we can have some fun."

"That was the plan." He smirked as he sat down next to her. "I want to see how much you can remember in the morning."


Sunday, July 2, 2028

Ellyria groaned on the bed, gripping her forehead. "Oh, Hell."

Zane chuckled. "Been there, didn't even get a t-shirt. Do you remember anything?"

"I remember seeing like nine of you, but I'm guessing it was double vision and a duplicate."

He laughed at that assessment and stood up to go make breakfast for her. "I will be back in a minute with some water for you."

She covered her face with a pillow. "Ibuprofen too, please."

"Coming right up." He grabbed the water and drugs before returning to give them to her. "Here you go." He kissed her on the cheek. "You relax, and I will be back in a bit with food."

"You are a gentleman and a scholar." She smiled and took the pills, washing them down with the water.

He left her in the room for a bit as he made breakfast for her. A secret smirk graced his features. He was excited about today. He received the keys to the penthouse yesterday while she was in a drunken stupor, and he planned to surprise her with a visit. First, he wanted to have some fun with it. He just needed to get her out of bed for his plan to begin. Coming back into the room about thirty minutes later with a nice big breakfast for her, he sat down next to her and placed the tray in her lap. "Here. This should help soak up the rest of the alcohol."

"You always know when to spoil me with a full English breakfast." She smiled.

"Years of practice." He smiled in kind.

She dug in. Her headache was still there, but improving. By the time she'd finished eating, she put down her utensils. "I don't remember eating yesterday."

He chuckled at that. "You demanded that you didn't want to lose your fun mood, so that is accurate. If you need more, just ask."

"Oh, no. I'm stuffed, but I will be just as hungry for lunch."

"Duly noted." He smiled. He looked her over for a moment before he enacted his plan. "That reminds me, we will need to go chat with the seller of the penthouse in a while. Something came up."

"Oh, no." She pouted. "What happened?"

He feigned a sigh. "Don't worry. We still own it. There was just an issue with the building. Something about things going too fast and corners being cut in the building process."

"Dammit. I knew it was too good to be true. When will it be done?"

"It's looking like early next year," he said, making a face.

She whined in distress. "Next year?! What happened to the keys in a week? That's a huge mistake!"

"Don't worry. I am taking care of it," he said in a soothing voice, giving her a tight hug.

She hugged him back. "Okay. We've got a meeting in New York then." She pulled away, heading towards the closet.

"Yeah," he said, smirking as she walked away. She'd taken the bait hook, line, and sinker. "It should be pretty eventful, so brace yourself for anything." He took a moment to let his human form shift into place.

"So, I'm hearing dress like a lawyer?" she asked.

He shook his head even though she couldn't see it. "No. Wear what's comfortable. I will take care of everything. Your demon is on it."

"Alright." She shrugged, coming around the corner wearing jeans and a t-shirt. "I'm ready."

"Good." He wrapped an arm around her. "Let's go get this sorted." He smiled as he led her to the door.

"Yeah. Let's get the pain over with." She sighed. "Who even works on Sunday? Other than land developers who screwed up a forty-million-dollar deal."

"Don't worry. I gave them an earful."

She deflated. "Sorry. I'm sure you handled it fine."

"It's okay." He gave her a kiss. "You have every right to feel annoyed by the whole situation."

She hopped into Shelby and closed her eyes. "If you don't mind, I think I'm going to sleep off the rest of this hangover on the way there."

"That is fine. I will wake you when we get there."

"Thanks." She yawned, settling in and relaxing to the hum of the engine.

"No problem." He smirked as she drifted off to sleep. He knew she would get mad at him when she found out that he lied. However, once she was inside the penthouse, she would forgive him right away. He chuckled to himself. This was the first time he had lied to her. He had a feeling he could do it after the soul binding, but there was no reason to do so until now. Why he wanted to do it in the first place, he didn't know, but he knew he wanted to give her a pleasant surprise. This would do the trick, so he got her there fast. He was looking forward to giving her this surprise.

Zane drove for about three and a half hours, enjoying the speed and hum of the engine. When he pulled into the underground garage, he turned to Ellyria to wake her up. One hand gave her a gentle shake, and he said, "Hey, we are here."

She sat up, gazing all about without seeing. "Hey."

He smirked and gave her a minute to wake up. "Come on. We have business to attend to." He hopped out of the car, walking around to get the door for her.

She looked around. "Where are we anyway?"

"At the meeting point," he said with a smile. "We need to go up and meet them."

"Alright." She shrugged as they found a room with a bay of elevators. "This is nice. It looks like they know what they're doing, at least."

"Yeah. It's not bad," he said as he led her to the last elevator and used a key to open it. He stepped aside to let her in first. "Come on. We are almost late."

Ellyria looked at the key in his hand. "They messengered over a key just for a meeting. Someone's feeling guilty."

"Yeah. They sounded embarrassed over the phone." He chuckled as the elevator rose. "They insisted we do this today."

She shrugged. "With how much money you wired them, they damn well better be sorry."

He smiled, knowing she was going to be in shock when the doors opened. "Yeah. It was a pretty penny."

"I know. A disgusting number of pennies." She rolled her eyes, looking at the lack of numbers on the elevator door panel. "What level are we even going to?!"

"I think it is pretty high up there," he said, looking up and trying to play the fool for just a moment longer as they neared their destination.

"Now they're just trying to make us feel bad." Ellyria rolled her eyes.

As they hit the top of the elevator shaft, Zane turned to look at her. "I don't know. I think the view may make up for it all," he said as the doors opened to their new penthouse.

Ellyria gasped, looking at what she was seeing and doing a double take. "Oh my God," she said without even realizing she'd sworn on the deity instead of Lucifer. "Wait a second. I thought you couldn't lie to me, you jerk!" She spun around and gave him a good smack on the chest as fiery anger burned in her eyes.

He brushed off the swat she gave him. It was nothing to him. If she wanted to hurt him, she could. A smile stole his lips, and he chuckled. "I realized I could lie to you not too long after the soul binding, but had no reason to do it. That is, until they delivered the keys yesterday and you were too drunk to remember it. So, I had a bit of fun. Sorry."

She looked at him with tears pooling in her eyes. "Okay." She jumped into his arms. "I like these sorts of lies."

He smiled and held her. "Don't worry. I will keep them to a minimum." He wiped away some of her tears, going in for a kiss.

She held onto him tight. "Well, show me around, you sneaky little demon."

He smiled and carried her around the house, showing her the different spaces. There was more than double the amount of room here than at the house, so they had plenty of space to grow. He showed her the much larger kitchen, which he knew was going to get well used before he brought her outside to the balcony. "The view is beautiful," he said, smiling as the wind blew her hair.

She kissed him before gazing around the city. "This is everything I dreamed it would be and more."

"Good. I'm glad you like it." He brought her back inside. "We will have to get a few things, but it won't take too long. I can do most of that stuff while you are at work as long as you don't mind me leaving you be for a few days."

"That's fine. Things have been boring." She sighed. "You can take time to do whatever we need." She leaned into him.

"You will want to ward the place first."

"Of course, I will. I don't want Section Seven to sense anything that comes out of here."

"Then it looks like we have a busy week ahead of us." He gave her a hug.

She groaned a little in frustration. "I have a busy three days. Starting now. I still have to work Wednesday through Friday." She summoned her wand and got to work drawing runes along the walls.

He watched her for a moment as she worked. "I can't wait to move in. It has been too many years in the making."

She grinned at his excitement, growing quiet for a while as she went about her task. As she was finishing the last rune, she said, "I'm going to channel magic now."

"Go for it," he said, leaving her to it. He wanted to figure out where everything would go. "I am going to see where the computers are going."

She smiled. "You do that." She rubbed her hands together and summoned her magics, touching the first and last runes and channeling as much of her energy as she could into the wards.

Zane came back a little while later with a few sheets of paper in hand. A quick glance over the pages was all it took to notice diagrams of the locations of their furniture and other items. "Okay. I have a good idea of where everything is going. I just need to put a sigil here, and then I can jump back and forth to make the moving go faster."

"I should be able to ley walk between places too," she said as she continued to focus on the magic. "Though that takes more energy than warding."

"You just focus on doing your work. As long as I have the sigil, it is like walking through a door for me. It takes almost no energy."

"I'm so jealous. Do what you need to do. I'll keep this up."

He smiled and kissed her. "I will." He walked into the primary bedroom and drew the demonic glyph that would allow him to travel the vast distance in mere moments.

Ellyria concentrated until she found her power waning about two hours later. She dug deep and used as much ley energy as she could get before calling it for the night as she panted, leaning against the wall. "Might've overdone it," she said, more to herself than anything.

Zane walked up to her and shook his head. "Of course you did." He sighed, pulling her into his arms. "You got excited to have the place, so you wanted it done sooner rather than later."

"It's not even done yet." She sighed, leaning into him. "They still need more."

"We can worry about it tomorrow," he said as he walked her into the elevator, pressing the button for the garage. "Let's get you to the house so that you can get some rest."

"I don't want to leave."

"I know," he said, holding her a little tighter. "But you will complain more if you sleep like garbage," he said, knowing her too well.

She closed her eyes, feeling the elevator come to a stop. "Fine. There's always tomorrow."

"Of course." He smiled. "Tomorrow I can jump back and forth. It will make getting here faster." He got her into her seat and walked around to his.

She looked over at him. "I'm fond of the private elevator. I don't have to deal with people after a long day."

"It is nice." He nodded in agreement and rested a hand on her leg.

Her mind whirled as she realized she owned the penthouse she'd wanted for so long. "I've got to talk with Steve and Daniel about the New York office." She leaned into him, enjoying the comfort he brought her. "I have done nothing but sleep today."

"There is nothing wrong with that. You had a long day and weekend."

"I'm sure I had fun." She giggled. "Even if I don't remember it."

He gave her a soft smile. "We will try to redo it at a different date. Then you can remember it."

"I look forward to it." She yawned. "I'm exhausted."

"You used too much magic. Of course, you are. Get some sleep. I will get you home safe."

She nodded. "Goodnight, Zane," she said as her head rested on his shoulder.

He smiled as she rested against him. "Sleep well."

# XI



Winter vacation started for Ellyria after a long workday. After a romantic dinner for two, things were getting heated. Caught up in the moment with Zane, she was ready to enjoy her first vacation for far too long. As Zane was leading her towards the bedroom, she opened her eyes to look up at him and froze. Something she saw out of the corner of her eye caught her attention. "Zane! Behind you!"

Zane turned to see where she was looking. He looked at the intruder and froze in place. "M- my king?"

Lucifer lounged on the couch in the living room, looking far more human than the last time they saw him. He assessed the situation and smirked at the two of them. "Oh, don't mind me. Continue as you were. I can wait until you finish."

Ellyria looked at Zane, unsure of what to say or do and turning bright red with embarrassment.

Zangrunath looked at Lucifer and then towards Ellyria, who grew more embarrassed by the second. He felt rage build within him, but knew there was nothing he could do about it given who was on the couch. He stepped in front of

Ellyria to help cover her up. "We were just-" He couldn't finish the lie in the literal sense.

"Oh, really?" Lucifer asked with a grin. "Because that looked like the beginning of the fun." He chuckled at his general.

Ellyria covered up. "You choose now of all times to lie?" she asked Zangrunath before turning to the Dark Prince. "It was the beginning of my first vacation in a very long time." She sighed in frustration.

"I figured as much." He shrugged, looking at Ellyria. "You don't have to cover up. Be comfortable around me. I am the Devil. I work with Lust herself. There is nothing I haven't seen before." He chuckled, trying to lighten the mood.

Ellyria sighed again. "I think I'm good like this."

"Do you feel more comfortable?" he asked with a knowing smile.

"I would feel better returning to where I was about two minutes before you appeared, but I'm about as comfortable as I'm going to get at the moment." Her blunt honesty surprised her, but she figured the Devil himself possessed magic she couldn't comprehend.

He shrugged again. "As long as you feel relaxed." He turned to look at Zangrunath. "What about you? Comfy?"

"Pissed," Zane said.

"Why is being comfortable important? It's obvious this isn't a social visit."

Lucifer gazed at Ellyria and nodded. "You are a smart one." He sat upright. "I want you to be comfortable because, in my experience, all job opportunities should begin as relaxed and laid back as possible." He smirked at the pair, in complete control of the situation at hand.

Ellyria shook her head and took a seat on the couch, looking at Zangrunath. "Job opportunities," she said as her mind whirled with possibilities.

"Well, this is more of a promotion for Zangrunath, assuming you can do it," he said, glancing at his demon with palpable amusement.

"A promotion?" Zane asked in confusion.

"In the simplest of terms, one of your superiors thought it would be *funny* to try besting ol' Lucy and went rogue." He chuckled for a moment before his face grew stern. An aura of danger grew around him. "So, I want the two of you to go destroy him so well that even all of God's angels couldn't put him back together again."

Ellyria went pale at the look on the face of the Devil himself. He was far too close for comfort; she gulped as fear washed over her, turning to Zane. "What do you want to do?"

Zane stared at the King of Hell and sighed. "I don't think we have much of a choice in the matter."

"You always have a choice. I guess I shouldn't beat around the bush. What do you want out of this? We're doing it."

"I get a promotion, but what I want is to spend time with you," he said, gesturing to the room. "You are what I want."

"Do I need to write a contract for this, or are you going to handle it?" Ellyria asked Lucifer, knowing her contract with the Devil already covered her own lifetime.

He waved a hand. "That will be easy enough."

Ellyria nodded, taking a breath and tapping the leys. Her eyes turned black and her skin became a more demonic red. "Where was his last known location?"

He raised an eyebrow at the changes he saw in the other fallen angel. "Brazil," he said in a quick and factual manner.

She searched the leys, sensing for any oddities. "Well, he's not there anymore," she said before feeling a blip of magic even farther off. Her eyes opened. "I think that was Argentina." The odd demonic changes reverted as she shook her head and blinked several times. She saw the baffled look on the Devil's face. She sighed, trying not to roll her eyes. "There's not much information we can find on living fallen angels. The best we can figure, I can't control the back and forth the same as you and others, since I'm half. Instead, for me, it comes out when I use powerful magic."

"Clearly." Lucifer chuckled. "I don't understand why you don't use it all the time. You would be quite formidable if you did."

Ellyria glanced at Zangrunath. "If I wanted to end the world, I could. It wouldn't be difficult. I'd much rather watch the light fade from people's eyes when they realize they didn't read the fine print."

"I think I can understand that." The Dark Prince nodded once, humming as he thought. "I prefer the world the way it is, so thank you for not doing that. Still, don't be afraid to stretch your wings a bit." He chuckled again, back to his usual confident self.

Ellyria shivered as the memories of her one experience attempting to fly with her spectral wings washed through her mind. "Been there. Done that. I don't think I like to fly that way. I'll settle for ley walking."

"Well, it was worth the shot. Thank you for doing this for me. I would do it myself, but much like yourself, the earth doesn't like it when I have fun." He barked a laugh and calmed himself a moment later. His eyes pierced into them. "You can go back to your fun. Just be sure to get that done for me soon. Ta-ta for now." With those last words and a wave goodbye, he vanished into the air, nowhere to be found.

"I suffer from severe word vomit around that being." Ellyria sighed.

Zangrunath nodded and sighed. "He has that effect on mortals. They want to express their deepest desires in front of him."

"Does it ever go away? In Hell, maybe?" she asked.

He shrugged. "I tried to lie to him there, but between that ability and the code, he is exceptional at seeing through deceit. I think it is his divinity."

After thinking about his words for a moment, she nodded. She often forgot about the demon code, which was a problem. She needed to think about that first and foremost when dealing with demons and the Devil. It was a bad habit that she needed to break sooner rather than later. "That would make sense. Huh." She paused in thought. "I never considered which abilities were from my father and from my mother. It's obvious that I can combine them, so I'm not sure which is part of my divinity or not."

He waved a hand, looking and sounding a little annoyed. "Well, whatever it is, have fun with it."

"Are you okay?" she asked.

"You are lucky. You have the powers of both humans and angels. I just have the borrowed powers that come with being a demon. I will never get that in my entire eternity. That is something you and the Prince of Darkness have in common." He gestured to where Lucifer sat moments before.

"Why couldn't you?" she asked out of nowhere. "We share a soul."

He shook his head. "That would break the code. Only a person born of divinity can wield those powers. I wasn't born with them."

She conjured a ball of magic that glowed in her hand and placed it in his. "I know that, and I didn't mean the divine powers."

"This is just magic," he said as she placed the ball in his hands. "It's like holding a candle to an inferno."

She sighed, looking down, and feeling like she was taking something he wanted away from him. She wanted to give that to him. As she shuffled off to their bedroom, she felt like less-than. He'd never rebuffed something she'd suggested so hard before. "I think I'm going to sleep before we go to Argentina."

He nodded and looked around the room. "Yeah. I will get this flight arranged and clean this place up while you sleep." He sighed as he tidied up after the visit. "Sleep well."

"Thanks," she said, heading into the bedroom and hearing the door click closed behind her. She slid down the wood there. "I just want you to be happy with your footing. Whatever it takes," she said before crawling into bed. "Count on the Devil himself to turn a vacation into work and cause our first actual fight."

As Ellyria went to bed, Zane cleaned up before he sat at the computer. Why did Lucifer have to show up? He had planned a fun vacation for Ellyria, and in less than an hour, the Prince of Darkness ruined it.

He thought about the disagreement; he didn't mean to get mad at her. It was mere jealousy. Envy. It was difficult not to be jealous of something you couldn't have, and he didn't want to think about what would happen if he ever got his hands on the destructive power Ellyria had. Some things shouldn't happen, and this was one of those things. He shook the thought from his head and booked the flight. He hoped tearing the rogue general into a fine mince would help him clear his head.


**Tuesday, December 25, 2029**

Zane awoke Ellyria early in the morning. When she looked outside, it was still dark enough to see the city lights. She leaned in for a kiss, but he didn't move the rest of the way in to join her. She sighed. "I'm assuming you packed our bags?"

"Yeah." He nodded. "We will need to get going soon in order to keep up with this one."

She got up and changed clothes. "I'll be ready in five."

He nodded, heading to the kitchen. He made her a sandwich to eat on the way to the airport. As she came out of the bedroom, he handed it to her and led her to the door. "Alright, let's get going."

She took the food and followed. "This feels like those first days of college," she said, looking at him. She frowned when he didn't look back.

"How so?" he asked, moving by muscle memory at this point.

She looked at him and shook her head. "No reason," she said, but she remembered dancing around him and their feelings. She thought the fly-by-night breakfasts and his cool attitude were a thing of the past. She was wrong.

Zane led them to Shelby; he got in and started her up. He waited for Ellyria to get in and get herself situated before he drove them to the airport. The streets were almost empty at this time of night, and he could rev the engine a bit, weaving between the other, much slower vehicles.

Ellyria finished her meal and looked at him. She felt her heart sink, but her gut coiled tight with anger as well. "Look at me, Zangrunath."

He turned his head to look at her and then back to the road to make sure they were safe. "What?" he asked, sounding impassive.

"What's wrong with you? I know there's a lot going on, but you haven't looked at me. You didn't kiss me good morning, and you didn't open the door for me. This is stupid. Dammit all to Hell. I don't care about anything else. I love you, and I won't let this screw up what we have."

Zangrunath continued to drive, letting out a sigh. "I love you, too. I do," he said, glancing over at her.

"But," she interrupted, "you were about to say but."

"*But*," he said with a growl, putting more emphasis on the word. "I am jealous of you. Alright?" He sighed as he drove, shaking his head like he was trying to forget about the last few hours in their entirety. "I just want to get this over with so that we can go home and be together. Okay?"

Ellyria took his hand. "I'm sorry," she said in a quiet, watery voice. "If it's any consolation, I don't want power or standing or any of it. I just want you. You can have it. All of it and me."

"Don't be sorry. I know you don't want any of it. You would have preferred a normal life over all of this," he said, knowing the truth deep in his soul. "I want you, but I can't have that power you have. If I were to have it," he trailed off. His mind raced before he shook his head again. "It would be better if I didn't." He finished, leaving the details out. It was best if he left that as vague as possible. He didn't want to scare her with the darkest parts of him that Hell had brought to the forefront.

She squeezed his hand, curious but too emotional and exhausted to pursue the lead. "I would make every single mistake and choice again if it meant I could be with you." She stroked the back of his hand with her fingers. "Use me as a tool if you need to. If I'm at your side, I don't care."

He pulled her hand to his lips and gave it a kiss. "I would never use you like that. Given the ritual and your deal, it should be the other way around." He chuckled, but no mirth came with the sound. "I would go through Hell several times over if it meant that I get to end up beside you." He smiled at her.

"Mine."

He squeezed her hand. "Mine."

They arrived at the hangar, and she stole a kiss from him. "I love you, Zangrunath," she said before they hopped out of Shelby. "Let's go get you a promotion to lead general or whatever. What would that make you?"

"Well, I won't be one of the seven lead generals, but I would be right under one. So, it would be like a human lieutenant," he said as they got onto the plane.

"But the guy we're after is one of those generals. Isn't he?" she asked. As she thought about the different ranks and why she could never understand the system in Hell, her curiosity grew. Who were they going after? Was it a good or a bad thing that the Devil was vague? She shivered as the realization struck. He didn't strike her as the type to omit something by accident; he kept his words vague on purpose.

"If he were, we would have much bigger concerns. We would need more help than just the two of us if that were the case."

She considered his words. "I thought your boss said someone above you needed handling. I'm confused."

"Yes, but he never said which one." He sighed. "There is a hierarchy of who runs what. Lucifer is at the top, and he has seven demons under him who oversee everything. They rival him in power, and he also didn't say who ticked him off. Fuck." Zane groaned, coming to the same realization she had moments before.

"That's what I thought." She nodded. "We'll figure it out. You're strong. I'm strong. Together, we could end the world. We can beat one demon."

"I admire your enthusiasm. We will, but it is going to hurt." He nodded and gave her a soft smile before he sighed, taking his seat on the plane.

She gave him a peck on the cheek. "It's not so much enthusiasm as understanding that we're kinda screwed either way. I expect pain."

"There will be, but I will try to keep it to a minimum."

"As long as I have it made up to me after this is done, I'll be fine." She leaned into him, taking his hand. Her thumb rubbed the back of his hand as she saw her demon frown. "I will help any way I can to make this go well for you."

He leaned his head on her. "Thank you. The sooner we get this done, the sooner I can make it up to you. So much for my gift to you." He sighed.

"I know. It was a nice vacation idea." She pouted.

He shook his head. "No. Believe it or not, I got you something. I was going to give it to you later today since you like this day for gifts so much," he said with a serious expression that turned into a soft smile. "I just never had the chance to give it to you."

"I thought today was just another stupid Pagan holiday the Christians converted when they took over." She chuckled as she used his words.

"Oh, it is, but I still wanted to get you something."

"You're so sweet." She smiled, kissing him as they both laughed some more. "I got you something, too."

He put an arm around her and rubbed her shoulder. "Then when we are done with this, we can exchange them."

"I look forward to it." She closed her eyes and leaned her head on his shoulder. "I'm going to get some more rest. Seems like the crazy will kick into gear as soon as we land."

He nodded. "You do that. We will go until we put him down when we get there, so do your best to be at one hundred percent."

She nodded. "Nothing quite like demon slaying on Christmas."

"Paint the halls with blood and gore," he sang.

"Grandma got sacrificed in a blood pact," she sang back, finishing with a yawn.

He chuckled and gave her a kiss on the forehead. "Sleep well. Love you."

"Darling," she said before falling asleep.

Zane held Ellyria's hand as she rested. His mind focused on the task ahead for a while, but turned back to the woman beside him. She surprised him. They had disagreed before, but today she had deescalated him from a fit of jealous rage. This was a new feeling for him. He had never had somebody that could do something such as that before, proving yet again that his witch was special. He knew he would protect her, his perfect other half, with everything that he had in him now and forever.

Several hours later, Ellyria ate a bland meal of airplane snacks. It wasn't great, but it was something. She would need to have fuel in her system for whatever would happen tonight. The pilot's bell rang to inform them it was five in the afternoon local time. She looked at Zane. "Demon hunting after dark."

Zane nodded. "I would much rather be doing this during the day, but we will work with what we have." He looked out over the city of Buenos Aires, trying to see any sign of the demon as they descended and said, "Where are you?"

"Do you want me to check again? It's been a few hours," she asked.

"Yes, please. I don't want him sneaking up on us."

She nodded and tapped the leys. "He's heading north by northwest. Feels like there's something big that way. Maybe a ley convergence like Stonehenge."

"He is trying to get stronger, then. We need to cut him off before he gets there."

"We can do that. I can still ley walk. I don't know why we didn't come that way in the first place, but you were already chartering the plane." She shrugged. Her eyes were still black, and her skin changed colors, starting at the eyes. "I'm just going to take the big guy's advice and keep it going for now."

"Good." He nodded as the plane landed. "I chose this because you needed the rest. We can't go into this half-cocked and tired."

Ellyria nodded. "It's fine. We've got the money, anyway." She unbuckled her seatbelt and sat up. "Let's do this."

Zangrunath smiled and turned into his demonic self. A growl escaped his lips. "Let's." He opened the door to the plane and picked Ellyria up, shrouding them in mist. He started flying in the direction she pointed out a few moments ago.

Ellyria continued to concentrate, pointing for him like a dowsing rod. "At least I'm helpful on this adventure."

"You are always helpful." He smiled. "As long as you are by my side, you are helping."

She kissed his cheek, pointing due west after feeling an oddity a moment later. "Okay, that was weird. He, like, jumped."

He veered in the direction she pointed. "I don't know how he did that. He might have used a sigil to go between points."

"You're the expert." She shrugged. "You like to keep all the demonic secrets close to your chest, even though I'll be like you one day."

"I don't do it on purpose. It is out of habit. Mortals aren't supposed to know how we operate. You are the exception because we are bound. When this is done, I promise I will explain it to you," he said, rubbing her back in soothing circles.

"Thank you." She smiled, leaning into him. "It would be nice to know what I'm in for besides reading about the whole making demons thing." She shivered.

He nodded. "I won't be able to help with that. The process weeds out the weak and makes sure the strong thrive. Hell thrives on strength."

She nodded. "I get it. It's just a lot of blood."

"You will be fine. You are strong. I know you will become a powerful demon." He smiled.

"I will," she said with more confidence than she felt. "Either way, I'll be yours forever." She pointed due north a moment later. "Okay. He's gotta be screwing with us."

He growled, changing directions. "He better not. This needs to end fast."

Ellyria sighed. "I can expedite by ley walking if you want to try."

Zangrunath thought it over and sighed. "Let's do it. I don't want to, but I want this over with. I just have a bad feeling."

Ellyria nodded, understanding how he was feeling. "I would prefer to be on the ground for this, then."

He nodded and flew towards the ground, setting her down gently as he landed. "Let's get this done."

Ellyria looked at the setting sun. "Yeah. Let's finish this before it's too dark for me to see the fight." She took his hand, concentrating hard before a flash of light and a jerking motion brought them into the center of a clearing. She looked around for a second. Her gut sank. Her eyes met Zane's before she pushed him out of the circle they'd jumped into with a wave of magic. "Get out! It's a trap!"

Zangrunath flew backwards out of the circle, seeing a magical barrier enclose Ellyria inside. He almost toppled backwards before he caught himself and landed square. His eyes darted around the clearing, checking for any danger, before he ran up to the wall of force and pounded against it. "Elly!"

Ellyria ran up to the wall and found it to be solid. Her eyes panicked. "Zangrunath," she said. "It's in my book. This circle, it's a magic siphon." She dropped to her knees as she felt the magic leave her. It started as a trickle before growing stronger and faster with each passing moment. Her eyes flickered between black and her normal brown.

"Fuck!" His eyes darted around for the demon they were after. "Where are you, you coward? You're a poor excuse for a demon!"

There was a long moment of silence before a flash of light appeared next to Zangrunath. "I am right here." The ex-general grinned as he drove his fist into Zangrunath's face, throwing him several feet away from the circle. He licked the demonic black blood from his hand and chuckled. "I was expecting something stronger, but," he paused, gazing at Ellyria instead of the demon. He licked his lips as he found himself filled with a sudden feeling of hunger. "You are the reason for him being here, aren't you?"

Ellyria stepped back. The pain in Zane's cheek throbbed in her own. This unknown demon disgusted her, and she decided that engaging with him wasn't worth the little time or energy that she had. Instead, she ran to the center of the circle. She looked all about before wrenching as much energy from the earth as possible. The leys came to her aid, and she felt a surge of power. She stomped, and the surrounding wall flashed with bright light. She did it again before she realized this one was already weaker. Stealing a glance at where Zangrunath landed, she bit her lip. "I love you," she said, pouring as much of her magic as possible into him as fast as she could.

Zangrunath felt his wound close in an instant, and his gaze focused on Ellyria. "No." His eyes widened as he lost sense of his usual calculating nature for a moment, dipping into his wrathful side. He shot towards the demon. Now that he'd seen their enemy, he shouted to get the demon's attention. "Sathanas, let her go!" His arms turned into blades, and he unleashed a flourish towards the general.

Sathanas took the blows with practiced ease. They were nothing but flesh wounds against his power. He chuckled as he felt the wounds close faster than Zangrunath could make them. A Cheshire smile dominated his lips as he gained the upper hand. Sathanas raised a foot and kicked Zangrunath square in the chest, creating distance between them. He heard bones crack in the other demon's chest as he turned towards Ellyria. "No. I want the power to overthrow Lucifer.

She has it. I'm taking it, annihilation ritual or not." He laughed like the megalomaniac he was.

Ellyria fell to the ground in pain as Zangrunath's ribs cracked. "Ah!" By some miracle, she was still conscious enough to send him the magic he needed to heal the wounds and then some. She could feel the magic of the leys weakening. A tiny voice in the back of her mind told her she took too much. Desperate to end this, she saw the other demon and reached out a hand, concentrating hard between sending Zangrunath power and using it. Blood came from her ears as she tried to tear him to shreds with her power; a small wisp of matter sloughing off starting at his sharpened horn.

Sathanas noticed Ellyria's attempts at helping Zane and growled. He made a quick series of hand motions, sending spikes from the ground into her legs in a manner eerily similar to how she'd killed Larry years previous. "You can stop that. Just let me take the power already. It will be easier on the both of us if you just give in." He smirked.

Zangrunath felt the pain shoot through Ellyria and into his legs. He released a roar. His wings became wreathed in flames. He blazed towards the target of his wrath. "You will die!" He grabbed Sathanas by the arm and ripped it off in one quick, fluid motion. Now that he disarmed the other demon in the literal sense, he stabbed him several times.

Ellyria screamed in agony. Her focus on everything external faded. She cut the spikes from her with two swift hand motions and healed herself, gasping in pain. Her breaths came in heavy pants; her movements grew sluggish. She curled up and let out a sob before giving Zangrunath everything she held back from using. Her magic was running out, and she couldn't let the other demon have these things. Her energy manipulation and matter creation. The connection to the leys. She felt her heart skip a beat, as it was all torn from her. She choked and sputtered.

Sathanas sneered at Ellyria and felt that she was all but spent. He could feel power coursing through him. A smirk pulled at his lips before his gaze met Zangrunath's. "And so it is done." He laughed as he waved a hand, sending several spikes shooting up and through Ellyria's chest and torso.

Zangrunath released a strangled noise of loss and heartbreak, not unlike a whimper, though he would describe it as a gasp of surprise. He watched as he felt the moment Ellyria died, helpless to stop it. He died countless times before, but this time was a million times more painful than anything he had ever experienced. Feeling the other half of his soul leave this plane, he fell to his knees and wailed in grief. He held his head in his hands for all but a moment, and in the few seconds that passed, something snapped inside of him. He glared at Sathanas, standing up and stalking towards him. "You are dead." His voice rumbled in a low timbre as he used Ellyria's powers with instinctive intuitiveness to create armor made of pure, holy light around himself.

Sathanas froze as he noticed golden tears falling from Zangrunath's eyes. They flowed upward and formed what looked like a shattered halo above his head. He shook his head as he backed away. "N- no. No demon should be able to wield the powers of divinity. That breaks the code."

"Fuck the code," Zangrunath said with a growl, creating a greatsword of light in his hand. "I am going to eviscerate you and spread your atoms across space time. To Hell with the repercussions!" he yelled to the Heavens as, in an instant, he appeared next to Sathanas and swung the sword with practiced precision. The strike knocked Sathanas back into the barrier, shattering it as he flew through the force field.

Sathanas tried to cast a spell, but found that nothing happened. His eyes went wide as he saw Zane appear next to him again, striking him down into the ground. Thanks to the massive amount of power being used and their durable demonic bodies, a massive crater formed where the battle raged on, with Sathanas at the bottom of the growing pit. He attempted to stand up. The magic he'd taken from Ellyria already waned, thanks to the injuries he'd sustained. He got to a knee before Zangrunath jumped onto his back and a cracking noise rang out through the clearing. "Please, no," he said, trying in vain to get away.

Reacting fast, Zangrunath's hand moved almost impossibly fast. Above them, what looked like miniature black holes appeared. Small stars formed around them. Zane drove the sword through the base of Sathanas's spine and wrenched his head back by the hair. He turned the body to look him in the eyes. A symphony of sickening squelching sounds sounded out in the moments before Zane ended his existence. "I have been around for over three thousand years, and in that time, I have done countless rituals, none of which ended like this." He paused as tears welled up in his eyes again. "Then you tried to overthrow Lucifer himself, broke the code, stole Ellyria's power," he trailed off, and his voice broke. "The woman I love! You killed her right in front of my eyes." He went from yelling to eerie quiet. He leaned forward to snarl the next words into Sathanas's ear. The earth below them rumbled as he seethed. "I sentence you to death. No amount of magic, holy or otherwise, is bringing you back."

Zangrunath tore Sathanas into small pieces with quick and violent movements. He completed the task with practiced ease, as if he were ritualistically dismembering the demon for the millionth time in his life. With each chunk of rent flesh, he hurled the pieces of Sathanas into the inky black voids that hovered above them. When there was nothing left of the demon to destroy, he stood up. His back arched as he cried to the Heavens at the loss of his Ellyria.

Ellyria's eyes opened. She breathed easy. Looking around, she found the room unfamiliar, but comfortable. Art decorated the walls, and an elegant Victorian style decorated the room. She sat up and jumped when she saw the familiar form of Lucifer. "Ah, shit."

Lucifer sat at a desk a respectable distance away from her. He leaned back in his chair, turning to gaze at her. His usual unruffled expression was missing. Instead, he looked annoyed and dismayed, almost beyond recognition. He looked at Ellyria out of the corner of his eye, and his hand moved to cover his face. "Calm down. I already have enough to deal with after this. I don't need any problems from you right now." He waved a hand at her as he muffled a groan.

"I'm just realizing that even though I died before my deal was done, I still went to Hell. I think. To be honest, I expected tormented souls, fire, and brimstone. This ain't bad."

"The souls wouldn't shut up." He sighed, sitting up to look at her better. "As for this," he gestured to the room and shrugged, "it is what I desired. So, I made it be. Then there is your deal." The King of Hell paused, trying to process the oncoming nightmare ahead. Even he didn't want to bring up the failure of epic proportions.

"Oh." She covered her face and groaned. The sound filled the room. "I worded that amendment the way I did for a reason, but didn't take unnatural death into account. Crap."

"Yes, indeed." He nodded. His eyes gazed at her and through her, piercing into her soul. "Not to mention the annihilation ritual that had yet to be completed. Both of which I messed up by sending you on a suicide mission without knowing what he'd done."

She nodded, feeling her magic missing. It was with Zane. Zane who wasn't here with her. She grew still. "Dammit." The feeling of weakness made her growl in frustration.

Lucifer sighed and stood up. "Because of my mistake of epic proportions, congratulations! You get to go back," he said, walking up to her with an unreadable expression in his eyes.

She stood up, staring back into his dark and terrifying eyes. She gulped. "I'm not staying?"

"No. Not yet," he said, gazing down his nose at her as if inspecting something that he intended to purchase or destroy. "You still have a ritual to finish, and I need to deal with the aftermath of what your other half just did." He shook his head. "My brother will never let me live this down."

"W- what did Zangrunath do?" she asked, panicking and ignoring his last sentence. "Is he okay?"

"Oh, he is fine," he said with a dark chuckle. His annoyance was once again growing by the moment. "He used your powers to become one of the four horsemen of the apocalypse in order to make Sathanas no longer exist." As he processed the words, he stared at the wall behind her for a moment. "He got the job done though," he said, trying to look at this disaster with the thinnest of silver linings.

Ellyria closed her eyes tight, and let out a sound of frustration. "I stop using magic before I get to that point."

"Thank you for that. Though Zangrunath could control what he was doing, I doubt he could've stopped himself. Demons don't normally fall in love, so they go overboard when they see the person they are bound to die in front of them." He sighed, looking her over with that assessing gaze again. "Go up there and take your powers back, please. I need to go have a chat with the council."

Ellyria opened her lips to respond. She wanted to ask more questions. She always had more questions. Instead, she awoke in a great deal of pain. Blood trailed down her skin. She blinked several times, gazing up at Zangrunath. She coughed. "Zane," she said in a weak voice as her heart beat a slow, steady rhythm.

Zangrunath jumped as he heard Ellyria's voice and felt her body move again. He pulled away, seeing her wounds healing. He looked at her face when he heard his name. Pulling her against his chest, he held her, crying as he did so. "Elly."

"Not so tight. Everything hurts," she said with a pained groan. "Boss man sent me back."

He chuckled at her words and loosened his grip. He didn't want to hurt her more than she already was. "I thought I lost you forever." He sniffled.

She shook her head. "Should've checked Hell before you got that far."

He gave her a kiss. "I wasn't sure I could find you," he said, wiping away his tears. "I never failed to protect someone, so I thought-"

She noticed the physical changes about him that her magic created. Somehow, they made him more beautiful to her. "Shh." She wiped away a golden tear. "We. Are. One." She leaned into him, wanting to cry with sympathy just at the look of him, even though she knew it would just make matters worse to cry herself. "Can I get my magic back?"

He nodded and placed a hand on her chest, channeling her magic back into her. "That power; I shouldn't have used it. It wasn't mine to use. I'm sorry."

"I wanted you to use it," she said, breathing a little easier now. "I stop before I let it get that far."

"I know. That is why you should have these. Seeing you-" He didn't finish his sentence, but he continued with the rest of his thoughts. "Made me snap. I didn't care what happened as long as he died."

She cried in pain and emotional anguish then. "Can we sleep, please? I'm exhausted."

He felt a few tears fall and nodded, knowing how she felt better than anybody in the universe. "Yeah. Let's go to the plane and sleep," he said, flying towards the airport, leaving the devastation he caused behind them.

"No." She shook her head. "I ley walked us to Chile. Just find a hotel. I don't care."

"Okay," he said, giving her a kiss. "That is fine by me." At her order, thanks to demonic magic, he learned the location of the nearest city, flying her towards where his instinct directed him.

He kept looking down at her, making sure that she was okay. He watched as Ellyria's eyes closed, and she drifted to sleep in his arms, snoring. Her soft, warm breaths reassured him she still lived. Zangrunath smiled down at her. As he flew, he stroked her hair. The simple action became a comfort for both of them.

He arrived at a hotel in short order, waving a hand to disguise them with demon magic, and rented them a room. He brought Ellyria to the room and closed the door behind them. The full force of both his and her exhaustion hit him. He laid down in bed, holding her in his arms as he passed out.

# XII



Ellyria took all but a second to realize she didn't recognize the room she was in. Where was she? She groaned in pain. She felt the form of her demon beside her, and she turned to look at him. "Zane?"

Zane stirred awake when he heard Elly's voice. "Yes?"

"Where are we?" she asked. Her stomach growled with ravenous hunger.

"A hotel in Chile," he said as he let go of her. "You asked me to fly somewhere close instead of heading back to the plane."

She got out of bed and ran to the bathroom, returning a minute later wearing clean and repaired clothing. "The poor pilot needed a break, too."

He let out a sigh. "We pay him enough so that he doesn't mind working a holiday. He wouldn't mind."

She slid into his arms, holding him close. "Regardless, I didn't want to fly."

"I don't blame you," he said, holding her in kind. He groaned. "I am still sore after that."

She nodded and tried not to cry at how much it hurt to breathe deep. "We are sore. Let's get room service and relax until we're better. I don't think I can do much more magic than I already used to fix my shirt today, but I came up with a plan to get home."

Zangrunath nodded. "I am fine with that. I don't want to go anywhere right now." He rolled over, grabbing his cell phone. "I will let the pilot know he can head back whenever."

"Sounds good." She lounged on the bed. "I want to visit as many countries as we can on the way back home."

"I will never say no to that." He smirked, knowing what she had in mind, and dialed the pilot before ordering room service for her.

Ellyria waited for Zane to be off the phone. Then she said, "Now you know firsthand that I can end the world. Would've been kind of cool to see the fireworks."

Zane rested next to her and looked into her eyes. "I never doubted that for a second. Though you might see the aftermath." He chuckled.

"Well, it's either scorched earth or a crater," she said.

"Yes. Wasn't thinking. Just kind of did."

"I don't need to see it then. I'll just look it up next time one of the online satellite maps refreshes." She giggled.

"Or check the news." He laughed before his countenance changed. He sighed and wrapped an arm around her. "I don't want to lose you again."

She cuddled into his chest. "You can't," she said. "My contract amendment screwed the Devil over."

He looked into her eyes. A chuckle bubbled up in his chest before spilling into a fit of laughter. "Of course, you would beat the Devil at his own game." He gripped his side from laughing so hard and groaned. "Ouch."

"I know. I feel it too." She gripped her side as well, stifling a similar groan. "You've got me like this for the rest of my natural life. I used the good words." She smirked.

He leaned in to give her a much-needed kiss. "I wouldn't change it for a second."

A knock came from the door. "Room service!" a voice said through the door.

Zane sighed and stood up. He walked to the door and answered it. Once he got the food from the man, he shut the door again. He came back to bed a moment later and sat down next to her, offering a tray of food. "Here you go. Sorry, it's not my cooking."

She took the plate and shoveled the meal into her mouth. "Too hungry to care."

He smirked, watching her eat for a moment as he relaxed. "That's okay."

A few minutes later, Ellyria finished her meal and laid down on the bed beside Zangrunath. "I love you," she said.

He smirked and turned into his demonic form. He wrapped his tail around her waist, pulling her close to him. "I love you."

**Thursday, January 3, 2030**

Ellyria and Zangrunath held hands, walking the streets of Mexico City. They chatted until they happened across a bar that seemed out of place. Zangrunath stopped, assessing the building with confusion and wonder. "That doesn't seem right."

She glanced over at the building and did a double take. She reached out a hand, feeling the energies there. "Huh. It feels magical."

"Yeah, but that wasn't what drew me to it," he said, looking at her instead of the building. "It was the name."

"Dilrith. That's not Spanish."

"No. It is closer to the Spanglish version of demonic," he said, giving her a serious look. "It means demon slayer."

She looked up at Zane. "Hard to pass, then? Though I admit I'm curious."

He chuckled. "Oh no. We are checking this out." He smiled and led the way to the entrance. "I doubt they know what the name means."

"I doubt that. I would bet on it."

"You're on. The usual wager?" he asked with a smile.

She thought for a minute. "Double it."

He chuckled and nodded, holding out his hand as they entered the bar. "Deal."

She shook on it. "Agreed."

As the two entered the building, they saw license plates from across the globe decorating the walls. There were a few patrons idly chatting. A country song ended and rock music picked up afterwards. At the back corner of the room, a large man stood in all black clothing, eyes gazing around the bar for any signs of trouble.

Over at the bar, a middle-aged gentleman making drinks wore a fine and well-tailored outfit despite their surroundings. The slacks were designer. The button up might not have been, but the silk tie negated the thought that anything he wore was cheap. "Hello," the man said with a thick European accent. He didn't look up from his workstation as he did. He had medium brown hair that could have either been blonder or darker when he was younger, but patches of white there now made it difficult to tell. It was just long enough to pull into a small tail at the base of his neck and slicked back. His goatee made him look even more distinguished. He finished wiping a spot on the counter and looked up, revealing icy blue eyes.

Zane looked at the man for all but a second. "Fuck," he said, knowing in an instant who was tending the bar.

"What?" Ellyria asked, tensing at Zangrunath's reaction.

He gazed at the man for a moment longer, and the bartender gave him a curious look in return. He turned his attention to Ellyria for a moment to address her question, but he never turned his body away from the man behind the bar, keeping him in his sights in the corner of his eye. "Have you ever heard a ghost story and thought to yourself that there is no way that could ever happen?" he asked, seeing the bartender come around the counter to approach them. "Well, there is a ghost standing in front of us."

Ellyria looked the man up and down. He didn't seem like a witch, but she sensed some sort of magic. She thought fast before asking Zane quiet enough for only him to hear. "Is that ghost you're mentioning us or him?"

"To be honest? Both," he said as the man stopped right in front of them.

"Is everything alright? Do you need anything? A drink or maybe some food?" he asked with eerie calm as he assessed the pair. His voice sounded concerned, but it felt like much more happened behind the stoic gaze the man leveled them with. He seemed to size up each of them in an instant, looking them in the eyes for a moment as he did.

Zane nodded. "Yes, everything is fine. Just wasn't expecting the place to be quite like this. That is all."

Ellyria broke the piercing eye contact of the bartender and glanced at Zane. "Well, I think I'm in desperate need of alcohol after the last few weeks."

The man smiled and waved a hand towards the bar. "Well, that I can help with." He moved back behind the bar. "What can I get you?"

"Whiskey and cola. Double whiskey," she said, taking a seat on a stool. "What is this guy?" she asked with telepathy.

"I will take a double of what she gets," he said with a sigh before sitting. He watched the man make the drinks and replied in the same manner. "He was Section Seven's number one demon exterminator before he up and vanished one day," he said, continuing to eye the man. "No one knows why he left. Everyone thought he was dead, but it's obvious he wasn't."

Ellyria nodded, assessing this former magic hunter. She stiffened. "I think I found why he quit," she said into his head. She pointed at the gold band on his left ring finger. "Who's the lucky lady?" Ellyria asked, trying to sound conversational.

The man smiled and handed them their drinks. "Her name is Lily," he said, leaning on the bar as he did so. "She is devilishly beautiful." He smirked at the double meaning of his own words. His mind working through the facts and trying to figure out what this was all about. The weight of the holy weapon on his hip was heavy on his mind.

Zangrunath coughed around his drink and took a moment to calm himself. "Oh, I bet she is," he said, realizing who the man was referring to.

Ellyria took a drink and realized it wasn't as cold as she liked. She focused for a second and froze the glass without moving her fingers, taking another sip. She looked up to find the bartender's eyes boring into hers.

"You know, miss," he said, a smile growing on his lips. "If you wanted a colder drink, you could have asked." He chuckled, turning towards Zangrunath. Now that all the moving pieces slid into place, he could relax into the situation more. "Yes, she is, but you already knew that. Didn't you, demon boy?" he asked, leaning against the bar.

Ellyria was dumbstruck. "How did you do that so fast?"

"You or him?" he asked, pointing to Zane.

"Yes."

He chuckled. "I could smell him the second he walked into the door." He looked at Zane before regarding Ellyria for a moment. "I could also smell demon coming off of you, but it wasn't until you cooled your drink that I realized I had a witch here with her demon."

Ellyria searched all about. Nobody looked startled by those words. "Okay. I'll bite. Are we all weird here?"

The bartender laughed. "It's a matter of perspective, but the ones here right now know what's up."

Ellyria sighed. "Well, this trip just got a lot more interesting."

"Yes, it did." Zane gestured to the bartender. "Ellyria, meet Tarso Helge, the demon hunter."

Tarso extended a hand. "Nice to meet you."

Ellyria shook hands with the man. "Retired I hope. I feel it if you take him out; that hurts."

"Oh," Tarso said, raising an eyebrow at her words. He noticed the annihilation ritual seal on her back. The details pieced themselves together as they came to light. He looked at the demon. "You two are soul bound. Interesting." He smiled. "What is your name?"

"Zangrunath." He sighed, holding out his hand to shake Tarso's.

She made a face. "You can just tell that?"

He shook his head. "Your scent has a stronger demonic smell than normal. That and I can see parts of the seal on your shoulders. It is a huge giveaway."

She looked at her outfit and realized people here could see and understand the sigils on her exposed back. "Oh. I'm so used to normal people that I forgot others could see it."

He waved a hand. "It's fine. I just haven't seen a seal that detailed in several years."

"Uh, yeah." She sighed, remembering the mark of the fallen in the center of the seal. She closed her eyes and concentrated on the shirt, knitting itself together to cover her upper back and shoulders.

Zane glared at Tarso. "Could you please stop staring at her back?"

Tarso chuckled and nodded. "Alright." He took a step back. "Would you care to go downstairs to have a more private conversation? There will be fewer prying eyes."

"I guess so." Ellyria shrugged. "I admit I'm curious."

"Then let's head downstairs." Tarso smiled, waving the bouncer in the corner over to run the counter for him.

Zane glanced at Ellyria before releasing a deep sigh as his body stood up without his permission. She'd already decided, and the ritual was taking over, soul binding or not. "Fine. Let's go."

"Sorry. We never see magical folks outside of Tom and Steve. I'm kind of invested."

"It's alright." He nodded. "We still have a couple of weeks before we need to head back home."

Tarso smiled at the pair as he led them down a set of stairs to the private portion of the bar. They walked down a long hallway with several doors that each had strange symbols on them. At the end of the hallway, a set of heavy doors dominated the space. He swung them open and brought them into an area that looked like the one above. Now it contained far more exotic patrons. Two demons flanked the doors, standing guard as they walked in. There were creatures of varying shapes and sizes sitting around the bar. Each one eyed Ellyria, who seemed out of place among the group of weirdos and misfits.

Tarso brought them to a private booth and gestured for them to sit down before he closed the shutters behind him. "So, what brings you two to Mexico?" he asked, sitting down across from them.

"Christmas Day demon slaying became a vacation trip." Ellyria shrugged.

Zane chuckled. "You make it sound like that is a casual thing."

"Why are demons killing demons now?" Tarso asked.

"Because someone asked us to." She didn't realize how much her vagueness spoke in volumes.

He gave her a curious look, but nodded. "I won't pry too deep then." He looked like he was about to ask something else, but his manners overrode the question. "Are you hungry? Can I get you something?"

Zane shook his head. "Don't need to, but she might."

"I could eat." She nodded.

"Alright." Tarso smiled. "What can I get you?"

She didn't need to think. "Well, we are in Mexico. Tacos."

He chuckled. "Alright. I will be back in a moment." He stood up and left the two of them alone. The shutters to the booth remained open when he walked away.

Ellyria looked out of the private booth. "Okay. I think I saw someone with scales out there."

"That wouldn't surprise me. I saw a few people out there who I wasn't expecting to see." He eyed the odd fellow in the booth on the opposite side of the bar. "Pretty sure there is a dragon in here," he said with surprising nonchalance.

"Excuse me, but a what?" Her expression was between amazed and baffled.

"A dragon," he said with a chuckle. "You know angels and demons exist. Did you think dragons didn't exist?"

"I- uh, ugh. I should've realized when we met Tom."

"It's okay. The general population doesn't need to know. Secrecy was one reason behind the crusades, so most creatures went into hiding." He took a sip of his drink.

After hearing that, Ellyria took a large gulp of her booze, remembering one battlefield from their trip to Europe over her graduation. "Especially the other weapons of war," she quoted his words. "Oh, you jerk."

He smiled. "All is fair in love and war."

"I love you," she said. Then she cringed, switching to mental speech. "You don't have to say it out loud. I'd hate to ruin your demonic street cred."

He leaned down and kissed her. "I love you," he said out loud. "I don't care what they think. You are the only one that matters to me."

She smirked, taking a drink and staring down a demon that was watching them. "This has been the weirdest vacation of my lifetime. So far."

"I don't plan on them getting any weirder, so this should be the pinnacle." He nodded at Tarso when came back with a plate of tacos in hand.

"Here you go." Tarso smiled, setting the food down in front of her and sitting across from them again. He pulled the shutters to the booth closed to allow them privacy. "Enjoy."

Ellyria breathed in the delicious scent before digging in. "Yum."

"I am glad you like my wife's old recipe. *Grazie*." He gave a respectful nod.

Between bites, Ellyria asked, "So no offense, but how does one go from what he called you," she pointed to Zane, "to all of this?" She gestured to the bar. "Sounds to me like an interesting story."

Tarso chuckled at her words. "Well, it is interesting. I started by working as a soldier. After that, they chose me to join the Pontifical Guard when I killed a demon. Section Seven was my employer for over twenty years before I met somebody on a mission that I couldn't find the wherewithal to kill. I fell harder than Lucifer from the pearly gates in love with her." He smiled at the memories. "It wasn't easy getting out by any means, but I did. Now I live here, making sure that others like myself have a safe place to relax away from prying eyes."

Ellyria almost had her drink come out of her nose at his mention of Lucifer, but she kept it together. "I would imagine that getting out was much harder than you make it sound. Section Seven is persistent." She suppressed a groan.

"They are." He nodded, knowing what she meant better than anybody. "It helps when you have friends in both high and low places. You don't work for Section Seven without making some friends."

"Say no more. Of all people, I know about all of that best." She thought about the rather obvious marks on her back that he'd seen.

Tarso smiled and nodded. He was going to speak again before a loud commotion came from the main bar, making him stand at attention, ready to receive the signal for an oncoming fight. His eyes narrowed, and the booth doors swung open. Two children with bat wings sprouting from their back flew in, jumping into his arms. "Daddy!"

A demon woman sauntered in a moment later. She smiled, releasing a sigh. "Sorry, dear. They woke up from a nap, and their wings had come in. They insisted we come see you." She looked at the two people in the booth with him. "Sorry for the intrusion."

Ellyria bit her lip and shook her head. "No. It's alright. Kids will be kids." She smiled at the half-demons and looked at Zane with teary eyes. "I'll be right back."

Zane saw the look in her eyes and nodded. His gaze followed her for a moment as he watched her walk to the bathroom. He didn't see any demons follow her. There would be Hell to pay if they even tried to touch his woman. When she was out of sight, he sighed and looked from the blond-haired and black-eyed boy and girl to Lilith's disguised form, which was as statuesque as any model or actress and just as blonde. "I didn't expect settling down and motherhood to be so inviting to you."

Lilith gave Zane a serious look and shook her head. "Be quiet, mister-to-Hell-with-the-repercussions. Don't think that even though I am here, I haven't heard about that little adventure you had in Chile."

Zane sighed. "It is a long story that isn't suited for children." He nodded towards the twins, who were flying above their father, who were trying to catch them as giggles filled the air.

Ellyria returned with puffy eyes mid-conversation and started listening to catch up on what she missed. Her eyes kept darting over to the children. She took a deep breath and tried her best to relax.

Lilith leveled a gaze at Zangrunath and smiled. "It is alright. I was only teasing. Don't get your tail in a twist."

"I will try not to." He smirked.

Tarso paused what he was doing and turned to Lilith. "Alright. I think it is time we went home for the day." He smiled at the kids, who looked overjoyed at the idea of their father coming home early. He gave Zane a nod. "It was a pleasure to meet you, general." He gave the demon a mocking salute.

Zangrunath chuckled and gave him the finger. "Get out of here. It was nice to meet you, too."

Ellyria shook her head and laughed. "Oh, boy. Someone teased you while I was away."

He shrugged. "I managed."

Tarso smiled, leading the kids away. "It was nice meeting you Ellyria. Have a great evening. Don't worry about the food and drink. It's on me." He waved as he left.

"I'm still paying," she said under her breath, turning her attention to Zane once the happy family was out of sight. "Sorry I bailed on you there."

"It's fine. I figured you needed to get some air."

She sighed, looking at where the family had just disappeared. "Yeah."

Zane moved a hand to hold Ellyria's. "Are you alright? It's abnormal for you to lose your composure."

"They have what I want." She shrugged. "Hellish desires and all that."

He sighed and nodded. Of course, she put it in terms that he could understand. "I'm sorry. If there was a way, I would give that to you."

She leaned into him. "I know."

He squeezed her hand, realizing something important. "I owe you on our bet."

"I'll collect tonight." She looked at a few bar patrons. Every demon in the place gazed at them unabashedly. "I think we're going to be busy."

He nodded and looked around at the patrons. "Yeah. They look like they have questions."

"Well, it can't be worse than meeting your boss. Bring it on." She finished the sentence a little louder for their benefit.

Zane sighed at the shutters of the private booth. The only thing private about it was that people couldn't always see the occupants. He waved for the few people who were watching them to come over.

Three demons crowded the booth, body blocking the exit. One of them had shoulder length black hair. His hazel eyes regarded Zangrunath, ignoring Ellyria. "You got a promotion while in the middle of a ritual?"

"Yes, Zorron. It is possible to multitask." Zane smirked, wrapping an arm over the back of the booth to rest on Ellyria's opposite shoulder. "Enjoy your time here while you can, because I will not let you slack when I get back."

Zorron shivered, knowing of Zangrunath's reputation despite the softer side he'd already presented today. "Yes, sir," he said with a little squeak of fear before stalking off. That was all he was really interested in. His comrade became the new general and his boss.

"Wrath, sir?" a second demon who had a large, pointed nose and aristocratic cheekbones asked. His human disguise was pale with brown, shaggy hair. He licked his lips, eyeing Ellyria before bowing at the waist towards Zane. "Ozmong, sir. Can you tell us the tale of what happened in Chile?"

"No. Sathanas won't be coming back ever. The rest will remain between myself, Ellyria, the council, and the Dark Prince."

Ozmong nodded, regarding Ellyria like she was about to become his next meal. "And you. You're the one who summoned Wrath?"

Ellyria tried not to raise her eyebrow or show any sign of surprise. She could only hope that she succeeded. A few years of being a lawyer helped, if nothing else. She realized that there were seven generals, but she hadn't put the puzzle pieces together until someone shoved it into her face. The seven generals were the seven deadly sins, and Zangrunath, *her Zane*, was one of them. Wrath himself. She recovered fast, given her revelation, and smiled. "Yes. Of course, I did. He wouldn't be here to make you look like you're about to wet yourself otherwise. Stop simpering," she said with a sneer. She glanced over at Zane, surprised by her own reaction.

Zangrunath smirked and gave her a silent nod of approval. "Ellyria is the most powerful witch that has ever existed," he said, pulling her closer against him. "And she is mine." A growl rumbled in his chest, making Ozmong step back in fear. He cowered behind the third demon that had approached their table.

"At your service." The last demon bowed. His hair was a striking red color, and his eyes were emerald green to go with it. "Thyneakas," he said with a respectful nod, but no bow or other sycophantic behavior as seen with the previous demon. "I came to introduce myself to the infamous Wrath and his lady," he said, seeing another figure walking towards their booth that gave him a shock. He nodded at the man before finishing what he came here for. "May I ask what led you here to your visit today?"

"Curiosity about the place," Zane said without missing a beat, watching as both Ozmong and Thyneakas backed away from whomever was approaching.

Thyneakas nodded, flipping a gold coin in Ellyria's direction. "Have a drink on me."

Ellyria caught the coin, looked at it for a second before duplicating it and flipping the second back at the demon. "I can pay for myself. Thanks."

With that, the demons scurried off, shooed away by a singular man who wore a finely tailored suit. He grinned, nodding as he looked them over. "Oh yes. Tarso likes to keep eyes on his kind." He gazed at Zane when he said that before copying the same procedure for Ellyria. "It is odd to see a nephilim in here though," he said so only the couple could hear it. His short, wavy hair was black and a piece of his bangs fell into his face. Intense eyes, one of honey brown and the other black, stared back, and a well-built physique hid beneath the vest he wore, made even more obvious by how tight the clothing clung to his form.

Ellyria sighed. "It's odd to see any of us ever. I've never met one."

"Who are you exactly?" Zane asked.

The man chuckled and bowed. "My name is Azazel." He smirked at the demon. "I have seen many people. But a fallen? You are the first I have seen here." He sat down across from them without bothering to ask if he was welcome.

Zangrunath noticed the telltale signs of another demon. The haughtiness and smell of brimstone being chief among them. However, there was something off about it. He gazed back at Azazel. "To what do we owe the pleasure, mister nephalem?"

Azazel smiled and looked at Ellyria. "I wanted to come meet my kin. There are few of us around these days."

Ellyria took a drink, looking between the two. "Well, besides you and Lucifer, I'm the only other one I know of, and I'm not a demon. Yet." She shook her head. Even though she wanted to remain conversational, he brought several questions to mind. "I'm sorry, but did you just say nephilim and nephalem? Could you explain the difference?"

"You won't become a full demon. You will gain some features, but you will still look the same. The only exception being when you tap into that power that you hide. As for the rest, you are half angel, half human. I am half angel, half demon. Thus, the similar yet different names."

"Good to know."

"It seems you already know most of what to expect." He chuckled, looking at Zane. "You're lucky. You get her like that for eternity."

Zane released a low, possessive growl and pulled Ellyria closer to him. "Don't look at her like that."

"Okay." Azazel shrugged, putting his hands up in the air. "I was only commenting. I meant nothing of it."

"Stop," she said. Her resulting growl rumbled throughout the room as she glared between the two of them, eyes going dark. Nobody could question that she belonged in this part of the bar now.

Zane nodded and went quiet, the order from the ritual kicking in. Azazel just smiled, as if he knew he'd just learned something or otherwise gained the upper hand. "I am glad to find I am not the only one around anymore." He stood, nodding at Zane. "Keep her safe," he said, excusing himself from the table.

"I will," Zane said, gazing into Ellyria's eyes as he spoke the words.

Ellyria's eyes faded back to normal. "Sorry. Lost it for a second there."

"It's alright. You can get angry sometimes," he said, understanding better than anybody. He was Wrath, after all.

"I swear that, ever since the whole birthday thing three years ago, it happens more and more." She shook her head. "Doubt I'll need much of a ritual by the time I go."

"He just confirmed it." Zane smiled. "It's okay. You are still perfect to me."

Ellyria chuckled. "I know. You're thrilled, proud, and possessive about it." She kissed him and shook her head at his antics.

"I am yours and vice versa."

She chuckled at him and winked. "Let's go get a room. You owe me tonight."

He smirked, standing up and offering a hand. "Doubled, as I recall."

"Yes, indeed." She smirked, taking his hand. "I know you'll make it worth my while."

"Yes. I will." He led her out to the front to go pay for a room for the two of them.

When they were alone a few minutes later, Ellyria asked, "Would you mind if we stay for a day or two?"

"We can stay as long as you want," he said with a kiss.

"If it weren't for everything back home, I'd feel tempted to stay much longer."

"Relax and stop thinking. When we have time, we can always come back," he said before helping give her their agreed upon prize several times over.

Saturday, January 5, 2030

Ellyria was enjoying a hearty breakfast of huevos rancheros with green sauce in the bar when Tarso, Lilith, and their kids walked in. She glanced over at them and felt jealousy overtake her. "I'm such a bitch."

Zane tilted his head to the side. His back was to the door, and he hadn't noticed the latest visitors yet. "Why do you think that?"

"Envy."

He turned to look at the family. He sighed and gave her hand a squeeze. "I love you no matter what."

She nodded. "I love you. Maybe we'll adopt once the ritual is over. It shouldn't be a problem."

"We can do that." He smiled. "We will just have to explain a lot of weirdness to them."

"Yeah." She sighed. "We'd have to explain a lot regardless, but-" She paused, looking at the little ones. Tears welled up in her eyes. "I want to be someone's mom."

He rubbed her hand with his thumb. "You will be. And I know you will be great at it. You do whatever it takes to achieve your goals. You'll even make a deal with the Devil."

"Been there. Done that. All I got was a stupid seal." She laughed. "Sorry. I know we've been over it. I don't mean to keep rehashing it."

"It's fine." He kissed her cheek. "You just overthink things sometimes."

"I know." She sighed, seeing the kids testing out their new wings still. The boy was near the bottles at the bar, and she saw him knock one over. Thinking fast, she caught it with magic. "Woah there, buddy. That was almost a huge mess."

The young boy turned and smiled at her. "Sorry. I wasn't paying attention." He flew over and gave her a hug. "Thank you. My name is Adrian. Will you be my friend?" he asked, getting distracted by his sister playing with a demon over by the doors. "Lacey!" he said as he scampered off.

Ellyria looked at Zane and placed a hand on her chest. "Might've just melted a bit."

"You are still in one piece."

She leaned into him. "Maybe we should leave."

"You want to go home, then?"

"I don't know. I bet it's better than torturing myself through staying."

"We still have a couple of weeks before you need to go back to work," he said, doing some quick math in his head. "We can either go somewhere else and have fun or we can go home and relax. I have a late present to give you."

"Yeah. I do too." She nodded. "I guess it's time to go home."

"Home it is, then. Am I calling the plane or are we going Air-Elly?" He chuckled.

She laughed. "I will ley walk. I'm not feeling like flying right now."

He smiled and helped guide her out of the building. "Well, whenever you are ready," he said, allowing her to lead the way from there.

"It feels like there's a ley right behind the building." She shook her head. Why wasn't she surprised?

"Of course, there is." He held her hand as they strolled to the back of the building.

When they got around to the other side, Tarso was waiting. Ellyria jumped in surprise. "How did you do that?"

"I own the bar. I know every way in and out of the place, and I wanted to know why you didn't say goodbye before you left." He leaned against the wall and chuckled at her surprise.

"Uh." She looked at her toes when she saw Lilith and the kids nearby. Her eyes cut from them to him.

He glanced from the kids to Ellyria. "Oh." The levity about him from moments before disappeared as he realized what was going on. "I'm sorry."

"It's fine." She tried to sound flippant. "I want what I can't have. If you ever need anything, look me up. The law offices of McDonough, Hannon, and Grant. Cambridge, Massachusetts. We should open an office in New York soon, too."

"Well, if I ever need a lawyer, I will do that," he said, looking the two of them over. He saw her glance at the kids again and smiled. "You will be a great mother one day. You might not be able to have them, but there are plenty of kids out there who would be happy to call you mom."

Ellyria looked away with a bitter smile before looking back at Tarso with black eyes as she connected with the ley. "Thanks," she said, holding a hand out for Zane.

Zane took her hand and smirked at Tarso. "Stay out of trouble."

"Same goes for you." The demon hunter chuckled, but his eyes were on Ellyria as he spoke.

"I stay out of trouble, but it comes to me." She sighed, ley walking them into the penthouse living room. She took a deep breath as lethargy hit. "That might be the longest one yet."

"Are you going to be okay?" Zane asked her as he held her upright.

She nodded. "Yeah." As she spoke, her head spun. "Just need to lie down for a bit."

He nodded, picked her up, and brought her into the bedroom. He laid her down on the bed. "There you go. I am going to replace the food in the fridge." He made a face. "You rest."

"M'kay," she said, passing out.

He smirked as she fell asleep, going to take care of the house. When he finished, he came back to the bedroom, laying down next to her. He wanted to be close to her for a while.

Sunday, January 6, 2030

Ellyria slept until an early hour the next morning, finding Zangrunath watching her when she awoke. "Hey."

"Hey." He smiled, kissing her nose. "Are you feeling better?"

"Like I'm hung over, to be honest. I should've built up to that."

He rubbed her shoulder. "It's alright. We are home now. We don't have to go anywhere unless you want to. Besides, we have Shelby."

She smiled and stretched. "I'm glad we're back. I think I want to be lazy today."

"That is fine by me." He nodded, looking at the clock and chuckling. "Would you care for some brunch in bed then?"

She checked the time with him and giggled. "If it can be called brunch at two thirty in the morning."

He shrugged. "It's brunch time somewhere. Want anything in particular?"

"Not Mexican. I had my fill."

"Alright. Bacon and eggs with pancakes, it is." He smiled, getting up to go make her food.

When Ellyria was alone in the room, she looked up to the ceiling and prayed to any entity that would listen. "Please, let me be a Mom when this deal is over." She closed her eyes and got some more rest while she waited for her meal.

A long moment of quiet hung in the air before Ellyria heard a sound like a silver bell. The room grew silent again, and a few minutes later, Zangrunath came in with the food. "Here you go."

"Did you just ring a bell?" she asked, sitting up to eat.

He looked at her with a strange expression and laughed. "No. Why would I do that?"

She gazed back at him and frowned. "I guess I'm just so tired that I'm hearing things."

"Hey." He reached out, holding her chin so she would look at him. "As long as it's just a noise, it's fine. If it's voices, we have problems."

"If I'm hearing voices, it might be a new power." She shook her head at the thought, digging into her meal. She didn't want to imagine any other powers coming her way.

"Kill them all," Zane said into her head in a dark yet whimsical tone.

She winked at him. "I could, but one or both of us are becoming horsemen to do it."

"Both." He nodded. "I want you by my side."

"Do you know which one you were for that fight?"

"I am not sure, but if I had to guess, I think I was War."

She thought about that. "I'd end up being famine since I can tear matter into shreds."

He nodded, looking off into the distance. "You would cause a plague of destruction."

"Probably. Let's not find out for a good long while, though. I think that might kill me to try."

"Agreed." He shook his head to get rid of the thought, turning to look at her after a moment. "So, what do you want to do at three in the morning? The sun won't rise until about eight."

She smiled, finishing her food. "Let's go relax in the hot tub, assuming we left the heat on while we were out."

"Alright, but let me go check if it is warm first." He smiled.

Ellyria looked around the room and sighed. "I don't know what that ringing was, but I hope I didn't make another deal with the Devil," she said to the otherwise empty room.

Zangrunath arrived back a few minutes later. "It's good."

"Great." She smiled, getting out of bed.

He walked over to her and wrapped an arm around her. "It's cold out there. Below freezing. I want to make sure you stay safe and warm."

She chuckled. "I will keep close to you, then. My fiery demon."

He nodded, holding her close as he opened the door. He helped her over to the hot tub, which was steaming. "My lady," he said, waiting for her to get in before he joined her.

Ellyria stripped down and slipped into the heated water with a little shiver. "Cold, but so worth it." She sighed.

Zangrunath followed behind her. He let out a sigh of relief and sat next to her. "This was a good choice."

Ellyria curled up against his side. "The deal's done this year. Call it intuition or what have you. We're so close. I can feel it."

He wrapped an arm around her, holding her close. "I am a little curious to see what happens when this is all over. I have never been around after a deal's completion. This will be a first."

"We'll find out together." She smiled. "I'm glad I could make that deal when I did. I don't know what I would've done or how I would react if you disappeared without a trace."

"Violently and with extreme prejudice." He smirked, knowing her too well after so many years.

"I would make you come back."

"You would summon Lucifer again in order to do it too."

Ellyria grew quiet for a long time. They were both enjoying the companionable silence. "I don't know what the next milestone is after this."

"Everyone has the same feeling around this time," he said. "Pretty sure that you will know what it is when it happens."

"For right now, I just want you." She smiled. "Maybe in a few years, I'll figure out the rest."

"That's fine. I am okay with this right now." He smiled, kissing her forehead.

She looked out at the sky. "I think I'll miss this most one day- when I die." She sighed at the thought. "Seems like you don't get good views in Hell."

"It depends on where you go," he said. "This is nice, but there are some things that beat this by a huge margin."

"Oh?" she asked, turning to look at him. "Tell me about it."

"It depends on the time of year, but if you go at just the right time, you can see the souls come down like snow." He smiled. "It is quite the sight."

She kissed his lips. "Somehow you make something that should horrify me sound beautiful."

He ran his hand down her back. "You need to see the beauty in things you wouldn't consider."

She held onto him tight. "Thank you, Zangrunath. I love you. Can we continue where we left off on Christmas Eve after we get our gifts?" she asked.

"Of course we can." He chuckled. "I love you."

"Thank you. My gift is-" She burst into laughter. "Well, I dug deep. You're hard to shop for since there's a lot you don't need, and we buy whatever we want all year."

"Thank you." He gave her another kiss. "I would have settled on time with you. You are a pretty great gift."

"Thank you," she said, pulling away slightly. "Let's get this late gift giving show on the road before I turn into a prune."

Zane smiled, lifting her up and out of the hot tub and bringing her inside. He got them both situated with nice warm towels before carrying her to the couch where they both sat. "Well, I am not sure how this is all done, so why don't you go first?" He smiled.

She smiled and stood up. "Close your eyes please, and no peeking." She returned holding an elegantly wrapped package the size of a sweater a few moments later. She placed the box in his hands. "You can open your eyes now," she said while sitting beside him.

After opening his eyes, he looked down at the box before glancing back at her. He smiled as he unwrapped the box. He opened it up and saw a set of well organized and typed documents detailing a business deal in which Grant Construction had won the bid to demolish a parcel of decrepit buildings. "Damn," he said in shock before he looked back up at her. "But what do you want me to do with it?"

She chuckled. "I want you to have fun destroying them however you please."

A grin pulled at Zangrunath's features. He laughed hard, leaning in to give her a kiss. "Thank you. No one has ever done that for me before."

She smiled as they gazed into each other's eyes. "I want you to be happy." She held his hand. "And I know pulverizing things into dust does just that for you."

"Thank you. Now you close your eyes," he said, standing up and getting her gift. He came back a few moments later, placing a crimson red box in her hands. "You can look now."

Ellyria opened her eyes, trying not to laugh at the look of the packaging. "It's wrapped exactly how I imagined," she said as she undid the paper, revealing four metallic rings, each one with demonic runes on them. She looked up. "I don't speak enough demonic to know what this is." She looked up at him.

He chuckled. "That would make sense. I wanted to give you some closer, more personal, time with me, starting with your vacation."

She placed the box down and kissed him. "Thank you. You thoughtful, amazing demon."

"I am glad that you like it." He smirked into the kiss. "Love you."

She looked into his eyes and sighed with relief. They were home and on vacation. They could relax. "I love you, darling. Now where were we before the Dark Prince interrupted?"

# XIII



The alarm hadn't gone off yet, but Ellyria was awake and stretching. She looked over at Zane, who was typing away on a laptop, and smiled. "Hey. Today's the day."

Zane set the laptop to the side and leaned down to give her a kiss. "Morning." He smiled in return. "Excited?" he asked her as he went back to working on the laptop.

"I am." She smiled, rolling out of bed and getting dressed. "It's going to happen today. I can feel it."

He watched her for a moment before he closed the laptop. "Well, let's get this started." He got up, going to make her a big breakfast.

Ellyria walked into the kitchen, wearing a red dress that cinched at the knees. Her heels were black, and she looked out the penthouse window, observing the city. "Thank you, Zane. You took my idea from a decade ago and made it a reality. It's better than I imagined."

"You did most of the work." He shrugged. "In all honesty, I didn't do much on this deal short of the money and taking out a few people. Most of my other deals involved bloodshed and carnage. You had the easiest deal by far." He smiled as he cooked.

"Regardless, thank you for helping me make it happen." She moved into the kitchen to make herself a drink. "I know it's early, but I'm going to make a celebratory mimosa."

He chuckled. "That's fine. I don't mind driving you to work," he said as he plated up the food.

"Thank you." She smiled as she poured the drink into a champagne glass. She moved back over to the window, taking a sip. "Now this is perfect."

He placed the food on the kitchen island for her. "Enjoy."

She kissed him on the cheek, sitting down and eating. She hummed. "You always know when to go all out."

"I know you." He smirked. "A decade of being together will do that."

"The best, most crazy decade of my life so far." She chuckled, taking her time to eat. After a little while, she finished her meal and stood up. "Let's clean this up and head to the new office."

"I will get this going. It won't take long," he said, cleaning up the mess.

Ellyria helped with the dishes before she grabbed her things. "Let's go complete a ritual." She smirked, tossing her dark hair over her shoulder.

He smiled and took her hand. "Let's." He led them to the elevator. "I am curious to see what happens after this is done."

"I'll feel it. Won't I?" she asked. "Seems like a Hellish thing to do."

"You will." He nodded. "I don't think it will be painful, though. Just a gut feeling," he said as best he could since he had never been around for the aftermath of a deal before.

They walked to Shelby. She took a seat on the passenger's side. "I knew this would happen ten years ago, but I didn't expect to know when my soul was about to be forfeited. And believe it or not, I'm not worried. I know it will be in Lucifer's able hands."

He sat down and started the car. "I will also be here to keep you safe. You won't die anytime soon."

"I hope not." She glanced over at him. "I've been doing some research on my mom."

"Oh? Have you found anything of note?" he asked as he drove them to the new building.

Ellyria nodded. "One of her domains is the longevity of life, so I might be around for quite a while."

"Well then, be ready for a long and interesting life." He smiled.

"It could never be boring with you by my side."

He chuckled at all the fun ideas he had in mind for their future together while he pulled into a parking spot. "Here we are."

She took his hand and squeezed it. "I want you by my side today, Mister Grant." She laughed about their inside joke from the time her assistant thought they were married.

"Of course, my darling wife." He laughed, giving her a kiss.

She hopped out of the car. "Let's go open the New York office." She smiled, strolling towards the door slowly so he could catch up.

He got out of the car, walked up beside her, and took her hand. "Lead the way. I want to watch you complete this deal."

She nodded, walking into the building. She stopped at the receptionist's desk. "Good morning, Gloria. Could you please call for a meeting at nine thirty? I'd like to gather the team to start the day."

"Of course, Missus Grant. I will let them know as soon as possible." The middle-aged woman responded, picking up the phone and making the calls.

Ellyria waited for Gloria to get off of her first call. "Just Miss. Thank you."

Gloria blushed, glancing at Zane. "Sorry. I saw you were together and assumed."

"It happens all the time. Just be careful about assumptions. They can get people in a lot of trouble," Ellyria said before walking towards her office. She walked by Yvette's empty desk. "Did my assistant make it in yet?" she asked.

"Yes. She is out getting coffee at the moment."

"Great. Thanks." Ellyria smirked, closing her office door behind Zane. "Every damn time I bring you, I swear."

Zane nodded. "Sorry that I am devilishly handsome."

She laughed. "I don't care what they think. We are one. I feel married to you. It's just the principle of the matter at this point."

"Well, if it ever becomes a problem, we can make it real," he said with a smile. "It wouldn't be too hard to get done."

She raised an eyebrow as she unpacked her briefcase. "That is not something I ever expected to hear from you."

"I don't care if we are. I just want to make sure you are happy."

She thought about his words as her computer booted up. "There's just one problem."

"What is that?"

"The one I'd want to marry us is very difficult to summon." She laughed.

He chuckled. "Then, I guess, we will just have to send him a letter."

"Might as well make it official with the only one that matters." She shrugged, responding to an email and taking a deep breath as she readied herself for the meeting. "Alright. Time to finish this."

Zane smiled and gave her a kiss. "Alright. I will be right beside you."

Ellyria stood up and started walking towards the conference room. As her office door shut, two staff members stood from their computer desks and ran in front of her. She heard noise coming from the room when one of them opened the door.

Her assistant, Yvette, said, "She's coming," in a quiet but urgent voice.

Ellyria pulled the door open and stepped in, looking over at Zangrunath with a smile seconds before he disappeared. Her smile became a frown. "Zane?" she asked both aloud and with telepathy. There was no response from Zane as she stood by the door.

Ellyria turned to the office staff all gathered around and realized they were all waiting for her. This is what she'd wanted, but it was wrong. She took a breath and gritted her teeth. She had to get through this meeting first, and then she could figure out what had happened. "Good morning!" she said with false happiness, trying to get through this while her mind raced with thoughts and ideas about making Lucifer pay for lying to her.

Ellyria pulled out her phone and texted Steve. 'I need you to give me an emergency phone call in five minutes. I need an excuse to get out. Something just went wrong. Magically so.'

'Sure thing,' McDonough said.

The five minutes were too long for Ellyria. Grueling and agonizing were feelings that had nothing on how she was feeling right now. She tried not to sigh with relief when Steve's call came in.

"Hey. Something's wrong. Get out of there and explain what just happened."

Ellyria covered the receiver uselessly. "I'm sorry. This is McDonough. You can go about your days. Thanks, team." She stood up and marched to her office on a warpath. "Zane's gone."

"What?" he asked in confusion. "Didn't you add an addendum to your deal?"

"Yes. An ironclad one with the King himself. He and I are going to have some words."

There was a nervous sigh on the other end of the line. "Please don't go overboard."

Ellyria growled, trying not to let the demonic changes of being a fallen angel overtake her. "Too late," she said. She could feel the heat Zangrunath was feeling all over her body. She imagined it was like what hot flashes were like. "I'm getting my soul bound back."

"Just don't get seen." He sighed. "Good luck," he said as the call disconnected.

Ellyria pocketed her phone and grabbed her things. "I'm sorry. This is an emergency," she said to Yvette on her way out the door. "Call me if I'm needed for anything."

"Will do, Miss Grant," the other woman said, watching Elly march out with a fiery passion in her eyes.

Ellyria hopped into Shelby and sped home. She parked, taking the elevator up. When she got to the penthouse, she flipped through her grimoire. She reread her contract three times. "I don't get it. You should be here." She grabbed her chest, feeling the loss. "You should be here."

She gulped, trying hard not to cry. This wasn't right. Zane should be here. The air crackled with electricity as she struggled to contain the anger and turmoil inside of her. "Screw subtlety!" She screamed to the Heavens, stomping hard on the ground. For once, she took everything. Her eyes darkened to black, skin became red and spectral bat wings dominated her back in seconds. Magic pulsed around the warded penthouse, writhing around her like it would break free. A dangerous and volatile combination of power and loss of control. She cloaked herself in the palpable magic around her, disappearing from New York and reappearing inside of the towering pillars of Stonehenge.

Behind nearby stanchions, people screamed and darted away in fear of the devilish woman that appeared out of thin air. She didn't bother even looking at them. Her sole focus was on what she came here for. Zangrunath. He belonged here, and she needed to have him. "Mine!" she shouted in a language she didn't know. *He* never taught her demonic. They thought there would be time for that.

A burst of magic rolled out from her location with so much power that it caused a tremor and thunder to crack. She channeled for as long as she needed. The ground shattered and remade itself over and over. Gravity lost hold at the hands of the fluctuating magic. Bodies, cars, and anything not battened down lifted into the air before Ellyria disappeared from the scene. Moments later, a sonic boom rang out, setting off car alarms and dropping all the lifted objects back down onto the ground.

Zangrunath sighed when he realized where he was. He didn't think that he would be back here so soon, but now he knew he wouldn't be able to see Ellyria for at least a few days. Their contract terminated. The ritual ended. He didn't want to do this, but his job demanded it. Making his way to Lucifer's familiar tower, he nodded as he walked past the demon manning the desk. This was official business. At the bottom of the ancient stairwell, he found the Keeper of Contracts. "Did it all go through properly?"

The blind demon nodded and turned to Zangrunath with a toothy grin. The clank of his keys a dissonant melody. "Yes. The ritual completed. We collected her soul. Now we just wait for her to die."

"There will be some time before that happens," Zangrunath said with a growl. He made his way up the stairs, feeling bitter solitude for a moment as he stepped out of the basement of the tower before he felt a quake ripple through Hell. His eyes darted all around before he looked upward. From here, the spire where the Dark Prince resided loomed above him more than usual. The shaking returned a moment later, and Zane noticed the magic forming at the top of the tower. He spread his wings and flew with haste. Someone or something was attacking Hell itself.

As Zane flew up the dark spire, he found Lucifer already waiting at the area where the magic was forming. Unlike their last meetings, he was not his usual angelic self. This time, he embraced his power over the underworld. His skin was crimson red and dripping blood. Replacing black feathers, the leathery material of his batlike wings looked tattered. White-hot flame made it near impossible to look directly at the wings. Ten horns raised from his head and a flaming crown hovered just above them. He gazed at the portal that was forming with mirthless eyes that seemed to damn a person with a look alone.

He glanced over his shoulder as he saw his legions and generals amassing around the tower. "Go back to your stations!" he said, causing shock waves to emanate from his person at the power of the order. He glared at Zangrunath. "Except for you." His low growl made Hell itself shudder. "This is your doing." He jabbed a finger towards the portal.

"What?" Zangrunath asked, trembling at the sight of his King.

"Ellyria is doing this," Lucifer said as his gaze focused on the portal, waiting for the one who had earned his ire to arrive. "No one breaks into my domain unannounced."

After a moment of pressing darkness and cloying heat, Ellyria looked upon a landscape she'd never seen before. Out of the corner of her eye, she saw the figure of the one she came for. She reached out a hand, dragging him to her as the area nearby disintegrated. "You took him! That wasn't the deal!"

Lucifer growled and flew into her face. He grabbed her by the wings, throwing her onto the roof of the tower. She hit hard. Wind knocked out of her, and the ceiling crumbled below them. "I took no one! He would have returned in a few days!" He landed on top of her, pinning her to the floor of his office. "You couldn't be patient, could you?"

Ellyria pushed him back with magic. A beat of her wings had her standing. Her control was waning. It wouldn't take much for her to lose it. Running amok in Hell became a real possibility in her mind. In her periphery, everything she touched or approached disintegrated; Lucifer himself the only exception. "Give him back. He is mine. Not yours."

"Calm down before I make you regret your next sentence," Lucifer said. His tone promised pain and misery. "You have violated laws you cannot fathom against Heaven and Hell. I can promise you that this is not the answer. Do you want your precious demon back?"

Ellyria glared at Lucifer. His warning growl forced her mind to catch up, registering the change in his appearance. She recoiled, and she inhaled a breath of air. She shook. What had she done? She shook her head. "If I stop now, I pass out," she said, sounding human again, and with the change came something new. The feeling of defeat.

He stared her down. "Go home before I make you. I can't kill you, but I can do other things. You broke into my domain and that is not to be taken lightly." He pointed a finger at Zangrunath. "He is going to stay here. Before you see him again, you and I are going to have a chat."

Ellyria glared back at Lucifer. Her eyes were fiery and defiant like their first meeting. "Fine," she said, disappearing with a booming wave of pressure. Ellyria appeared in the penthouse. As soon as her feet hit the floor, she passed out cold.

Lucifer growled and turned to Zangrunath. "For your sake, I hope she is worth it, because you won't be seeing her for some time." His form shifted back to his usual angelic form. "I will make her life a living Hell while you are here, and you are going to suffer as well."

Zangrunath made a face. The earlier fear still lingered in him, but now annoyance grew in his chest like a cancer. He nodded at the Prince of Darkness. "I expect nothing less." He sighed, wishing that Ellyria had waited instead of losing her head.

Lucifer smirked evilly at Zangrunath. "Of course, it is what I do." He chuckled. His gaze bored through Zangrunath as he said, "One year of hard labor. Now I will see to her."

"Of course, my King." Zangrunath bowed. He flew down into the ash and lava pits of Hell, beginning the grueling process that awaited him.

Lucifer smirked. He appeared in the penthouse. A flash of light, the only harbinger of his arrival. He saw the woman on the floor and kicked her side. "Get up. You and I are going to talk."

Ellyria didn't move, but a second, harder kick woke her. She rolled over, coughing with wide eyes. The room spun. She gripped her head in pain as she groaned. "Ouch."

He stared down at her, walking a slow arch around her and sitting down on the couch. "You are in a lot of trouble."

Ellyria sat up. Her wings were fading in and out of existence. She looked into his eyes in defeat. A sigh escaped her. "I lost control." She clutched her chest as she felt Zangrunath's pain. "It's my fault. Punish me, not him."

"Oh no, you two are one. The punishment goes both ways, and if you think that is bad, wait for what I have in store for you." He shook his head and stared back with cold eyes.

Ellyria nodded. "I don't understand what rules I broke."

"For starters, you went to Stonehenge, and looking like a demon, ripped a portal to Hell in broad daylight. People saw you and were recording videos with their phones." His chest rumbled with a growl. "That is six things right there. Not to mention declaring war on Hell itself," he said. He set his face into a stern grimace.

"Do I get bonus points for channeling famine?" she asked, slumping back onto the floor with an exhausted groan.

"Then there is that. Mortals shouldn't access the horsemen." He shook his head. "By all rights, you should be dead right now, made to suffer for all of eternity in the deepest pit of Hell, with Zangrunath as your punisher."

She sobbed. "I understand. Just get it over with, then."

"I can't. Your deal with me made it so. You must die of natural causes. I have to keep you alive."

Ellyria cried. "I can't even die right."

"Be quiet. You could have done nothing. Everything would have been fine. But you- instead of thinking," he paused, allowing the words to sink in, "something a lawyer should do, you went off the deep end." His tone fluctuated between scorn, judgment, and mocking.

Ellyria couldn't help but sob. She'd made so many mistakes in the past, but this was the worst. Her lips opened, and she spoke; it was a compulsion to do so. Zangrunath explained Lucifer's divinity to her once before, but she wasn't thinking straight. She didn't realize what it was causing her to do this. Every deep thought and secret that lingered in her heart and soul came out of her at that moment. "I want him. He is mine. We wanted you to marry us. I want children of my own, but since we can't have any, I think we'll adopt-"

"For fuck's sake, be quiet," Lucifer said. "You will get him back, but it will be *after* you've received your punishment. He is going to be working his demonic ass off while you are going to be here in a Hell of your own making. Then I might let you get married."

Ellyria nodded, curling into a ball as Zangrunath's pain washed through her. She let out a little yelp as torment rolled through her, becoming a hollow husk of her former self in that moment.

Lucifer stood up and strode forward, looming over her. "Stand up. If you want him back, this is the price."

Tears rolled down her cheeks. The room grew silent as she struggled to stand, stumbling until she was vertical. She wobbled in place. She met his eyes, all the changes brought on by her tirade gone. It was just Ellyria, much the same as a decade prior when she'd summoned a demon by accident. "Yes, my King."

"Good." He nodded. He traced a sigil into the air, forming a complex pattern that hovered in the air in front of her. It glowed with the searing color of a brand without giving off heat. He stepped to the side, staring her down. "For the next year, you will go about your business as normal, feeling everything Zangrunath feels doubled over." His eyes assessed her reaction with a careful, calculating look.

She looked back with dull, soulless eyes. "Yes, my King."

He crossed his arms over his chest. "Place your hand on the seal and bear your punishment."

Ellyria's right hand became a fist at her side. Her left opened, moving to touch the seal. She saw tremors coming from it. She expected tantamount pain at any moment. Seconds before she touched the sigil, she gazed at him, tears still falling. "Zane's going to feel this too, isn't he?"

Lucifer shook his head. "No, only you. That is your punishment: knowing that his torment is your fault and bearing it doubled over." His tone sounded like that of a judge, jury, and executioner.

She nodded and moved her hand the remaining inches to touch the magical brand, which wrapped around her hand, twisting up her arm where it blackened, burning into her flesh. Her lips formed into an O shape. The pain forced her to gasp before she wailed in agony. Her body convulsed, and she fell to the ground with a thud.

Lucifer watched with disinterest for a moment. His stony gaze looking through her. "Enjoy your time alone," he said, disappearing in a burst of light.

Ellyria writhed and twitched on the floor. She wished she could pass out, knowing that the embrace of death or unconsciousness wouldn't come. She chanted the words, "I did this," over and over, like a mantra. Whenever she could muster up the energy, she crawled to the table where she left her phone.

It took half an hour on the floor as her voice grew hoarse from her screaming, but she texted Steve McDonough. 'Home. Not good.' Her fingers refused to function after that. She sent the message, tossing her phone aside. Rolling onto her back, she cried while staring up at the ceiling.

An hour later, Steve knocked on the door of the penthouse. "Ellyria! Is everything alright?"

The door swung open for Steve, and the sounds of agonized screaming greeted him. Ellyria writhed on the ground in a pile of her own sick, sweating bullets. "Help."

He ran over and picked her up, moving her to the bathroom. He set her down in the tub. A worried gaze studied her. "What happened?"

Ellyria lifted her branded arm as she kicked and flailed in the tub. Another round of chanting began. "I did this." She sobbed like a small child, crying for their mother.

Steve eyed her arm and sat down on the floor. He sighed. "You pissed off the Devil." His whispered statement hung in the room, leaving no room for question. Even he could hear the annoyance in his tone.

"T- t- they're," she stuttered out, "torturing him."

"And you're feeling it, aren't you?" he asked rhetorically.

She nodded, tears running down her cheeks. "I m- messed up."

He nodded. "I bet. If you can, focus on me and explain what happened."

"I broke every rule there is."

He pinched the bridge of his nose. "How bad?"

"Search demon in Stonehenge on the internet," she said, clutching her chest.

Steve groaned, unlocked his phone, and pulled up a search engine. His mouth popped open in shock as he watched the shaky mobile video in horror. He saw the demonic visage of his business partner and did a double take, looking between her and the screen for a moment. His eyes glued to the screen as a portal opened, taking her with it, and the video came to an abrupt stop. He locked his phone, growing quiet for a long time as he processed the information. He knew from Ellyria's insistence that she was powerful, but this- "What the fuck?"

"I'm sorry."

"How are you not dead? That should have put a mile wide target on your back."

Ellyria pointed. Her arm shook. Her voice hoarse still, but powering through the words. "There's a copy in the first drawer on the right side of my desk."

He got up and marched over to her desk, finding the copy of her contract. He read it over several times before shaking his head. "This deal says he can't kill you. But he can torture you." He groaned as the puzzle pieces clicked into place. He understood the problem now.

She released a sob. "I should've died. I should've just died. It hurts."

He leaned against the wall and slid down. "Dammit, Elly. Why did you do it?"

"They took him. He wasn't supposed to go."

"So the contract ended, and he went back." He sighed again and looked at her. "You went through all of that, and you still didn't get him back?"

Ellyria held up one shaking finger. "One year."

"One year?" he asked. "What does that mean?"

"I get him back in one year."

His eyes went wide. "You are going to be like this for a year?!"

"Yeah," she said, grunting as she forced herself to stand on wobbling feet. "I'll get used to it."

He stood at a much faster speed and pushed her back down. "Don't force yourself. Take your time. I will cover for you. Family issues."

She shook her head. "I got used to the last seal. I can deal. Give me a week."

He looked nervous. "Okay, but please don't overdo it. I want you to take as long as you need for this. Don't come in if you can't think straight."

Ellyria's eyes closed. "I'm more concerned about sleep right now."

Steve nodded. "If you need me to get you something to help with that, I know some people that can get you potent stuff."

"Please," she said. "I'm such an idiot."

He nodded and sighed. "No, you just didn't think." He offered a hand to help her out of the tub. "You go lay down. I will be back as soon as I can," he said, moving towards the door.

"Thank you." Pain lanced through her back, and she gritted her teeth together to keep from screaming. It came out as a grunt instead. She looked over at Zangrunath's desk and frowned as she stumbled her way to her bedroom, where she fell into bed and prayed for an end to the suffering. "I'm sorry, Zane."

# CASTING A DIFFERENT TYPE OF SPELL

Do you wish you could cast spells like Ellyria? Well, dear reader, now you can! Reviews are the kind of magic authors live or die by, and you have the power in your hands. It doesn't take an Annihilation Ritual to help out this humble author. Just head over to your favorite review website, or the vendor where you purchased your copy of Deadly Deals, and cast a few spells of your own.

# ABOUT THE AUTHOR

The Deals of the Damned series is fantasy author M. W. McLeod's debut series in The Veil setting. She currently resides in Washington state, but she was born and raised in Arizona. After years of writing fanfiction, she branched off from borrowing a spark of others' worlds to casting her own type of spells. She is fascinated with tall ships, and is a self proclaimed caffeine addict, flavored coffee being the poison of choice. My other pen name is Maria Caiazza, but be warned, I don't guarantee a happy ending when writing under that name.

https://beacons.ai/mwmcleodandmariacaiazza

# ALSO BY
# M. W. MCLEOD

DEALS OF THE DAMNED SERIES

# OTHER BOOKS BY THE PUBLISHER

MODERN TALES OF OLD SERIES

*Heartless by Maria Caiazza*
*Seven Ravens by Maria Caiazza*


*Be Still My Undying Heart by Maria Caiazza*